PLAY YOUR HEART OUT

A Sinful Serenade Novel

CRYSTAL KASWELL

Also by Crystal Kaswell

Sinful Serenade
Sing Your Heart Out - Miles
Strum Your Heart Out - Drew
Rock Your Heart Out - Tom
Play Your Heart Out - Pete
Sinful Ever After – series sequel

Dangerous Noise
Dangerous Kiss - Ethan
Dangerous Crush – Kit
Dangerous Rock – Joel
Dangerous Fling – Mal
Dangerous Encore - series sequel

Inked Hearts
Tempting - Brendon
Playing - Walker
Pretend You're Mine - Ryan
Hating You, Loving You - Dean - coming summer 2018
Breaking the Rules - Hunter - coming fall 2018

Sign up for the Crystal Kaswell mailing list to get the *Play Your Heart Out* alternate POV scene.

For Karine. I hope you've become the person you always wanted to be.

Chapter One

❦

"*Oh. Ohhhh. Ohhhhhhh.*"

The entire bar echoes with the sounds coming from the single-stall bathroom in the corner.

"Jess, that one is yours." Rick points to the shaking bathroom door and hands me his set of manager's keys. "You're off after that."

Great. I'm off after I tell the people fucking in the bathroom to break it up.

"*Ohhh. Yes. YES. GOD, PETE. OHHH.*"

"Now, Jess." Rick's voice is dripping with irritation. His gaze is fixed on the cleavage of the copper-haired woman leaning over the bar.

What does he have to be irritated about? He's getting laid tonight. Sure, he's not going to get the woman screaming as loud as this Pete guy is, but he's not going home alone.

I press my eyelids together. Only two more weeks working here. My loan will go through. I'll quit this hellhole and officially enroll at USC Law.

Life will be under control.

My lips curl into a customer service smile. Rick is my boss. I have to be polite. "Of course, sir."

I take a deep breath and turn towards the bathroom.

It's late enough that the bar is down to a dozen customers. Half of them are lost in drunken misery. The other half are staring at me, licking their lips in anticipation of the drama about to unfold.

Attention from concerned strangers, my favorite. I steel my nerves. This is nothing compared to standing in front of a jury. If I want to be a trial lawyer, I need to learn to project strength and confidence.

"*Oh, God, Pete you feel so good. MMM.*"

A sigh escapes my lips as I tap a knock on the door. Must be nice to be that uninhibited.

Is it even possible to enjoy sex that much? It's not like the guy is at an ear piercing volume. I can barely make out his grunts.

Okay, that's enough of listening to the strangers having sex. I knock again. "Excuse me. You can't—" I'm a grown adult, I can say the word—"engage in sexual activities here. Please get dressed and leave."

This does nothing to quiet them.

I knock again.

"*MMM. PETE DON'T STOP.*" The woman squeals.

Rick is watching me with that same stern *do my bidding* expression. Dammit. Our bouncer only works weekends. I'm the last cocktail waitress on the floor. Either I take care of this or I escalate to calling the police.

Deep breath.

I pound on the fucking door. "I have the key. I'm opening the door in five seconds." My hands are so sweaty I can barely grip the thing. "Five. Four." I slide the key into the lock. "Three. Two." I turn it. My fingers curl around the door handle. God help me. "One."

I open the door.

A tall, broad-shouldered man has a thin brunette pinned against the wall. Her red dress is at her waist. His jeans are at his feet. Even in the dim light of the bathroom, the hard muscles of his ass and legs are clear as day.

He's still pumping into her. She's still screaming. No more words. It's a collection of incomprehensible sounds. She claws at the wall, shaking and panting with orgasmic bliss.

The guy, Pete I guess, waits until she's finished. Then he stops pounding and he turns to me.

My cheeks flush as our eyes connect. He's handsome.

And familiar. Really familiar.

He's not a regular. Certainly not from Long Island.

I don't know anyone in LA. Why do I recognize him?

I shove my hands into the pockets of my apron. I'm here to accomplish something and it's not checking out the manwhore with an exhibitionist streak. "Excuse me, but you can't do that here. Please take a minute to get dressed and leave or I'll have to call the police."

"Can you make it two minutes?" he asks with a deep, even voice.

He's ballsy. I'll give him that much.

My gaze is drawn to the tattoo curving around his hip and thigh.

Get a grip, Jess. Six months is a long dry streak but you don't need to stoop to being some player's sloppy seconds.

"Uh..." I can negotiate too. "Two minutes if you keep it down."

"Thanks." He turns back to the woman. One hand plants on the wall in front of her. The other stays over her mouth, muffling her groans.

He has the decency to wait until I close the door to resume fucking her.

Pete.

I know him.

But how?

I do a mental run through of every dark-haired man I know as I add up my tips. Time to close out with Rick. And to plead for an extra weekend shift.

He's sitting with the copper-haired woman, his arm around her waist.

Great. I'm interrupting his flirtation. That will put him in a good mood.

Someone bumps into me. Hard. It's her—the woman from the bathroom.

She scowls at me. "Thanks a lot."

I bite my tongue. Telling her to go to hell is above my pay grade. Better to step out of the way and let her storm off. Besides, she looks embarrassed. I'm not going to rub salt in the wound.

I try to step aside. Her eyes narrow. She goes out of her way to bump into me again.

Shit. My balance falters. I land right on my ass, my glasses sliding off my face.

I can't make out any of the details of her expression. But I can hear her frustrated sigh, her loud stomping steps, the cracking of plastic.

Dammit. I know that sound. There's no chance my frames are still in one piece.

Her footsteps get quieter as she storms out of the bar.

Where the hell did my glasses go? I'm about to swallow my pride and launch into a full on hands and knees search when I hear his voice. The man from the bathroom. Pete.

"You okay?" He kneels next to me and offers his hand.

I stare back at him. Does he really think I'm going to take that hand? God knows where he was touching the girl in the red dress. "Where has that been?"

"Just washed and scrubbed."

Not clean enough.

He's close. I can make out his expression. Concern. About me or something else?

"Your friend ran off." I push myself to my feet. "You should hurry if you want to catch her."

He looks up at me. "You were wearing glasses."

I rub my eyes. It does nothing to help my vision or my comprehension of the situation. His voice is even, his posture is confident. Three minutes ago, he was screwing that girl in the bathroom. Now, he's worried about my glasses.

I can't help but laugh. "You noticed what I was wearing while you were pounding the screaming brunette."

"Stopped pounding when you opened the door," he teases.

"I guess you did."

He reaches for something on the floor then pushes himself to his feet. "These *are* yours?"

He holds up my glasses. I squint to make out the damage. They're broken at the bridge. Damn.

"You have tape?" he asks.

I nod. "Yeah. It's through here." I lead him to the back room. After two months taking every shift I can get, I know the bar well enough to navigate sans corrected vision.

Supplies are in the Manager's Office. Booth against the wall is the only place to sit. I point everything out to him and slide into the bench seat.

A few moments later, he slides into the booth next to me with a roll of tape. My heart beats faster. A flutter builds below my stomach.

This beautiful image pops into my head—the two of us in the bathroom, him pressing me against the wall, one hand tugging at my long blond hair, the other sliding under my skirt.

I want to be lost in pleasure the way that woman was.

Is it even possible for sex to feel that good?

5

"Here." His deep voice pulls me out of my thoughts. He holds up my now taped together glasses.

"You're good with your hands."

He chuckles. "True."

"I didn't mean it like that."

His laugh gets deep. "Years of playing the bass guitar does good things for your dexterity."

The bass guitar.

No. He can't be Pete Steele, the bassist of the alternative rock band, Sinful Serenade. They're Madison's favorite band. Her wall is covered in pictures of them and especially pictures of the enigmatic bassist.

"These will hold for tonight." His deep brown eyes meet mine. "I'll buy you new glasses tomorrow."

"You're going to buy me glasses?"

"My fault these are broken."

"What if I never want to see you again?"

"Then you wouldn't have let me help you."

I bite my lip. I can't afford new glasses and I can't work with these for long. But seeing him again is dangerous. His proximity has my body buzzing. Will I really be able to resist him?

Last thing I need is some player breaking my heart. Even if he is rock star bassist Pete Steele.

"What if I have a policy of rejecting players who get into fights?" I ask.

"You getting at something?"

"Have you ever heard of asking?"

He nods. That's it, a nod.

I wipe my hands on my apron. "Are you going to ask?"

"If it will make you feel better about how badly you want to say yes."

Damn, he's cocky. I usually hate that kind of thing, but on him, it's sexy. I swallow hard. "It will."

"Will you allow me to buy you glasses?"

"Yes."

His fingertips skim my temples as he slides the frames back onto my face.

Now that I can see, there isn't a doubt in my mind. "You're Pete Steele."

"Unfortunately." His eyes meet mine. "And you are?"

"Jess."

"Nice to meet you." He shakes my hand. "Where's your phone?"

My heart is beating too fast. I need to tell him to get lost, to pull back so I won't get hurt.

My body won't allow it. My hands and arms move of their own volition. Before I know it, my phone is in his palm.

He taps his number into my cell then sends himself a text. "Jess what?"

"Jess James. Technically Jessica," I say. "People called me Jessie James all throughout elementary school."

"Sweet, innocent blond on the outside. Outlaw on the inside. I see it." His lips curl into a smile.

I melt. It's the most beautiful smile in the history of the world.

He texts me an address. "Meet me at one."

I wait for my judgment to kick in, but all I can feel is the flutter of desire in my stomach. "Okay."

His eyes meet mine. "You gonna be alright, Jess? You look a little flushed."

"I'm not used to breaking up sex in the bathroom." I play with my skirt. "That girl was screaming loud enough to wake the dead."

His smile turns cocky. "I've heard louder."

"Really?"

"Yeah." He pushes himself out of his seat. "I'll see you tomorrow."

"See you then."

I rub my eyes, pinch myself to see if I'll wake up from this daydream.

But I'm not daydreaming.

That's Pete Steele.

He knows my name.

And he's buying me glasses tomorrow.

What happened to my normal life?

Chapter Two

My tiny North Hollywood apartment is cruelly without air conditioning. Sixty seconds after my shower, I'm hot and sticky.

Screw pajamas. I plop in bed naked. Even my thin cotton sheet is too much. I try to sleep, but my thoughts weigh on me. *What if the loan doesn't go through? There's no way I'll pay for school. And Dad hasn't called back. Is he drinking again? I'm not there. How is he going to hold it together on his own?*

Just once, I want to forget how to think. I want to be like that girl in the bathroom at the bar, completely in my body, screaming in ecstasy.

Nathan never made me feel like that.

Mostly, I was worried if I was doing it right, if I was good enough for him.

But Pete...

I bet he could make me forget about everything besides his hands, his mouth, his cock.

My cheeks flush. I might as well work off some of this energy.

I'm hot but it's not from the temperature.

It's the thought of him.

I know it sounds ridiculous, but I usually have to try so hard to concentrate if I want to come. But thinking of him is seamless. I'm already halfway to an orgasm.

My eyelids press together as I slide my hand between my legs. I think of him, here, in the bed with me. I think of his strong hands trailing over my breasts, his soft lips on my neck, his hips rocking against mine as he pulls our bodies together, as he buries himself deep inside me.

৩১৯৩

THE AIR CONDITIONING POURS OVER ME AS I STEP INSIDE the coffee shop. A sigh escapes my lips. That feeling is heaven.

There he is, sitting in the corner, his long bangs hanging in front of his piercing brown eyes. Even in dark wash jeans and a light t-shirt, Pete is magnetic enough he glows.

But he's not alone.

There's a couple with him—a young woman with a cool, edgy pink ombre bob and a man with dark blond hair. He looks familiar.

Oh, shit, that's Tom Steele, the Sinful Serenade drummer.

For a second, I forget that Madison and I are not on speaking terms and I imagine her turning bright red and squealing as I explain that I not only met Tom and Pete Steele but actually had coffee with them.

Actually made myself the next notch on Pete's bedpost.

Then I remember and my stomach twists. My lunch threatens to make a reappearance.

I'm not sure what hurts more—that the only person in the world I trust betrayed me or that we're still not on speaking terms.

My shoulders tense. I miss her as much as I hate her.

"Hey." His voice cuts through the quiet room.

The deep, steady timbre makes my knees weak.

I nod my own hey and make my way to his table.

The woman with pink hair smiles at me. "Hi, I'm Willow." She offers her hand to shake. "We didn't mean to crash your... date. We just moved and um, we were picking up some stuff at Pete's place and he mentioned he was meeting someone here. It's not like we're spying. I swear. Just this place has the best mocha. Do you like chocolate?"

"Yes but not with coffee." I smile. She's obviously spying, but it seems like she has good intentions. "It's nice to meet you."

"Yeah. You too. It's nice to finally see Pete with someone... so um. Your dress is pretty. ModCloth?"

I nod.

The light haired guy laughs. "She means to say that it's nice seeing Pete with someone who isn't trashy."

"Tom! That's not it. And who the hell are you to talk?" She stammers. "Just... it's a really nice dress."

"Yeah, Aiden will be glad you're finally with a nice girl. He might shut up for a solid ten seconds." Tom scowls.

Pete cringes at the mention of this Aiden person. He clears his throat and points to Tom. "I'm sure you recognize Tom, my brother. He's known for his inability to mind his own business."

Tom mimes being stabbed in the gut. Willow laughs. Her gaze flits between her massive engagement ring and Tom. He stares at her with the same affection then his mischievous green eyes fix on me.

I know that look. It's the way I used to look at the guys who were interested in Madison. He's protective. Must be the older brother.

Though, come to think of it, the two of them look nothing alike.

Tom turns to Pete. "Did you get bored of casual sex or are you two meeting for an afternoon quickie?"

Pete looks at me. He raises a brow: *play along?*

I nod. I can deflect attention from nosy family members. I have a lot of practice.

"I have work tonight. I don't have much time with Pete, so we should really get going." I smile at Tom. "It's nice to meet you."

Willow takes the hint. "Yes. Enjoy your date. We were just leaving." She turns to Tom and whispers something in his ear.

He laughs and turns back to me. "Don't know what time you get off work, Jess, but I'll put you on the list for our show tonight. It's a soundtrack release party. Very exclusive. You should come." He laughs. "Well, I'm sure you'll *come*. But after that. If you want anything to do with Pete after he gets you off."

Willow shoots him a *don't start* look.

Tom slides his arm around her then makes eye contact with his brother. "Shit, this is fun. No wonder you assholes teased me so much about my whorish ways."

Willow rises to her tip toes to whisper in Tom's ear. Only it's not quite a whisper. "How about you get *me* off before my meeting?"

His eyes go wide. "Fuck yes." He smacks her ass playfully then pushes her to the door.

She giggles and throws me a goodbye wave. "Have fun."

The room quiets as the door shuts. The energy shifts. The playful, adorable couple is gone. It's just me and Pete and all the intensity in his stare.

"I'll put your name on the list," he says. "The club's a quick walk from your bar."

"I really do have work."

"We don't go on until ten." He motions to the menu. "What do you want?"

I wipe the sweat from my brow. "Something cold."

"Specifically?"

"Iced latte. Extra ice."

I need something freezing cold if I want any hope of spending the afternoon with him without melting into a pool of desire.

๑๕๑

THE OPTICAL SHOP IS JUST DOWN THE STREET.

Only it's closed. It's closed on Tuesdays.

Without a word of explanation, Pete pulls out his cell phone and taps a text message. He nods *I've got this*.

A moment later, there's a friendly sales associate unlocking the door. She smiles at Pete and shakes his hand eagerly.

"Mr. Steele, it's so nice to see you again. This must be your *friend*." She turns to me. "Jess, right?"

I nod. "Nice to meet you."

She doesn't introduce herself. "Let me know if you need any help. I'll be in the back finishing some bookkeeping." She blushes as her eyes meet Pete's, but she says nothing about it. "You can grab me once you've made your selection and I'll measure your prescription."

She disappears into the back room.

"You have the power to open closed retail stores?" I ask.

"I don't like to cause a scene when I shop," he says.

"So..."

"So I called ahead, promised I'd promote the place on social media."

"You do this every time you go shopping?"

"Only on occasion."

"You're a private guy for someone who fucks people in bar bathrooms."

His lips curl into a cocky smile. He's proud of himself. For the public sex or for getting that girl to scream at the top of her lungs? Hard to say. And contemplating the subject further will do nothing to cool me down.

I try to focus on the massive selection of glasses. There must be a thousand pairs in every shape and every color of the rainbow. I try a dozen, sorting them into noes and maybes.

Pete stays a few feet behind me, giving me space to browse.

My eyes catch his in the mirror. "What happened to that woman from yesterday?"

"She left when we were done."

"Do you—" I switch to a pair of rectangular frames. "Do that a lot."

He cocks a brow. "Depends on what you mean by *that*."

"Have one-night stands?"

"Last few months, yeah."

Usually, I avoid getting into other people's business. But I want to know more about him. "Can I ask you something personal?"

His voice is light, teasing. "If you look me in the eyes instead of looking at the mirror."

I turn and take a step towards him, so I'm close enough I can see all the details of his face. "It didn't seem like you were enjoying yourself."

"That's not a question."

"Were you enjoying yourself?"

He shrugs. "It was fine."

Just fine? That girl was screaming like she was having the best lay of her life.

My eyes catch his. I'd never, in a million years, ask anyone else this question, but I feel like I can talk to him. It's dangerous.

Again, I try to convince myself to pull back. It doesn't work. This tiny hint of intimacy feels good. I want more of it.

I stare back into his dark eyes. "Why didn't you enjoy it?"

"Wasn't good sex." Pete moves closer. His fingers brush my wrist. "There's sex where you're there, in the moment, all your attention on your partner, on the pleasure spreading over her face as she groans your name and rakes her nails across your back."

My knees go weak.

"Then there's sex where you show up, close your eyes, and stay in your head, focused on the idea of somebody." He leans in to whisper. "That woman wanted to fuck Pete Steele, famous bassist. She didn't give a shit about the actual guy, what I liked, what I wanted."

I swallow hard.

"I don't blame her. I knew what I was getting into. I made sure she came. But it wasn't good sex."

Holy fuck, can sex really be that good? I'm hot everywhere. I open my mouth to respond but my tongue refuses to move.

Okay. Glasses. Need to pick out glasses before I melt. I move to the next wall and try another twenty pairs. This time, I find three maybes.

"I do see your point." His voice softens. "I saw Miles and Tom fuck their way through fans and I swore to myself I'd never do that."

"Miles?"

"Our singer. But you already knew that."

My cheeks flush. Guilty as charged. Okay. Pete isn't bullshitting me. I won't bullshit him.

Somehow.

It must be possible to have an honest conversation that isn't couched in white lies that properly deflect attention.

"My sister has a crush on you," I say. I try to shrug off the tension forming in my shoulders but it doesn't work. It still hurts. "She talks about Sinful Serenade all the time. She has a dozen pictures of you on her wall."

"Anything good?"

"Good how?"

He cocks a brow and tugs his t-shirt an inch up his stomach. It's quick, a flash, but I can make out the v-lines just above his skinny jeans. Mmm.

"No. You're very modest. In photographs."

"Only in photographs?"

"I've known you for about twelve hours."

His stare is a playful challenge.

"You've mostly talked about what a good lay you are." My cheeks flush but I maintain most of my confidence. "I'm not saying you aren't, but—"

"You'd like to find out." It's a statement, not a question.

"Are you offering?"

He stares back at me. "I might."

My stomach flip-flops. It shouldn't upset me this much, him not offering to sleep with me. "What's stopping you?"

"Haven't decided if you're interested in me or my fame."

"What if I'm interested in your body and the other two don't matter to me?"

"That's cold, Jess, writing off my personality like that." He smiles but there's a hint of sadness in his eyes.

It's almost like he believes that I am writing off his personality, that I couldn't possibly be interested in anything besides his body or his fame.

He blinks and it's gone. Then he's close enough that I can't think anything.

His whisper sends goosebumps down my spine. "There's no question. We both know you're interested in my body."

Okay, that's as much confidence as I can muster for the afternoon. I bring my stacks of maybes to the counter in the center of the room and narrow it down to three pairs of glasses.

I try the pastel pink pair. It's pretty, sweet, feminine.

"Those are perfect," he says.

"My ex would always tell me not to wear girly stuff. That I needed to grow up."

"He sounds like an asshole."

"That's easy to say now that he's my ex. But I was with him a long time."

I was sure I loved him. That he loved me. He *was* an asshole, but he was charming too. Funny. He always could convince me he knew best, that he was looking out for me rather than trying to get his way.

Things were okay. Until I got into law school at USC. He asked me to choose—him or school. But he didn't even wait for me to answer him. Just started sleeping with my sister.

How could I have been so wrong about him?

My chest heaves as I exhale. I want to share this insight with Pete. It's not like me. Usually, I keep my feelings under lock and key.

It's safer that way.

I try to change the subject. "He was charming but he was a snob. Made fun of me for reading young adult. He couldn't stand that I had a poster of Katniss Everdeen in my room."

"Jess, I expect better from you. That's inexcusable. What kind of asshole doesn't love Katniss?"

I laugh. "You read YA?"

"I read everything." He cocks a brow. "Even the dirty stuff."

Another laugh escapes my lips. That flutter in my belly builds. I like him. Not because he's famous. Not because he's hot.

There's something about him, this steadiness to his voice, this confidence in his expression. I feel like I can be myself with him. It's dangerous, how much I want to reveal myself to him.

His eyes stay glued to mine. "You should read whatever you like. With all due respect, I've only known you twelve hours and I can tell you need to let your hair down."

"Should I come to your work and fuck a guy in the bathroom there?"

"Sure. But you're not going to shock anyone. I've heard every guy in the band and most of the people in the crew have sex."

"You wouldn't send a peon to break it up?"

"No, I'd listen. Nothing I like better than listening to a beautiful woman come."

My cheeks flush. He'd listen to me... That mental image returns—him pressing me against the bathroom wall, one hand digging into my hair, the other between my thighs.

Pete shakes his head. "Jess, if you're going to think about me naked, you could at least have the decency to describe the scenario to me."

Uh. I stammer something incomprehensible.

I suck down my iced coffee but it's no help cooling me off. I'm still melting. Better change the subject. "No, I, uh, I'm going to law school in the fall—" I cross my fingers. I know the gesture doesn't change the chances of my loan going through, but I'll take any ounce of luck—"and getting caught having sex in public is frowned upon."

"I'll make sure you don't get caught," he teases.

The flush spreads to my chest and stomach.

Must focus on picking out frames. That or I'm going to push him onto the couch in the corner, rip off his jeans, and take him right here.

Ahem. The pink glasses are cute. But are they too cute? I try them again and glance at Pete. "What do you think? Too librarian?"

"Sexy librarian."

"Really?"

"Yeah. Like you're gonna drag me to the erotica section and read aloud until I take you against the wall."

"You're trying to make me blush."

He shakes his head. "If I was trying to make you blush, I'd explain in detail."

"Go for it."

"You sure?"

I nod.

"I'd press you against the wall and take off your cardigan one button at a time. Then I'd tug your bra out of the way and drag my hands over your tits until you were licking your lips and groaning my name. I'd wait until you were begging to finally bring my mouth to your nipples."

My legs go weak.

He smiles. "Should I go on?"

"No thank you." Uhh... It takes me a solid minute to get my wits back. God damn, he's too fucking sexy. I can barely stand. Deep breath. I hold up my glasses. "I've decided. I want these."

He nods and calls the shopkeeper.

She pops out of the backroom and waves with a smile. "I can take your prescription back here whenever you're ready."

"Sure." I motion towards the back room.

He nods *go ahead*. His lips curl into a smile. "We'll have an hour to kill waiting for her to fill your prescription."

I nod.

"I have an idea about how to fill the time. I'll tell you when you're done."

Chapter Three

✦✦✦

I never thought I'd be so disappointed to eat ice cream.

We buy scoops at a shop across the street and take them to a beautiful park. The big yellow sun casts a glow over the half green, half brown grass.

The people here are as gorgeous as the scenery. It's not like Long Island. Everyone is fit with trendy clothes, fresh makeup, and recently styled hair.

I smooth my French braid reflexively. I'm sweating and my taped together glasses refuse to stay on my nose. I push them up but it does little good.

Pete leads me to a shaded spot under a tree. He sits, his back against the trunk, his legs spread wide with invitation.

I'm tempted to slide between them, to rest against his chest and soak in the comfort of a body against mine. It's lonely out here, by myself. Work has left me too tired to accept invitations to hang out. It's easier to stay home and read. Books never ask me to lie to them or stab me in the back.

Instead of giving in to my desire to mount Pete, I sit on

the grass. I take a generous bite of my mint chip ice cream. The sweet treat does nothing to refresh me.

My eyes fix on Pete. On his tongue specifically. It's fascinating watching him lick ice cream off the spoon.

He catches me staring.

I make the first excuse I can. "I've never tried that flavor. Green tea?"

He cocks a brow. "That's what you're thinking?"

I nod. He shakes his head playfully but doesn't press the subject.

Getting close is risky but I have to know more about him. I keep my eyes on his. "You've been sleeping around a lot."

"That a crime?"

"No. I'm curious. Do a lot of women act like the brunette did, interested in the idea of you?"

He nods.

"Any reason why you're sleeping around?"

"Wouldn't put it that way." Pete digs his spoon into his ice cream. "You didn't look me up?"

"No. Seemed rude. I can't quite remember the gossip. Didn't you have a serious girlfriend?"

He nods. "We broke up a few months ago."

"Oh." That explains a lot. "Is that why you're sleeping around, to get over her?"

"Close your eyes."

"Excuse me?"

He nods to his ice cream. "I want you focused on the taste."

"Sounds like a line."

"Don't need a line. You already want to fuck me."

I say nothing to confirm this.

He stares back at me with a demanding expression.

Okay, I'll play along. I close my eyes. My lips part of their own accord. My tongue waters with anticipation. There. The spoon slides into my mouth. The cold, creamy treat is delicious. It's rich with an earthy flavor.

I swallow the dessert, blink my eyes open, and stare back at Pete. He's trying to hide the pain in his expression but it's there, clear as day. As clear as mine.

What would it be like if we let the walls around our hearts down and had an honest conversation? I've never done that before. Not even with Madison. I was always trying to protect her from how bad things were with Dad.

I deflect or throw out white lies without thinking about it.

It's scary, telling Pete the whole truth and nothing but the truth. But there's something intoxicating about it.

I finish my ice cream and stare at the big, bright sun.

A voice breaks my concentration. It's high pitched, a girl about twelve or thirteen.

"Oh my Gosh!!! I... Are you really Pete Steele?" she squeals.

Pete is a good sport. He nods hello and extends his hand. "What's your name?"

"Alexandra." She smiles at him and thrusts her phone into his hand. "Will you sign this?"

"You get permission from your mom?" He nods to a twenty-something woman sitting on a park bench and staring at us.

"That's my nanny," the girl says. "And it's fine. Please."

He pulls a marker from his jeans, signs her phone case, and hands the device back.

The girl stays put. She motions to me, clasps her hands together, and squeals. "Is this your girlfriend?"

Pete's lips curl into a smile. He looks at me and raises an eyebrow. *Play along?* The girl is excited. I'll play along.

I smile at the girl. "Yes. But it's a secret."

"Why?" she asks.

"Her father doesn't approve," Pete says. "You can keep a secret?"

"Of course," the girl squeals. She continues to stare at us. "She's really pretty."

My cheeks flush. Kids her age are not usually so complimentary. "Thank you."

"If she's your girlfriend, you should kiss her," she says.

Pete laughs. "Alexandra, you should be a lawyer one day. Like Jess. She's going to law school. And she's shy."

This does not please Alexandra.

"No, she's right." My cheeks flush. "You need evidence to support your claim."

"Future lawyers have to stick together?" He raises a brow.

I nod. Yes, that's my testimony. It has nothing to do with how badly I want him kissing me.

My heart thuds against my chest. My stomach flutters.

His hand slides around my neck. He's actually going to kiss me.

Pete's fingers dig into my skin as he pulls me closer. The strength of his touch erases every other thought in my brain.

His lips brush against mine.

Every nerve in my body fires at once. His lips are soft, sweet, and slightly sticky. He tastes like that green tea ice cream. And underneath that is something that is just Pete.

My hand digs into his thigh, into the fabric of his jeans. Heat collects between my legs.

But he pulls back. It's nothing. Barely more than a peck.

I want more.

I want him kissing me again, kissing me like he means it.

A lightness spreads through my chest. It's a terrifying thought—asking him to go home with me—but it's exhilarating too.

Alexandra blushes and runs back to her nanny.

He shifts back into his seat. "You made her day."

"*You* made her day." I play with my spoon, stirring the melting chocolate into the melting ice cream. "My friend back home, Kathryn, she has a lot of boyfriends. A new one every few months. Once I asked her why and she said 'the best way to get over someone is to get under someone else.'"

"I'd rather be on top."

My cheeks flush. "Really?"

He nods. "I can list my favorite positions if you'd like."

He smiles, reveling in my nervousness.

God, it's hot today. I shift into the shade but that puts me six inches from Pete. It doesn't help cool me down.

"Your friend sounds like Miles, our singer." Pete shakes his head. "You'd like him. He was going to be a lawyer."

"He's the one who tattooed his girlfriend's name on his chest?"

Pete sticks his tongue out in distaste. "You secretly a stalker fan?"

"My sister cried for a week."

"I thought I was her favorite." He winks. "Don't tease me like this, Jess. You're going to wound my fragile ego."

"Would you get a tattoo of a woman's name?"

"No." He leans towards me. "You have any tattoos?"

"None."

"Mine, I felt them, here—" He presses his palm against his chest, over his heart. "Knew I needed them. Felt it in my soul."

"You didn't feel your ex in your soul?"

"Never." His eyes cloud with something I can't place. His gaze goes to the grass, his brow furrowing with concentration. Then he's looking at me again. "You know all this gossip because your sister is a fan?"

"Yeah."

He raises a brow, assessing the veracity of my claim. He

must believe me because he nods. "You want to make her jealous?"

"We're not on speaking terms."

"Why?"

"That's personal." My stomach tenses. I want to stop thinking about her. I want my old life to feel like it's three thousand miles away.

He pulls his phone from his pocket. "You don't need to speak to her for this. You just need to trust me."

I scan his face for a clue to his intention but he's still a mystery.

"Jess, Jess, Jess." Pete shakes his head in mock outrage. "You seem like such a nice girl, but I see it in your eyes. You want to make her green with envy."

"Maybe."

"Do you trust me?" he unlocks his phone and opens the camera app.

I don't know him. I shouldn't trust him as much as I do.

The intensity in his eyes spurs me on.

I nod. "Yes."

Pete turns the phone to selfie mode and angles it towards us. His other hand goes behind my neck. This time, he's not delicate. He's not holding back. His fingers dig into my hair. They press against the back of my head as he pulls me into a kiss. His lips brush mine. Then his lips are parting, and mine are parting too.

His tongue slides into my mouth.

Then he's pulling back. It's only a taste. A hint.

It's not enough. I need more.

He looks into my eyes. "Here." His fingers go to my temples, curl around the edges of my glasses. He pulls them off and sets them on the ground behind him. Then his eyes are back on mine, staring into mine.

My eyelids press together. Yes. More. Now. Please. I need

this tall, dark, handsome stranger erasing every worry in my brain. I need his lips on me, his hands on me, his cock...

One thing at a time.

He pulls me into his lap. My knees plant outside his hips. They're muddy instantly, but I don't care. For once, I don't care about consequences. Only about how intoxicating Pete is.

He presses his palm between my shoulder blades. Heat floods the spot. Then his lips are on mine, his tongue is sliding around mine, and I'm hot everywhere. I clutch at his shoulders. My fingers dig into the cotton fabric of his t-shirt.

I was with Nathan for three years. We kissed a lot. And there were guys before—boyfriends in high school.

It was never like this.

Never close to this.

I'm panting and desperate when Pete releases me. His hands go to his sides. He leaves his phone on the ground. All of his attention is on me. The intensity of his deep brown eyes makes my thighs shake.

If that's how he kisses...

Having sex with him might actually kill me.

He brushes a stray hair behind my ear. "You want her even more jealous?"

Invite me back to your place. Hell, invite me to the backseat of your car. To the bathroom at that coffee shop. Tell me to skip work and spend the night coming with you. Anything. Anywhere.

I nod. Yes. I need this, need to forget everything except our bodies for a while.

If he doesn't ask, I will.

He stares into my eyes. "Play my girlfriend."

Chapter Four

❧

Play my girlfriend.

The sun is still shining. The breeze is still blowing. The air is still warm.

And Pete's eyes are still intense and impenetrable.

Play his girlfriend... that's ridiculous.

"You don't need anyone to play your girlfriend." I grab my glasses and shift off of him, suddenly apathetic to staining my dress with dirt or grass. There. I stare back at him as I slide my frames on. "You're rich, famous, and handsome. You could find a girlfriend in thirty seconds flat."

"I don't want a relationship."

Okay... "Why not hire a professional?"

His expression gets intense. "I'll make it worth your while."

My head is spinning. I try to tell myself to run a million miles away but my legs won't move. "What would it even mean? How would I play your girlfriend?"

"We tell everyone we started dating a few weeks ago, that we're just now making it official. I'll take care of everything you need. You'll come with me to all the events where I have to make an appearance."

I try to think up a response as he pushes himself to his feet. Nothing comes. God, he's so tall. I rise to meet him. Even in my wedges, I have to look up at him.

He moves close enough to whisper. Instantly, my senses are overwhelmed. All the nerves in my body make the same demand for his lips.

His breath warms my ear. "Tell me what you want, and I'll make it happen."

My thoughts crash together. Every night, I fall asleep worried about how I'll pay for law school. Then there's rent, food, transportation.

There's no way I'm going to find this kind of money elsewhere.

It would be stupid to refuse. Taking advantage of him is selfish, but don't I deserve a chance to be selfish for once in my life? He's offering. I can say yes.

I try to push the words to my mouth. *If you pay my tuition.* But my stomach clenches up. I can't take his money.

My knees go weak. It's a struggle to take a step backwards. "I don't know. I need to sleep on it." I need to figure out some better way to make school work. Something besides lying.

After ten years of lying for Dad, I barely know who I am. I finally have a semblance of a backbone. I can't throw that away.

"Your glasses." He motions to the optical shop.

"I, uh, I'll get them later. I need to get home and change for work."

"I'll give you a ride."

His eyes fill with vulnerability. Then he blinks and it's gone.

What the hell does he need me playing his girlfriend for?

I want to know. I want to know everything about him. Maybe there's some way to agree to this. To make it fair for both of us.

I'll try to figure it out. After my thoughts settle down.

I take another step backwards. "I'm in the mood to walk. Alone."

He nods with understanding.

I turn and get the hell out of there as fast as I can.

☙❧

TWO HOURS INTO MY SHIFT, I SNEAK INTO THE BACK ROOM to check my loan status on my cell.

I stare at the screen as the page reloads.

Damn. Pending.

It might not go through.

My stomach drops. I don't know what I'll do if I have to wait another year for law school. That will prove Nathan right. Prove to my mom that I'm another stupid woman who let a guy get in the way of her dreams.

If I'd studied harder, got better grades, I could have gotten a better scholarship.

For a second, I consider asking Dad for money. He makes a good living. But that would come with strings. I'd have to be the person he wants me to be. I'd have to go back to lying to hide his drinking.

I slide my phone into my pocket and take a few deep breaths. I've always wanted to be a lawyer. I don't want to keep waiting for my life to start.

I need to find a way to pay for school. And I'd love to spend more time with Pete. But how is lying for him different than lying for Dad?

Where the hell will I be in all that?

"Jess." Rick's voice booms through the backroom. He's irritated.

Great. I brush a few stray hairs behind my ears and make my way to Rick.

He's standing behind the bar, pouring a Moscow mule into a copper mug. His eyes are fixed on a pretty redhead. Not the one from last night. A new one.

Guy has a type. I'll give him that much.

His gaze stays on her chest as he talks to me. "Your boyfriend is here. He needs to buy a drink or get lost."

My boyfriend? "I don't have a boyfriend."

"Don't lie, sweetie, you're not the first waitress to have a quickie in the backroom. I don't care. It's slow. Chat if you want. As long as he buys a drink." Rick nods to a table in the corner.

Pete is sitting there, his eyes fixed on me.

I offer Rick my best customer service smile. "Of course, sir." It *is* my job to sell drinks. "Did you assign the Friday shift yet?"

"Yeah, gave it to Christina. She needs the cash."

"I need the cash too," I say.

"You'll get the next one." He motions to Pete. "Now, Jess."

Okay, there's no arguing with Rick when he's in *I'm taking this woman home* mode.

Pete is sitting in a black vinyl booth. It matches him— black t-shirt, black skinny jeans, black converse. Hell, he's even wearing black eyeliner.

It should be a crime, looking that good in eyeliner.

It should be a crime, looking that good, period.

His lips curl into a smile. The joy spills over his expression. His cheeks crinkle. His eyes brighten. There's even something different about his posture—more relaxed.

"You're staring," he teases.

My stomach flutters. "You're wearing eyeliner. It looks good." The guys I know back home wouldn't be caught dead in eyeliner. They're missing out, really. He looks fucking yummy.

"Stage makeup," he says.

"So you don't wear it normally?"

"Sometimes." He looks up at me. "You okay, Jess? You're bright red."

I let out a nervous laugh. "You must have steady hands. That line is even." Okay, so I want an excuse for why I'm staring at his dark eyes. They're inviting, deep. I want to drink them in.

He cocks a brow. "That's what you're thinking of my hands doing?"

The flush in my cheeks spreads to my chest as I think of his hands doing something much more exciting.

He shakes his head with mock outrage. "Jess, we covered this. If you're gonna imagine me touching you, you need to describe it to me."

"Uhhh." I swallow hard. "Rick, my boss. He thinks you're my boyfriend."

Pete stares at me like he's looking for meaning in my eyes. "Convenient you're already selling that story."

"No, I haven't decided."

He nods.

"But uh... he wants you to order a drink or leave."

"Whiskey, rocks."

"Well or call?"

He names an expensive brand. I motion *just a minute* then check all my tables on the way to my bar.

Rick is protective about the top shelf stuff. I repeat the request to him instead of pouring it myself. For once, he looks at me. He nods his approval of my supposed boyfriend.

Pete's eyes are still fixed on me. He's frustratingly unreadable, especially from a distance.

It's almost like he's checking me out.

Not almost. He is. When I adjust my much too tight skirt, his lips part with a sigh of desire.

I'm pear shaped to the extreme—not a lot of boob, very much in the way of butt. Usually, I'm self-conscious about my round bottom but the way he's staring makes me feel utterly perfect.

"Drinks up." Rick nudges me. His attention goes back to the pretty woman who is flirting with him.

With my most confident posture, I bring the drink to Pete.

He nods a thank you, takes a sip, and sets the beverage down. He motions to the plastic case on the table. "Your glasses."

"Thanks." I reach for them. "I should go."

"Try them first. Want to make sure they fit."

"In case I decide I never want to see you again?"

His voice is steady, even. "Would be a shame if you decided that before I got to hear you come."

My cheeks flush. I look to his expression for a sign he's playing with me, but there's nothing but desire in his eyes.

I want to say yes to his offer. I want more time around him. But is it really worth going back to lying to the world?

Pete motions to the booth. "Sit down."

Given the way Rick is flirting, I have plenty of time before I have to do another pass around the bar.

I sit close enough my knee brushes Pete's. The fabric of his jeans is rough against my bare skin. It sends shivers up my spine.

He turns so we're face to face. His fingers brush my temples as he pulls my glasses off. "You have beautiful eyes."

"Thank you." I swallow hard. There's something intoxicating about him. I want to soak it up.

He opens the case, takes out my new glasses and unfolds them. His eyes fix on mine as he slides my new glasses on.

His touch is gentle, caring, like we're old lovers instead of near strangers.

His fingertips brush my chin on their way to his lap.

This is a better prescription. I can see more details in his face. The flecks of honey in his dark eyes. The strong line of his jaw. The soft curve of his upper lip.

"You're staring," he says.

"Checking my new prescription."

He laughs, cocking his brow like he finds my claim implausible. "What's the verdict?"

His expression shifts, serious. He's not asking about the glasses. He's asking about the offer.

Right now, staring into his eyes, I want to say yes more than I want anything.

It's dangerous, how desperate I am to wipe his pain away.

I take a deep breath. I can't afford to say no. Even if I'm not sure I can live with saying yes. "I'm thinking about it."

I stare back into his eyes. They're vulnerable. Why does he need this lie? It doesn't make any sense. He's handsome enough he could find a girlfriend in thirty seconds flat, even without the whole wealthy celebrity thing going on. Even without the whole clearly a sex God thing going on.

I drop my voice to a whisper. "I need the money."

"You're starting law school in the fall."

I nod. "My scholarship only covers half my tuition. I'm trying for loans for the other half plus living expenses, but so far, I haven't had any luck."

He stares back with understanding.

Still my stomach clenches. "I don't want to take advantage of your situation."

"I have more money than I'll ever need."

"I don't want to lie to people."

"You like me."

I nod.

"I like you. It's not a lie. More of an exaggeration."

"It's a lie." I push myself back. My fingertips dig into my thighs. "Don't argue semantics with a lawyer to be. We'll be at it all night."

His lips curl into a half smile. "You don't want to go at it all night with me?"

Mmm. That flutter builds below my stomach. I do. But not enough to concede his point. I keep my voice low. "It is a lie."

"Yeah. But it won't hurt anyone."

"How do you know?"

He says nothing. That vulnerability flares in his eyes. He blinks and it's gone.

I can't decide until I have all the information. I press my palms together. "Why do you need a girlfriend?"

"Fame bullshit."

"That's not an explanation."

"It's complicated. A lot of egos that need stroking."

My cheeks flush. "You're trying to make me blush."

"You blush easy. I don't have to try *hard*."

My stomach flutters. "You're doing it again."

He smiles. "Yeah. I like a responsive woman."

God, how I want to be responsive with him. "You're a tease, aren't you?"

"Yeah. Should I keep going?"

I shake my head and check Rick's position again. He's still flirting.

If I agree to Pete's offer, I can quit this job. I can eat salmon for dinner every night. I can buy more cacti for my mini garden. Hell, I can even buy an air conditioner for my apartment.

It's tempting.

Is there really anything worse than missing out on law school?

"I get that you don't know me. That I don't know you. How about we ask each other a few questions," he says.

"Okay." That's reasonable. "You can go first."

"What's your favorite book?"

"Really? That's your question?"

He nods. "Want to make sure I still like you as my girlfriend."

"Isn't it pretend?"

"Guy's got to have standards."

I laugh. "And what book deems me unworthy?"

He smiles. "Can't tell you before you answer."

"*The Hunger Games* by a landslide. You?"

"*Jurassic Park*."

"Dinosaurs and man not knowing his own limitations. Not bad. Popcorn but not bad."

He cocks a brow. "Oh and *The Hunger Games* isn't popcorn?"

"Insult Katniss again and you're getting an instant no."

His laugh lights up his face. My heart sings. God damn, that's a nice laugh.

"You have your own standards." He smiles. "I appreciate that."

Mmm. Such a nice smile. I bite my lip, trying to get my thoughts to rearrange themselves into something I can work with. "You don't seem like you do things other people want."

"Not usually."

"So tell me the truth. Why do you need a fake girlfriend?"

His expression softens. It's earnest. He's thinking. He's going to tell me.

"It's complicated. Basically, my manager likes to throw his weight around. This is his current project. He's threatening to bury our next album if I don't agree."

"Oh."

"You won't be taking advantage. You can find money a million places. I can't find anyone like you."

"You barely know me."

"I know enough."

"Hey!" The guy at the next table over waves. "Aren't you in some band?"

Pete frowns. He shakes his head. "No."

The guy shrugs it off and goes back to his conversation.

Pete turns to me, his expression softening again.

He leans in close enough to whisper. "Whatever you decide, come to the show. I want to feel you come on my hand."

Chapter Five

✦❧✦

The music pours onto the crowded sidewalk. It's not Sinful Serenade. It's another band, one that is all over the Los Angeles alternative rock radio station, KROQ.

There must be a hundred fans who want in the club. The show is open to the public, but from the frustrated looks, I'm guessing there are a lot of people here without tickets.

I smooth my pink, fit and flare cocktail dress, and brush my hair behind my ears. This is the nicest outfit I own. My makeup is on point. I can go up to that bouncer and tell him I'm on the list. No problem.

Deep breath.

I dig into my purse and pull out my ID, then I march to the burly bouncer. He looks me up and down, assessing my potential. It's the same way I look at people who seem out of place at the bar. Not a good sign.

"I should be on the list," I say. "Jess James. Uh, Jessica technically." I show him my ID.

He looks to the clipboard in his hands then to my ID

then back to me. "You're in the VIP section. Stairs are on the right side of the club." He points to the door.

I'm in the VIP section.

How the hell am I in the VIP section?

The club is packed. It looks like it's meant to hold about three hundred people. There must be double that tonight. There are four guys playing on the small stage. I don't recognize them—I can't say I'm up on the alternative rock scene—but I've heard this song a hundred times.

The guys are cast in bright white stage lights. Except for soft purple lamps lining the walls, the rest of the room is dark.

Downstairs is a big dance floor and it's packed. I move around the edges of the club until I find the floating glass staircase.

I take careful steps. My balance in these wedges is questionable at best.

There's another slightly less burly bouncer guarding the VIP area. This time, I say nothing. I simply hold out my ID. He nods, looks to his clipboard, and lets me pass.

Damn. Upstairs is a lot more sparse—people sit at couches and arm chairs instead of packing onto a throbbing dance floor—but it makes up for it in sheer volume of beautiful people. A handful of teen soap stars, a top 40 pop-punk band, and a very famous lingerie model.

Suddenly, my department store dress and my comfort brand wedges feel insufficient. And to think I assumed a soundtrack release party would be full of people in band t-shirts and jeans. Downstairs, that's true. But up here, I'm clearly under-dressed.

"Hey, Jess!" Someone calls me over. Someone in the corner. Oh, it's Willow.

She's in Tom's lap and she's beaming. The girl couldn't be happier to see me.

How am I supposed to lie to her?

I nod a hello and walk over.

It's just her, Tom, and a tall, tattooed guy with dark hair and piercing blue eyes. He's not in Sinful Serenade.

"Sit, sit." Willow pats the cushion next to hers. "Pete is talking to someone about—" She turns back to Tom. "What was he talking about?"

Tom laughs. He stares at her with every ounce of love and affection in the world. "He and Drew are fighting over the setlist."

"Pete doesn't fight. I call shenanigans," she says.

The blue-eyed stranger clears his throat. His piercing eyes fix on me. "Jess, I take it?"

I nod. "Yes."

He extends his hand. "Ethan. Nice to meet you."

We shake. His piercing eyes pass over me. He's handsome. Incredibly handsome. The full sleeves of tattoos don't hurt. His lips curl into a cocky smile.

"You know that's Pete's girl," Tom says. "You better watch it."

I'm already Pete's girl? That's why they're being so nice. How would they feel if they knew it was all a bunch of bullshit?

There's no way they'd be this nice.

They might hate me as much as I hate Madison.

"Since when?" Ethan cocks a brow. "Saw him taking home a different girl last week."

Tom shoots Ethan a glare.

Ethan shrugs. He looks back to me. "Better to find that out sooner rather than later. Trust me on that."

I nod. "Been there, done that. I swore off men until recently."

The three of them are still looking at me expectantly, waiting for me to clarify the Pete x Jess relationship status.

"Uh... we're not labeling things." I smooth my dress. It's not technically a lie, but it's certainly not the truth, the whole truth, and nothing but the truth.

Willow's eyes light up. Tom is equally excited. I'm not sure why these two people are so invested in Pete's relationship status. Whatever the reason, I don't like the way my stomach is churning over this half-truth.

Ethan turns back to Willow. "Let me see that rock again."

She giggles and holds out her engagement ring. "Isn't it gorgeous?"

"Expensive." He looks up at Tom. "Fuck. Almost wish I hadn't dropped out of—what we were called—"

"Agents of Orange," Tom says. "Why you playing humble? Dangerous Noise is burning up the charts. You'll be bigger than us soon."

Ethan laughs. "Bigger than Sinful Serenade? Doubtful."

Tom looks to Willow with affection in his eyes. "We're old and ready to settle down."

He and Willow exchange a sweet kiss. Then they're both looking at her engagement ring.

Jeez. Do people really get this mushy? There's no sign they're faking it. Who would they be trying to convince?

Ethan looks to me. "They're cute enough to make you sick, huh?"

"You don't like it?"

"Never thought I'd see Tom settle down. Means I have to pick up the slack, but I'm game."

So Tom was a slut and Ethan is a slut now. Nothing wrong with that. It's sensible really, never getting close enough to anyone that their betrayal will tear your heart in half.

Ethan scans the room. "Where is your boy?" He looks at me like he's considering me as a potential hookup.

He's cute, but he's no Pete.

"I don't know," I say. "How do you know Tom?"

He looks to me. "I was in one of the Steele brothers' bands back in high school."

He leans to Tom and whispers something in his ear.

Tom shrugs. "Not sure, but I wouldn't test him."

Ethan whispers something.

"Your funeral," Tom says.

Ethan nods to someone behind me. It's Pete. He's talking to one of the models. My cheeks flare. She's gorgeous with miles of legs and a tiny, toned lower half. A tiny, toned everything actually.

It doesn't make sense. He can ask some model/actress to play his girlfriend. She'll be used to the constant scrutiny. She'll benefit from any media attention.

The weight on the couch shifts as Ethan sits next to me. It's a little closer than platonic. Okay, I can put the pieces together. He's trying to see if Pete will get jealous.

It's incredibly immature, I know, but I want to know if it will work. If Pete has any interest in me beyond as his faux girlfriend.

I nod a *go for it* to Ethan.

He scoots a little closer as he hails Pete over. "Hey, Steele. You ever showing up to this party?"

Pete turns towards us. His eyes catch mine and stay there. It's like the model disappears. The way he's looking at me, I'm sure he's not interested in any of the other women in the room.

My cheeks flush. My breath picks up.

"You look amazing." He slides onto the couch and hugs me hello.

My lungs empty. It's the first time he's really hugged me. It's the first real hug I've had in a while—my family doesn't hug—and it makes me warm all over.

For a moment, all the sounds and sights of the club fade

away. I feel nothing but Pete's arms around me, his hard chest against mine, his breath on my neck.

When he pulls away he shoots Ethan a *get lost* look.

Ethan moves to an empty chair with a smile. He's an instigator. I can tell.

He and Tom exchange a series of meaningful looks. I'm not sure how to parse them, but it's clear they're referring to us.

This lie is a big deal.

"Ethan give you trouble?" Pete slides his arm around my waist protectively.

"No. I was about to get some dirt about what you were like in high school out of him," I say.

Pete pulls me closer.

Ethan laughs. "Steele is secretive. Not sure I have much. Besides the emo glasses."

"Damn. I miss the emo glasses," Tom says.

Tom and Ethan spar. I can't say that their conversation interests me. Not with Pete's body next to mine.

His hand slides to the curve of my ample hips. Mmm. The fabric of my dress is thin enough that I can feel all the heat from his palm. He smells good. I bet he tastes better.

My head fills with all sorts of delicious mental images. I want to take him up on his offer.

Once I've decided what I'm going to do.

If I can get over how awful I feel lying to his friends.

A nasally voice cuts through the room. "You're due backstage now Tom. Mr. Steele."

Immediately, Pete pulls back. His posture stiffens. His eyes flare with frustration.

"Why am I never Mr. Steele?" Tom's voice is half teasing, half tense.

They're looking at a short, balding man with a ponytail.

He's wearing a too tight suit in a shade of bright blue straight out of the 1980s.

"Cause you've got no class, Sticks." Pete's trying to joke but he's not selling it.

He stands. I stand too. It's a reflex, mirroring his movements. I do the math again—it will be a solid half an hour before we can be alone.

Pete motions to the ponytail guy. "Jess, this is our manager, Aiden."

The guy throwing his weight around. I study him in hopes of finding enough clarity to decide. There's something slimy about him. He's not a trustworthy person.

He seems like the kind of guy who makes due on threats just because.

"Nice to meet you." He leers at me as we shake. His gaze turns back to Pete. "Glad we're on the same page."

Tom's ears perk. His expression hardens. "What was that?"

"About the setlist," Pete says. "Drew wanted to test our new song."

Tom isn't buying this but he says nothing on the matter.

Aiden leers at me again. His gaze is slimy. He's judging my T&A. He nods, deeming it acceptable.

Gross.

He keeps his gaze on my ass as he speaks to Pete. "Glad you didn't go the model route. It's more—"

"Yeah. Jess has a fantastic ass," Pete says. "I understand why you want to stare, but she's mine. I get a little protective."

His glare says *back the fuck off.*

Aiden smirks, somehow pleased about this turn of events.

Pete turns to me with a forced smile. He opens his mouth like he's about to speak. Instead, he pulls me into a kiss.

Mmm. I'm sure it's for the sake of slime-ball Aiden, but it

still feels good. I soak in the taste of Pete's lips. The feel of his tongue in my mouth. He moans with pleasure as his palm presses against my ass.

He really does find it fantastic.

"Break a leg," I breathe.

He nods goodbye and follows Aiden towards the upstairs stage entrance. Tom joins them a moment later. The brothers whisper over something but they both keep calm expressions.

Chapter Six

ish

Willow scoots next to me. "You do have a nice ass." She laughs. "I see a lot of them. I'm a photographer. Mostly shoot boudoir."

"Oh. Thanks." I guess.

"I'm all shoulders." She motions to her small hips. "But, uh..."

Ethan laughs. "Everything Tom says about you is true." He turns to me. "Think she wants to say that Pete looked like he was gonna take you in front of all of us."

"I would not talk about him that way," Willow protests. "He's like a brother."

"No, your brother is a lot more protective." Ethan turns to me. "Willow's brother, Drew, is the Sinful Serenade guitarist. Actually, he was the original Dangerous Noise guitarist."

"Don't talk about how you're better than he is," Willow says. "I don't need him in a mood."

Ethan laughs. "Sometimes, the truth hurts." He turns back to me. "Where is your brother's girl?"

"She went backstage with him," Willow says.

Ethan raises a brow. "So he was warming up his hands the fun way."

"Gross. Don't." Willow turns bright red.

"It works." He winks at me. "Should work just as well for Pete. I'll give him the tip."

I turn the same bright red shade.

They're both incredibly friendly. Like I'm already part of the family, all by virtue of being Pete's potential girlfriend.

Will they stay friendly if I call this off? If I go through with it and we break up? I thought Nathan's friends were my friends. But after everything happened, they took his side. Didn't even consider that he cheated on me.

Only person I can still stand to talk to is Kathryn.

There's no way they'll be this friendly if they find out I'm deceiving them.

"Sorry, Aiden is gross," Willow says. "I shouldn't repeat gossip but... steer clear and you'll be okay."

I nod.

Ethan and Willow go back to teasing. From the sound of things, he's close with Tom and Pete.

The stage goes dark. Everyone in the room goes quiet. Then, like a burst, the lights go on, and Sinful Serenade starts playing.

The crowd goes insane. All conversation upstairs ceases. Everyone in this place must be cheering. The band plays their award winning mega-hit, *No Way in Hell*.

All the light is on the handsome, blue-eyed singer, Miles. The man croons. He sells every single line. Even with his hand wrapped around the mic, his emotionality at 11, he has all his attention turned on the crowd. He's a hell of a frontman.

When the song ends. He moves towards the front of the stage. He waves at half a dozen girls. I swear, I hear fainting.

"Been a while since we played LA. You miss us?" he teases.

The crowd cheers and screams.

He turns to the back of the stage, to Tom at his drum kit, and he motions *come here.*

Tom stands. He looks to the crowd, raising a brow dramatically and teasing pulling up his t-shirt.

And then the shirt is gone. Miles shakes his head but he's smiling.

"You hear the tragic news?" Miles asks the crowd. "Tom Steele is now engaged."

The crowd is a mix of cheers, awws, and boos.

Willow giggles. She grabs my hand like it's a reflex. Wow. We're fast friends. Or she's that excited about her engagement. It's sweet, really, how transparent she is about her love.

Tom too. He's looking in our direction, squinting like he can't make anything out. No doubt, the stage lights are far too bright for those details.

He blows her a kiss anyway. She squeals and blows back.

My attention goes to Pete. He's standing on one side of the stage, his guitar strap tugging his t-shirt down enough to expose a lot of chest. Mmm. He looks grander on stage. A presence. There's something inviting about him. But it's not like Miles or Tom. He isn't welcoming the crowd in.

He's like a cat. He's there. And I want his attention all the more because I don't have enough of it.

Miles is an engaging performer but my focus stays on Pete.

When the next song starts, he shifts into this amazing concentration. He's damn sexy playing, lost in music. He looks up, moves towards the front of the stage like he's teasing the crowd.

Girls cheer. They want him. Hard to blame them, but, tonight he's mine.

Then he's back, lost in the music again. I watch his shoulders flex and relax, his hands speed over his bass, his hips shift in time with the music.

Mmm. Those hips.

Damn. It's not like he's the only sexy guy in the band. I force myself to take a moment to watch each of them. Miles is already without his shirt, clawing at his tattooed chest like he can't help but touch himself. Tom plays his drums like a God damn animal.

And the guitarist—must be Drew—is intense, focused, and playful at the same time. His arms are thick with tattoos, his dark hair is short, his tight jeans show off a sculpted lower body.

I went to a Sinful Serenade show once with Madison. How did I not notice how hot these guys were? It was the night before finals. I was distracted, but still... how could I not have seen the way Pete's hips and hands and lips move?

৩৫৩

ETHAN DISAPPEARS IN THE MIDDLE OF THE THIRD SONG. My attention stays fixed on Pete until the band finally takes their leave.

A few minutes later, he's back. Tom too. And there's another couple with them—the tattooed guitarist and a short, curvy woman in a gorgeous cream dress. She's completely clean cut except for the tattoo of an ornate key on her shoulder.

She squeezes his hand. Oh, there it is. Another shiny rock. So she's his fiancée. They are a cute couple. He slides his arm around her waist protectively, pulling her body into his.

I bite my lip, trying not to get ahead of myself wishing Pete would touch me like that. Falling for him is out of the question. Falling for him is a surefire path to my heart being torn to shreds.

Pete joins me on the couch. He nods to the guitarist. "Drew—" then to the pretty twenty-something woman, "Kara, this is Jess. My *friend*."

My shoulders relax. The truth is such a relief.

"Oh. Of course." Kara beams as she shakes my hand. "Nice to meet you. It's great that you could come to the show."

Why does everyone keep looking at me like they're already sure I'm Pete's girlfriend?

His fingertips skim the edge of my skirt. It makes it difficult to think about anything but coming on his hand.

"You want to get out of here, Kendrick?" Drew pulls Kara into a tight embrace.

"That's her last name," Pete whispers. "It's their thing. Don't ask."

"After I see the ring." She bounces to Willow. "Show me again."

"You picked it out," Tom says.

"Exactly! Need to see if it looks as gorgeous as it did in my mind." Kara takes a long moment to check out the ring then she whispers something in Willow's ear.

Willow laughs. Motions *go*. Then Kara and Drew nod a series of goodbyes and descend the stairs.

It's bizarre, being surrounded by this much affection. Even before the divorce, my parents hated each other. I've never seen two people so happy in love.

It stirs something inside of me, this empty spot that wants to be filled. There's no one in the world I trust. The only two people I love are Dad and Madison and I can't talk about my feelings with either of them.

Madison doesn't care that she hurt me. Dad still expects me to lie for him.

My eyes find Pete's. There's an earnestness to his expression. I feel like I can trust him. Like I can talk to him.

That might be worth lying to everyone else.

His hand slides under my skirt. My thoughts fade away. My shoulders and back relax. I want to feel the way I did at the park, like there's nothing in the world but the two of us.

Sex first. Decision second.

I lean in to whisper. "Do we have to stay to talk?"

"Have to clear something with Aiden but I can do it *after*."

Mmm. After. I nod. "Yes please."

"Yes please, what?"

I can hear the smile in his voice. "Yes, please... will you... Do I have to say it?"

He chuckles. "I'll get you there."

His fingertips skim my thighs as he pulls his hand back to his lap. He pulls back enough he can stare into my eyes. I still can't figure out what the expression in his deep brown eyes means, but damn if I don't like staring into them.

They're gorgeous eyes.

That vulnerability returns. He blinks and it's gone. I shift backwards, breaking his touch. But it's too loud to think. Ethan's band Dangerous Noise is in the middle of their first song.

They're good. Ethan is quite the attention whore on stage. He holds up his guitar, tugging at the bottom of his t-shirt, teasing the audience with the promise to strip.

The audience likes it.

Pete stands and pulls me to my feet. He nods to Tom and Willow. "Excuse us."

Tom raises a brow. "This is a classy place."

Pete nods.

Willow whispers something in Tom's ear.

He smiles. "After Dangerous Noise."

"You have too many pet projects," she says.

"You work eighty hours a week, kid."

"Sixty," she protests.

Tom motions for us to go. He pulls Willow into his lap and runs his hands through her short hair.

Pete slides his arm around my hips, pulling my body next to his. It's almost like he's tense over the happy couple's PDA. But that doesn't make any sense. He's not looking at Willow with any kind of romantic or sexual interest.

The man is an enigma. I want to know more.

He leads me to the back of the VIP area. There's a roped off area with a NO ENTRANCE sign. He scans the room. A cocktail waitress has her eyes on us. More likely, she has her eyes on him. She licks her lips hungrily.

He could easily take her home. But he looks at her with apathy. He doesn't want her. He doesn't want any of the gorgeous models in this place.

He wants me.

Pete leans in to whisper. "Wait for me on the balcony. I'll lose her." He motions to the closed door in the corner of the roped off area.

He wants to do this on a balcony? Damn. First the bar bathroom then this. He has a thing for public sex.

I should say no. I'm going to be a lawyer. I can't get caught having sex in public.

I try to force the word to my lips but it refuses. "What if we get caught?"

"This is private property. They'll ask us to leave. That will be it." His eyes meet mine. "We can hold off till we get back to your place."

I shake my head. I don't want to hold off. I want him. Now.

I trust his assessment of the situation.

"No. Let's do it now," I say.

He nods.

I wait for him to grab the waitress's attention and I sneak past the velvet rope. The door to the balcony is frosted glass. You can't see in or out. I turn the handle and check my footing. All good.

We're overlooking the alley. No one can see us, not from the street, not from the club.

No one is going to catch us. Not on camera—it's too dark for that.

Thoughts swirl around my brain. I like Pete. Find him interesting. Hell, find him fascinating.

Can I play his girlfriend without falling in love with him?

I press my hands into the smooth metal railing. It's the only cold thing here. The sounds of the street—conversations and cars—flow into my ears, competing with the music coming from the club.

There's only one thing I know: I can't leave without being with him.

Period.

Chapter Seven

A soft breeze blows over my arms. It's still warm. The city lights blur together as I take shaky breaths. I've never been this nervous before.

The door pulls open and Pete steps onto the balcony. Already, the air feels several degrees warmer.

How can I want him this badly?

I barely know him.

He pulls the door closed behind him, and slides his hands over my hips.

Then he smiles and everything else fades away.

His hands go to my shoulders. They slide over the straps of my pastel pink dress, over the backline and neckline until one finds the zipper that runs parallel to my spine. He leans in close enough to whisper. "Turn around."

My sex clenches. His voice is deep and commanding. I want to comply.

I turn around. My back arches as a sigh escapes my lips. My thoughts fade away. Until the only thing I can feel is the tingle of anticipation.

Pete unzips my dress and slides the right strap off my shoulder. Then the left. The fabric collects at my waist.

His hands skim my hips, under the dress, just over the thin satin fabric of my thong. Then they're on my ass, on my bare skin. "Your ass is fucking fantastic."

My cheeks flush. "Thank you."

His fingers dig into my flesh. Then they're on my hips again, playing with the straps of my thong. "Look at me."

I turn so we're face to face. His expression is intense with desire.

It does something to me, the way he's looking at me. Makes it even harder to stand.

He moves closer, pinning me to the wall with the weight of his body.

Dammit, that feels so good I can barely breathe.

My eyelids flutter closed. I soak in the sweet sensation of his fingertips on my bare skin.

I barely know him. We're in a semi-public space. We might get caught. Right now, that doesn't matter. Right now, the only thing that matters is his hands on my skin.

His lips press against my neck. He kisses his way to my ear. My cheek. My lips. I rise to my tip toes, pressing my body against his.

He's hard. I can feel him through his jeans.

From the feel of things, he's massive.

I arch my back to rub my crotch against his. There's too much fabric in the way. It's not enough.

I groan as he slides his hand down my back.

He catches my lower lip with his thumb. The touch is intimate. Delicate.

I stare back at him as he drags his thumb over my lips. Then the digit is in my mouth. I press my tongue against the soft pad, sucking like I'm sucking him off.

He groans a delicious low throaty groan.

Pete pulls his hand to his side. "Close your eyes."

I do.

He plants a soft, wet kiss on my neck as he peels off my bra. His fingertips trail over my shoulders.

He's slow about exploring every inch of exposed skin. That same anticipation builds inside me. This isn't enough.

I know where I need his hands.

But I can't ask... I can't dirty talk. No way.

His kiss gets harder as he moves down my shoulders. His teeth scrape against my skin. He shifts lower, plants a kiss on my chest. Then lower. Lower. He's inches from my nipple.

Lower.

Almost.

But he moves away, does the same to my other breast. I reach for him, rake my hands through his hair.

The music from the inside of the club cuts off. The band is done. There's clapping then it's quiet enough I can hear our breath. Mine is more strained than his, but we're both panting.

It does things to me, knowing he's as needy as I am.

The way he's looking at me—he's teasing me.

Baiting me.

He wants me to ask.

Can I do that? I take a deep breath, arching my back and tugging at his hair. It does nothing to change his path.

"Please," I groan. My thighs shake with anticipation.

"Please what."

My cheeks flush. "Are you going to make me say it?"

"Hmm?" He plays dumb. Kisses his way back to my lips. Then his tongue is in my mouth, swirling around mine. He pulls back and stares into my eyes. "Say what?"

God, I'm burning up. I must be every shade of red.

He brings his lips to my ear. "You want me to suck on your nipples."

I let out a much too loud groan as I nod.

"Should've just asked," he teases. "Any other requests?"

"You're enjoying this."

"You aren't?" He presses his palm against my sex, over my panties.

My response is a low moan.

"You're wet." His voice is breathy, needy. "You want my fingers curling inside you?"

My sex clenches. "Yes. Do that. And the nipples too."

He smiles. "Close your eyes. I'll stop teasing. This time."

Thank God.

His lips sink into mine. Mmm. He tastes so good.

My hands find their way to the edge of his t-shirt. Then they're under it, on his taut stomach. His skin feels good against my hands, like it's meant for them.

Damn, he's a good kisser. He sucks on my lower lip as he pushes my thong off my hips. The undergarment falls to my feet. I step out of it and kick it away.

I'm half naked on a balcony. With a man I barely know.

I should care. I should be terrified. But I'm not. I want this more than I've ever wanted anything.

Pete breaks our kiss to press his lips against my neck. My shoulder. My chest. Lower. Lower. Lower.

This time, his lips close around my nipple. Pleasure shoots to my core. I sigh with relief as he sucks on me. Soft. Then harder. Harder.

I yelp from the pressure. It doesn't hurt but it's fucking intense.

He moves to my other nipple and does the same. I tug at his black hair, trying to keep my voice down.

His hand slides up my thigh. Closer and closer. My legs shake. I press my back against the wall to keep my balance. It's been too long. I need him touching me.

Almost.

Almost.

There. His fingertips skim my clit. He looks up at me, checking my reaction. I nod a yes. He needs to continue. All of this needs to continue.

He strokes me.

His hands are steady, the pressure light. I arch my back to pull him closer. Deeper. I need more. Need his fingers inside me.

My cheeks flush as I try to force the words to my tongue.

My hands go to his shoulders. "Please... Pete... I want you to... To do what you said."

He flicks his tongue against my nipple. Is he going to make me say it? I let my eyes close. I take a deep breath. Okay... I can do that.

In theory.

I dig my nails into his shoulder. "I want your fingers inside of me."

Immediately, one finger teases my sex. My body sighs with relief. I can do this. Can ask for what I want. Hell, I'm practically dirty talking.

Conscious thought falls away as his finger slides inside of me. I arch my hips, spread my legs wider.

I let his name fall off my tongue.

"God, Pete." I arch my back to drive his fingers deeper. "Please don't stop."

He kisses me hard. His tongue is aggressive, dancing with mine. I groan into his mouth. He needs to know how good this feels.

Tension knots between my legs. I'm close to the edge. About to spill. And kissing him back isn't enough to contain my pleasure. My lips break free of their own accord, part of their own accord.

No thinking. My hips shift, seeking the perfect angle.

There. Pete stays in time with my movements, going faster, deeper.

He's tuned to my body, playing me as expertly as he played his fucking bass guitar.

With the next stroke, all the pleasure wells up inside me. I go over the edge, groaning his name as I come. I can't help myself. I don't want to.

When I'm finished, he pulls his hand away.

He keeps me pinned against the wall with his hips. His lips hover over my ear. "My name sounds good on your tongue."

My cheeks flush. "Thank you."

"I want to hear it again." His voice gets lower. "Can you handle more?"

God yes. I want him inside me. I have to ask. Deep breath. I try to build the courage. But the silence of the song ending throws me.

There's another sound. Something familiar.

Oh no. It's footsteps.

They move closer. Closer. Then there's a knock on the balcony door. A woman clearing her throat awkwardly.

I turn, covering myself as quickly as possible.

"Ahem. Excuse me..." Her voice wavers as she pushes the door open.

"This is becoming a habit for you," I whisper.

He nods with a cocky smile. "Rain check." He steps into the club.

"Oh my Goodness. I didn't realize it was you..." She clears her throat. "If you need another few minutes, it's okay."

Damn. Being a rock star has its perks.

"We're finished." His deep voice echoes around the room.

My bra and panties are flung over the balcony. That's not happening. At the moment, I'm not concerned. I'm on a cloud. Everything is light and easy.

I zip my dress and step into the club.

The waitress stares at me like she's determining whether or not I'm good enough for Pete. Her gaze goes back to him. She does not even bother trying to hide the way she's gawking at the still very visible erection straining against his jeans.

"We'll get out of here," he says.

"Yes. Of course." She manages to look into his eyes. "Are you two... together?"

He looks at me for permission. When I nod he turns back to the waitress with a megawatt smile.

"Yeah. But keep it between us," he says.

"Of course." She looks Pete in the eyes, leans in close like he's a good friend. "I'm so glad you're moving on from that cunt, Cindy. You deserve better."

Pete steps back. His expression fills with discomfort. Still, he nods a thank you.

This woman has never met him and she feels comfortable calling his ex-girlfriend a cunt.

Being rich and famous has its drawbacks.

Chapter Eight

Tom and Willow are still cozy on the couch. They shoot us one of those *I know what you were doing* looks. I smile politely, feigning innocence as I grab my purse.

Pete doesn't feign anything. He shrugs as if to say *and so what if I was getting her off on the balcony?* Or maybe I'm getting ahead of myself.

No, the way the brothers are exchanging knowing looks—they're communicating something.

Again, the question nags at my insides. Why is Pete lying to his family? I understand him needing to maintain a public image. But why not tell his friends and family the truth?

I can lie to strangers. I'm not sure I can lie to people who clearly love him.

Pete pulls me into a hug. Mmm. It's difficult to think with his body pressed against mine.

I rise to my tip toes so I can whisper in his ears. "Can we talk somewhere private?"

He nods. "Give me ten minutes. Gotta talk to Aiden." He presses his lips to mine.

I'm breathless when he pulls back and leaves in search of his manager.

Tom and Willow have half their attention on me. The rest is on Ethan and another guy from his band. They're talking about music, but Willow keeps looking at me.

Could be the conversation bores her.

Could be she doesn't buy that Pete and I are dating.

Could be a million things. No matter the case, I don't like the scrutiny. I need to clear my mind. Alone.

"Excuse me. I'm gonna get some air." I point to the not off limits balcony. "Tell Pete I'm out there."

"Sure." She smiles then turns back to her fiancé.

Without my rock star faux boyfriend, I'm not a noticeable party goer. I have no trouble shifting through the crowd and stepping onto the balcony.

There are two people smoking cigarettes in the corner. One is a musician known for sleeping with reality TV stars. I had a crush on him back in high school but up close he's not nearly as appealing as Pete is.

Damn, is it my fate to compare every man I ever meet to the sexy bassist? If so, I'm doomed. It's going to be nearly impossible to find someone who stacks up.

I move to the empty side of the balcony and breathe in as much clean air as I can.

I can get used to lingering hugs from Pete.

I can certainly get used to mind-blowing orgasms.

I can even deal with the looks people shoot me when I'm next to Pete—like I'm not hot enough to be a rock star's arm candy.

Even though it means lying to his friends and family, his offer is tempting.

I pull out my phone to check my loan application. No wifi and my data connection is slow. I hold the phone up as high as I can. There! It's loading. Loading. Loading.

Denied.

No.

It can't be denied.

I stare at the ugly red letters. They refuse to change. This was the last loan with a decent interest rate. There are others but I'll be paying them off until I'm forty.

The half of tuition I owe for the semester—my scholarship covers the other half—is a solid six months of working nights and weekends at the bar. Twelve months for the academic year.

I'm not sure how I can down that kind of money. I'm not sure I can ask for it either.

I contemplate my choices but answers refuse to come. The energy of the air shifts, warmer and more inviting, and I know he's here.

Pete slides his arms around me, pulling my body into his, my back against his chest, my butt against his crotch.

"What's that for?" I ask.

"You don't like me feeling you up?" He slides his hand to my ass.

"No. I like it."

"Mmm. Me too." He pulls me closer. "You good?"

I nod. "Just hungry."

"You want something here?"

Deep breath. I barely know my name when he's touching me, but I know I want to have him again. I can ask for that. "Let's go somewhere quiet."

"You sound tired."

I nod.

"Let's order something at your place."

"Are we going to..."

He slides his arm around my waist and nods to the exit. "We're going to talk."

⚜

IT'S A QUICK DRIVE IN PETE'S QUIET AS A MOUSE BLACK Tesla. The luxury electric car is another thing I could get used to. It has cushy leather seats, freeze your ass off powerful air conditioning, and all sorts of fancy digital controls.

Actually, his car is too nice for this shitty neighborhood.

I turn to him as I unbuckle my seatbelt. "You sure it's okay to park here?"

He cocks a brow. "If you want to go to my place, ask."

"No, I just... this isn't a good neighborhood and this is an expensive car."

His deep brown eyes bore into mine. "You're worried."

I nod.

"You worry a lot?"

I nod a yes.

He shifts out of his seat then out of the car. I follow his lead, squeezing my purse against my shoulder reflexively.

Pete moves close enough to whisper. "You don't have to worry about me. I know how to handle shit. Don't come from money."

"Oh."

The look in his eyes tells me he doesn't want to discuss this. Anyone else, I'd back off right away. I don't push people's defenses.

But I want to know more about him. I want to tear down the walls around his heart.

I drop my voice to a whisper. "Where do you come from?"

His posture stiffens. "Lived in a shitty neighborhood when I was a kid. Inland empire. Riverside. It's nicer now. Back then it was meth central. We had drug dealers next door. I know how to defend myself."

"Oh. I'm from suburban Long Island. We don't have

much crime. We don't have much besides chain restaurants and Westfield Mall."

"There a non suburban Long Island?" he teases.

"Haven't you read *The Great Gatsby*? We have The Hamptons. Technically, Queens and Brooklyn are in Long Island."

His lips curl into a smile. "Guy who didn't go to college can't have read a classic piece of American Literature?"

"No, I just mean—" My cheeks flush. "Have you read it?"

He nods. "It's no *Hunger Games.*"

I laugh and lead him up the stairs, through the door, into my tiny studio apartment.

There's about two feet between the kitchenette and my twin bed and another two between my bed and the desk.

He shuts and locks the door. "You like Thai food?"

"Never had it. I'll eat anything but I'm allergic to peanuts."

He nods. "I know a place that's good with modifications if you want to try it."

"Okay..."

He moves close enough to run his fingertips over my shoulders. He pulls out his cell then stares into my eyes. "Trust me. I've got this."

I trust him a lot more than I should, what with us meeting twenty-four hours ago. I nod a yes.

"What do you like?" he asks.

"Vegetables."

He laughs. "Really?"

"Yeah. They're good. Red peppers are my favorite."

His cheeks crinkle as his deep, throaty laugh fills the room.

"What the hell is funny about red peppers?" I ask.

"Nothing. Just never met someone who loved vegetables."

"Let me guess. You have a manly love of red meat?" I tease.

"Wouldn't turn it down." He smiles. "Prefer shellfish."

"Expensive tastes."

He nods and motions *one minute*. Then he's on the phone, ordering delivery. It's nearly midnight but it's not a problem. We'll have our food in half an hour.

Thirty minutes with Pete. And there's my bed. It's a perfect situation, really.

But I can't sleep with him until I've made up my mind about this.

I'm not ready to decide. I reach for anything else I can discuss. "Do you really have expensive tastes?"

"Don't think about it like that." He motions for me to sit on the bed.

His posture is more *I'm going to take care of you* than *I'm going to fuck you until you're screaming*.

I sit anyway.

He moves to the kitchenette and opens the cabinets. "What do you have to drink?"

"You're supposed to ask permission to use someone's kitchen."

"Am I?"

I nod.

"You really want me to ask?"

"No. Just. You're kind of pushy."

"I know." He turns back to me. "What do you want?"

You with me on this bed. "Water. The only thing I have to drink is water."

He pours two glasses of water and hands one to me. Then he's next to me on the bed. My body likes where this is going. My head knows better—knows we have to reach an agreement before the fun naked on the bed part.

But my damn body has no patience. My heartbeat picks up. My knees press together reflexively.

Pete's expression is earnest. His defenses are down. It's

the first time I've seen him like this. I can't waste this opportunity.

He looks me in the eyes. "Guess I'd say I appreciate that I have money now. Want to use it to enjoy life instead of spending it on shit that doesn't matter to me."

"Do you save?"

He chuckles. "Should have known you'd ask that."

I fold my arms and tease back. "And why is that?"

"There's nothing wrong with taking the safe route." His lips curl into a smile. "Yes, I save. Do you need a figure?"

"No... that's none of my business."

"But you want one." He chuckles. "You act all sweet, but you're nosy."

"It's natural curiosity."

"I'm not gonna tell you unless you ask." The last hint of tension falls off his face. "You want to ask?"

"No. That's okay." I scoot a little closer. "What's it like going from having nothing to having everything?"

"A mindfuck."

I laugh. "You're so eloquent."

"Thank you." He takes a long sip of water then looks back to me. "You want the answer I give in interviews?"

"Do you get interviewed a lot?"

"Jess, you're breaking my heart questioning my fame like that," he teases. "You're gonna have to stroke my ego to make it up to me."

I laugh. And think deliciously dirty thoughts.

"We talked about that imagination of yours." His voice is still light, still teasing.

"It's just... you're the bassist. I can't even name another bassist."

"Can you name a guitarist or a drummer?"

Uh... maybe. "Dave Grohl!"

"That's cheating. He's a singer now."

"Um... Tom Steele."

"Guess I didn't preclude Sinful Serenade." He laughs. "That was a real lawyer trick. You're gonna be a shark."

My heart sings at the thought of law school. I close my eyes and try to push the rest of my thoughts away. What is it I want, besides Pete's body against mine?

It's law school. My future.

I take a deep breath. I can ask him to pay for school. Somehow. Even if I feel sick over using him.

His fingertips brush my thigh. "You're right. I'm not as famous as Miles or Tom—he took it upon himself to became a social media star. Leaked nude pics. Long story."

"Are there any leaked nude pics of you?"

He cocks a brow. "You'd really invade my privacy like that? Cold."

"No, I wouldn't. I swear."

"I believe you."

His smile spreads ear to ear. I want to reach up and trace the lines it makes in his cheeks.

"Okay, you want the answer." He clears his throat and adopts a more prim and proper posture. Shoulders back, hands in his lap. "I'm grateful for every fan, every ticket or album or t-shirt we sell, every time someone streams one of our songs, cause it means I can focus on music and not on paying the rent."

"Is that true?"

He nods. "Mostly." His brow furrows. His shoulders lock up.

There's something else he doesn't want to tell me. I set my water glass aside and move close enough I can run my fingers over his palm.

"What about that isn't true?" I ask.

"I landed with my adopted mom, Ophelia, when I was a teenager, after my dad died." He clenches and unclenches his jaw. "She's middle class. Always knew I had my room waiting."

He skipped right over what happened with his dad. I want to know, but I can read his posture and it's screaming *don't ask.*

He shifts backwards. "Have you decided?"

Okay, he doesn't like having this hanging over us. I'd like it out of the way too. But that means I have to ask for a hell of a lot.

Deep breath. I can do this. "Is it monogamous?"

He nods.

"There were a dozen models at the club who were picturing you naked."

"And?"

"And... it's not tempting?"

His brow furrows. "Don't understand the question."

"You have easy access to beautiful women—" I take a deep breath. I want to tell him. I want him to understand. "My ex cheated on me. We were days from breaking up but he didn't even respect me enough to tell me it was over before he started screwing someone else."

"I've been there."

Oh. That's why they broke up. That explains some of his *no way am I getting into a relationship attitude*. But now he's stuck in some ugly memory, his body turned away from mine.

"Do you want to talk about it?" I ask.

"Not really. Do you?"

I shake my head. "I guess I'm the one who is jealous. I'm not sure I can compete with a lingerie model."

He turns back towards me. This time, his eyes pass over me slowly. "You fishing for a compliment?"

"Just being honest."

"All due respect to whatever the fuck her name was—she seemed like a nice person—but I'd take you any day of the week. You have gorgeous eyes, responsive tits, an ass I can grab onto."

How can *responsive tits* feel like such a compliment? My cheeks flush. I've never been so flattered.

"You're fucking hot, Jess. And I like you. There's no competition. I don't want another girl." He stares back at me with a look that says *don't make me find another girl.*

Okay. This is it. Either I go for it or I tell him to get lost.

I take a deep breath, preparing my response.

Here goes nothing.

Chapter Nine

I stare into Pete's gorgeous brown eyes. "I want to do this, but I have terms."

His lips curl into a smile. "You want to do it?"

God, that smile. It does things to me. "First, you need to explain why you need me to play your girlfriend."

"The short answer is that Aiden is a piece of shit who can't be fired—his uncle's the head of the label. Only real option is keeping him pleased. Usually, he stays busy doing drugs, but he's fresh out of a rehab stint four and he wants to feel important."

I offer him my hand. Something to sooth the furrow in his brow.

"His latest idea is that I need a nice, sweet girl on my arm. According to marketing, I test best as the enigmatic guy who's good to his girlfriend. Usually, I'd tell him to go fuck himself, but he's threatening to bury our next album." His eyes turn to the floor. "We're obligated to record it but there's nothing in the contract that requires them to release it or promote it. If that happened... Tom would lose it."

"If you're doing this for your brother, why not tell him?"

Pete pulls back. "Out of the question."

"Why?"

"Just is."

"I'm not doing this unless I understand why we have to lie to your friends and family. They're nice people. And they clearly love you." I take a deep breath. It helps break up the tension forming in my chest. "It's not going to be easy to deceive them."

He stares back at me. "Tom would fucking kill Aiden if he knew. And he'd be too pissed to be smart about getting away with it." He lets out a laugh. "Guess that's a fucked up way of putting it."

I reach up and run my fingers through his hair. Again, the frustration in his brow softens. I do it again. Again. Until his eyelids are pressing together and he's letting out a soft moan.

He's practically purring.

"You can't tell anyone," he says. "Tom will find out."

"And you like him thinking you're happy, so he won't worry about your ex breaking your heart, or how much it sucks that you don't live with your brother, your best friend anymore."

"Is it that obvious?"

"No, but I know what it's like when you feel like you've lost your best friend." My stomach clenches at the thought of Madison.

His fingers curl around my wrist. Gently, he brings my hand to my waist. His expression gets intense. "What are your terms?"

"I'm going to be me," I say. "No pretending I'm someone else."

"Wouldn't ask. Like you the way you are." His eyes stay glued to mine. "There will be events, shit where you're expected to look a certain way. But you look fucking fantastic now. You'll be fine."

His eyes rake over me. Once again, my heartbeat picks up. My sex clenches.

Lust makes it difficult to concentrate. I close my eyes and focus on my breathing. This is a big ask, but it's the only way I can secure my future.

I pry my lids apart and stare at him with all the confidence I can muster. "I want you to pay my tuition for the entire year. Plus living expenses."

"Done."

"That's it, done?"

"Yeah. Anything you want besides money? I've got money."

"I don't have money, and I have a strict policy of not asking other people for it." I do nothing to swallow my irritation. "It means a lot to me, being able to go to school without worrying about making rent."

He nods with understanding. "I get that."

"I don't want to take advantage of you," I say. "I wouldn't ask if I had another way to pay for school."

"I know."

"How?"

"I can tell." He shifts closer. His eyes find mine. "I want you to live with me. I have air conditioning."

Tempting.

"And a pool."

More tempting.

"I skinny dip every night."

Incredibly, painfully tempting. But it's still out of the question. This apartment is mine. I spent hours arranging the flower decals on the walls. I perfected the cacti garden on the windowsill. This is the first time I've ever had my own space. I can't give that up.

"I'm sorry, but I'm not leaving this place without a good reason." I look Pete in the eyes. It takes great restraint not to crumble and beg him to take me to his place for skinny dipping under the moon.

"There's a lot of fame bullshit. You sure you can handle that?"

"No. But it can't be worse than giving up on law school." I offer my hand to shake. "Do we have a deal?"

"Yeah. I'll take care of the money tomorrow."

We have a deal.

I'm going to law school.

Screw the handshake. I jump into Pete's arms, pushing him onto my bed and knocking his glass of water to the floor in the process.

He laughs. "You want something, ask."

"I want a hug."

He looks at me like he can't believe my response. Still, he pulls me into a close embrace.

I can feel his heart beating against my chest. Hear his steady breath.

It feels right in his arms. Too right. If I keep holding him, I'm going to fall for him.

The doorbell rings. Our food. He goes to get it. By the time I've cleaned the spill, he's back and the room smells like hot sauce and ginger.

"What is that?" I ask.

He sets the food on the counter and unpacks it, checking each dish carefully. There's a vegetable curry in coconut broth and a colorful stir fry with chicken and a dark sauce.

We eat dinner on my bed. Both dishes are flavorful and rich. Pete even admits that the vegetables are fantastic.

After we're finished, he clears the trash, lays me on the bed, and plants a long, deep goodnight kiss on my lips. His hand slides between my legs, skimming the edge of my skirt.

Then it's at his waist, and he's at the door, wishing me

goodnight in a voice that says he knows I'm about to touch myself thinking of him.

&

THE MORNING IS BEAUTIFUL. THE AIR SMELLS BETTER. THE sun shines brighter. Even the graffiti plastered over my shitty neighborhood is more appealing.

I take a long jog. It's hot but even that feels good. I don't have to worry about money for the next year.

It's unreal.

After a quick shower and a bowl of cereal, I pick up my phone.

Pete: Check your admissions status.

I go right to my computer. USC website, login, loading.

There, in beautiful green letters: *ENROLLED.*

I'm a law student. Officially. My chest is light.

I'm a fucking law student.

I'm flying.

Jess: Thank you!!! You have no idea how badly I wanted this.

Pete: I have some idea what you look like when you want something.

Jess: That's different.

Pete: Still like thinking about you sighing and clutching at my shoulders because you're desperate to have my cock inside you.

My skin tingles with anticipation. I rub my eyes to check if I'm dreaming. It's right there, in text.

Damn, he's just as direct in text message as he is in person.

My phone buzzes.

Pete: I'll stop distracting you.

Jess: Thanks. I have a lot to do today.

Pete: How are you going to celebrate?

Jess: I don't have time. I have work. I have to pick classes. I have to call my dad.

Pete: Fuck that. We're celebrating. And you're quitting that job. I'll take care of you.

Jess: I don't want to take advantage.

Pete: You're not. I need you for those hours. I'm gonna work you hard.

Jess: Are you sure?

Pete: Yeah. How long have you wanted to be a lawyer?

Jess: Since I read To Kill A Mockingbird in eighth grade.

Pete: Really?

Jess: I know. It's too cute for words. That's what everyone thinks of me—blond hair, blue eyes, big glasses.

Pete: You dye your hair that color.

Jess: You're not supposed to accuse a woman of dying her hair.

Pete: Looks good on you.

Jess: Thanks.

Pete: I'm looking forward to dragging my fingers through it the next time you're screaming my name.

Jess: Are you trying to make me blush?

Pete: No. I'm making you wet.

Jess: I plead the fifth.

Pete: Stop dodging. We're gonna celebrate. I want to get you off after you get off.

Jess: Excuse me?

Pete: Try saying it.

Jess: It's too embarrassing.

Pete: At first. Then it's freeing. Try.

Jess: I'm going to have fun with you after I'm done with work.

Pete: That wasn't so hard, was it?

Jess: Let's hope it's hard.

My chest heaves as I inhale. God, this is beyond embarrassing. But once I see the words on screen I feel exhilarated.

Pete: Go on.

Jess: It's too embarrassing.

Pete: You want my cock hard. What's embarrassing about that?

Jess: You know what's embarrassing about that!!!

Pete: Do I?

Jess: You're a tease.

Pete: Yeah. We covered this.

Jess: But it's alarming how much of a tease you are.

Pete: You've seen nothing.

Jess: Really?

Pete: Don't tell me you don't like it. I'll have to prove you wrong.

Jess: I admit nothing.

Pete: Guess I'll have to prove you like it. Do me a favor.

Jess: What?

Pete: Skip the underwear tonight.

Chapter Ten

After work, I change into a cocktail dress and wedges in the backroom. For a second, I consider doing as Pete asked and skipping the underwear, but I can't muster up the nerve.

He's due to pick me up in ten minutes. I boot up my phone to pass the time.

Damn. I have a hundred new texts, a few dozen missed calls. My Facebook is slammed with people who want to get in touch. There are lots of questions and comments but most of them boil down to the same thing:

Oh my God, Jess, is that you with Pete Steele? No fucking way! He's so hot, you lucky bitch.

All of a sudden, all the friends who chose Nathan over me desperately want to talk to me. One measly video making out with a rock star and I'm Ms. Popularity.

My thumb hovers over my cell screen. I should feel powerful, victorious—my old friends, the ones who were perfectly happy to ignore me, are desperate to talk to me now that I'm a rock star's girlfriend.

My stomach churns. I don't feel powerful. Instead, my

head is heavy and my shoulders are tense. Those friends felt real, once upon a time. But they don't care about me. They never did. I'm still a tool to them.

How the hell am I supposed to know who I can trust when I can't trust my sister?

My phone buzzes in my hands. Pete. He's here. I wipe my misty eyes. I'm celebrating tonight. No matter how much the thought of Madison still makes my stomach clench.

I shove my phone back into my purse and shoot Rick a goodbye forever wave on my way out the door.

There's Pete, leaning against the passenger side door of his black Tesla. He's wearing black jeans and a black button-up t-shirt. He's wearing eyeliner again. A hint. Just enough to make it impossible to avoid staring into his deep brown eyes.

The smile falls off his lips as he takes me in. "What's wrong?"

I shake my head and smooth my cocktail dress. "Nothing."

He squeezes my hands and pulls my body into his. "Let's try again. What's wrong?"

"All my old friends want to talk to me."

"Fuck. I forget to tell you I posted those pictures from the park." He tilts his chin so he's looking down at me. "I'll make it up to you."

"I knew you would. That's not the problem."

"It killed me when I first realized it." He presses his palm between my shoulder blades. "That people are willing to use you like that—" He snaps his fingers.

There's an ocean of sadness in his eyes.

The feeling of dread in the pit of my stomach deepens. I'm using him to get what I want. He's using me to get what he wants. Is either of us really any better than the friends who want to talk to me because of my access to a celebrity?

"You aren't using me, Jess." He stares back at me. "I offered you a rate for a gig. You accepted."

"So that makes me a contractor?"

He chuckles. "You're gonna be a fantastic lawyer."

"I want to get everything straight." I want to be sure where he stands with this whole *don't want a girlfriend, my heart is closed* thing.

"Guess so. But we're still friends. We're not going to fall in love, but we're gonna fucking enjoy ourselves."

I nod. I don't like love being totally off the table, but it's better that way. Safer.

Pete opens the car door for me and helps me inside.

"Have you ever had to keep up appearances because of your fame before?" I ask.

"Can't make a scene. But that's not my thing. Don't have to work at it."

"How old were you when you became famous?" I ask.

"Was nineteen the first time somebody stopped me on the street 'cause she recognized me. Twenty-one when it became a regular thing."

"How old are you?"

"Twenty-three."

"I'm twenty-two." I play with my purse. "I can't imagine anyone stopping me on the street because they recognize me."

"It'll happen. People will forget the gossip soon, but the next month or two you'll be famous by association."

"What do I do?"

"It's like customer service. Smile, nod a thank you, get on with your day."

"Did you work, before you became a rock star?"

He cocks a brow. His lips curl into a half smile. "Being a rock star isn't work?"

Mmm. That smile. It takes great effort to avoid melting.

I half-smile back. "You know what I mean."

"Do I?"

I nod. "You're giving me a hard time."

Again, he cocks a brow. "Not yet. But I will."

My cheeks flush. "Oh. That's good." I smooth my skirt. It's hot today. Really hot. "Did you work a regular job before you became a rock star?"

"At a music shop. Talked a few people into picking up the bass."

"What's the difference between a bass and a guitar?"

"Jess, don't do this to me. We're getting along so well," he teases.

"Is that a deal-breaker, me being bass illiterate?"

"Absolutely."

"Then explain it to me."

He smiles. "Most people see the bass as some less cool guitar. No solos, can't sit on the curb playing songs acoustic for tips. Can't get laid wooing women with Dave Matthews Band."

"You play guitar too?"

He nods. "And the piano. Bass will always be my favorite. It's the backbone of a rock song. It doesn't call attention to itself, but the song feels empty without it."

There's so much passion in his voice. It makes it difficult to contemplate the boundaries of this relationship.

I clear my throat. I have to think about something besides how much I already like him. "How did you pick it up?"

"My father played it." Something in his voice changes. "He always encouraged me to pick it up. I wanted to make him proud."

"Is that your prepared answer?"

His brow furrows. "Guess it is."

"What's the truth?"

"Dad was an asshole. Learned guitar, bass, and piano trying to impress him but he never gave a fuck."

My chest pangs. My family isn't exactly sunshine and roses, but I always feel like my dad is proud of me. "I'm sorry."

"Don't be. Play three instruments well now."

"Why'd you stick with bass?"

"Like the way it feels in my hands."

"Can we make a deal?" I ask.

He cocks a brow.

"Let's agree not to lie or bullshit each other. Even if the truth hurts."

"You sure?"

"Why? Does my hair not look good this color?"

He laughs.

I nod. "I'm sure. I need honesty right now." How many times did I lie covering for Dad? Must be a few thousand. More even.

He bites his lip like he's thinking it over. Finally, he nods. "Okay."

We shake on it.

Already, I'm nervous over the potential to reveal myself. Okay. Need to grab something. I like him talking about music, like the passion in his voice.

I look up at Pete. "Tom, your brother, he plays drums, right?"

He nods.

"What's that like?"

"We create the rhythm together. There's a connection when we play—it's like nothing else."

"What about sex?"

"Nothing is better than great sex."

Mmm. I'm flushed and sweaty just thinking about being with him. But we need to talk more. I need to know more about him. "Can you believe that woman at the club? She called your ex a... a c-word right to your face."

"Not the first time I've heard that."

"You never think that?"

"A cunt is a beautiful thing, not an insult."

My cheeks flush. He looks at me, his lips spreading into a smile. He enjoys teasing me.

I like it too.

"So you really don't hate her for cheating?" I ask.

He takes a long moment to compose himself. When he speaks, his voice is low. Vulnerable. "You must know what's it like. Still hurts that she betrayed my trust. We were on and off that last year. Would have been easy for her to keep things off, but she chose to lie to me instead."

I nod. "Why do people do that?" It would have been easy for Nathan to send me an *it's over* text before he slept with Madison. It would have been easy for Madison to say *no, let's wait until it's official.*

But neither one of them cared how I'd feel.

Nathan hurt me, fine. He didn't owe me anything.

But Madison... we've always been allies. I took care of her most of the time, but she had my back when I needed her. I thought I could count on her. I thought I could tell her anything.

"Hey." His voice is steady. "Where are you going off to?"

I look back at Pete. "My ex-boyfriend cheated with my sister. They're still dating. I don't think about him, but she hasn't apologized. And I haven't told her how much she hurt me. We haven't spoken since I found out." My eyes go to my bare thighs. "I don't want to upstage you."

"It's not a competition." His fingers brush my cheek. "You're still hurting?"

"Yeah. She's the only person I've ever trusted."

"You want me to call her and tell her she's a bitch?"

I let out a laugh. "I think she'd take her own life if *the* Pete Steele called her a bitch." I run my fingertips over the back of his hand. "Do you still think about your ex?"

His voice drops to a whisper. "Not about her but about what happened."

My heart pangs. I want to touch him, to hold him, to wipe the memory of his ex away with my lips.

৩✕৩

THE CLUB IS SMALL AND DIM. ALL THE LIGHT IS ON THE stage, on a four piece jazz band. At least, I think it's a jazz band. I don't know much about music beyond *I like it* or *I don't like it*.

The host greets us with an *oh my favorite regular* smile. "Nice to see you, Mr. Steele. Take any empty table."

There are ten cozy, round tables in the center of the main room and about that many booths lining the edges.

Pete takes a booth in the far corner, out of the way of any prying eyes, and slides in next to me.

A waiter stops by our table. "For you, Miss?"

"Just a coke."

He nods to the waiter. "Same for me." Once the waiter is out of earshot, Pete scoots close enough to whisper. "You don't drink?"

"Not usually."

"Any reason?"

My self-preservation impulses fire away. "No."

"Jess—"

This honesty thing was my idea. I'm going to tell the truth, even if it kills me. "Yes, there is. Someone in my family has a drinking problem, but I don't want to talk about it right now."

He nods. Scoots closer. "You ever listen to jazz?"

"Never."

"Most people, their first reaction is that it doesn't make any sense."

I close my eyes and try to find some logic in the music. There's no pattern. It skips all over the place.

"It's not like a pop song. No chorus, bridge, verse." His fingertips slide over my chin. "That's the beauty of it. You can't predict where the song goes. You have to forget your plan and feel the music."

Forget my plan? Not a chance in hell. "Sounds terrifying."

"It can be." His fingers curl into my hair. "Close your eyes."

I don't. Instead, I stare back at him. "Is this your thing—taking girls to strange places and asking them to close their eyes so you can assault their senses."

"Assault?"

"You know what I mean."

"It's my thing taking you places and asking you to close your eyes. Yeah."

"Why?"

"I want to know everything there is to know about your body, every place I can touch to make you purr."

My sex clenches. The man can talk.

His fingertips skim my temples as he pulls off my glasses. Gently, he folds them and sets them on the table. "Try it."

I close my eyes.

His fingertips brush against my inner thigh.

Almost.

He strokes my inner thigh with his thumb. I reach for something and get the soft fabric of his shirt.

His fingers brush the sides of my panties. "Jess, we talked about this. Now I'm going to have to tease you twice as hard."

My skin tingles with anticipation. "Really?"

"Yeah." He moves closer. His fingers brush against my clit, over my panties.

I sigh with pleasure. I need more of that. Need him to continue.

"Stop guessing what's gonna happen," he whispers. "Take it in, one thing at a time."

I try to stop guessing. To feel every note of the music. To feel every brush of his lips against my neck, every stroke of his thumb against my thigh.

The song fades into an outro and one of the musicians steps up to the mic. There are footsteps coming our way. The waiter.

I press my lips together, feigning innocence. It's clear Pete's got his hand up my skirt but it doesn't seem to bother the waiter.

He drops off our sodas with a smile, turns, and disappears.

Pete leans close enough to whisper. "Did it work?"

I shake my head. "I don't like jazz."

"It's not for everyone."

"I like knowing what's going to happen." I press my cheek against his as I bring my lips to his ear. "I like girly pop music."

"So you aren't a fan?" he teases.

"You're not bad."

His lips curl into a smile. "Jess, you're going to break my heart."

"I mean, you're no Pearl Jam, but you're solid," I tease.

He laughs. "Who's your favorite artist?"

"Amy Winehouse. Her songs were so raw, the way she'd put the ugly parts of herself in her lyrics. I wish I could do that."

"Most people can't."

"Are you good at it?" I pull back so I can look into his eyes. "At forgetting your plan and being in the music?"

"Better some days than others."

"I don't know if I can do that."

"You can." He runs a hand through my hair. His expression is attentive, curious. "Right now, there are things weighing on you. They're going to keep weighing on you as long as you keep running from them."

I swallow hard. It's disarming, how easily he sees through me.

"What are you running from?"

"The person everyone wants me to be."

"Who is she?"

"I don't know. But she's not me." I grab my soda and take a long sip. It's too sweet, too sticky. I barely know Pete. But I'm tired of bullshit. "She's an enabler."

"Who do you want to be?"

"Someone assertive. Who gets what she wants. Who doesn't let people push her around."

He leans in to whisper. His voice drops an octave. "Right now, what do you want?"

"To celebrate."

"Then let's cut the heavy shit." He nips at my ear. "What else?"

"Is this your thing—having sex in public?"

"Yeah."

"It's not a good idea for me. If I get caught, that will screw up my reputation. Lawyers don't get caught having sex in public."

"You want to wait until we go home?"

"No."

Again, he nips at my ear. "What do you want, Jess?"

"Are you going to make me say it?"

His voice drops. "You want to be assertive."

Damn. I did say that. I take a deep breath, allowing my eyelids to flutter closed. I move closer to him, so I can whisper. "I..." My cheeks flush. I can't say it yet. "I want to know why you chose me. You could have asked a million girls to do this and you asked me."

"Because you like *The Hunger Games.* And you wear sexy librarian glasses."

"Really?"

He presses his lips into my neck. "You haven't once tried to bullshit me or use me."

"Oh."

"If the answer to that question is all you want, I can move to the other side of the bench."

I can hear the smile in his voice. Okay. Deep breath. I can do this. I can ask for what I want. I bring my lips to his ear. "I want to fuck you."

Chapter Eleven

M y lungs empty as I exhale. Nerves rise up in my stomach. My heart thuds against my chest.

It is freeing asking for exactly what I want.

He presses his fingertips into the back of my head. "After you come on my hand."

Warmth spreads through my cheeks and chest. "Here?" I blink my eyes open, suddenly acutely aware of every single person in the room. At least thirty. Maybe more.

"Here." Pete plays with the hem of my skirt as he sucks on my earlobe.

"What if someone sees?" A shudder runs down my spine as his fingertips brush my thigh. I'm quickly losing interest in potential consequences.

"Won't let that happen."

He pushes my panties aside.

But he doesn't touch me. Not yet.

My thighs shake with anticipation. I need him touching me. It's terrifying how badly I need him touching me.

I nod a yes. Mumble some collection of vowels that doesn't sound anything like a word.

His expression gets intense. He wants this as badly as I do.

Yes. Here. Now. A deep breath pushes my anxiety aside. I care more about him touching me than I do about the consequences.

I spread my legs wider. He slips his hand into my panties, his fingers skimming my sex.

Yes. I sigh with relief.

"Lift your hips," he whispers.

I do. His eyes fix on mine as he pulls my panties to my knees.

My sex clenches. I need to do something to contain myself or I'm going to scream all sorts of things. I untuck his button up shirt. Then my hands are under it, my palms against the hard muscles of his stomach.

His free hand goes to my wrist. He drags my hand to his knee. Then up, up, up, until I'm cupping him over his jeans.

He's hard.

"Keep it there." He groans as his fingers skim my sex. "Close your eyes."

This time, I don't object. I want what he's offering. I want all my senses tuned to him. I want every other thought erased.

My eyelids press together. The sounds of the room—the guitar, the trumpet, the conversation—blur into white noise. Our breath comes into focus. His is smooth. Mine is strained.

He groans against my neck as he slides his thumb over my clit.

God yes.

I shift, leaning towards him, turning my back to the room. I'm defenseless. No way to tell if someone is approaching. If we're going to get caught.

I trust him to make sure that doesn't happen.

It's terrifying how much I trust him.

He strokes me. I kiss him. Rub my palm against his erection. The jeans are in the way.

His touch gets harder. Harder. There. It's perfect. I bring both my hands to his shoulders and tug at his crisp black shirt. The fabric catches between my fingers. It's soft. It's practically magnetic.

Pete groans into my mouth.

I groan back, sucking on his tongue as the tension in my core knots tighter and tighter. There isn't a single part of me that wants to hold back.

His next stroke pushes me over the edge. I dig my nails into his skin as I come. My orgasm is intense. I shudder. I barely manage to keep from screaming.

His deep brown eyes fix on me, watching me like I'm a masterpiece.

I hold his gaze for as long as I can. It does something to me. Makes it hard to keep track of my breath.

When I finally get a handle on the whole inhale exhale thing, his lips curl into a smile.

That's the only thing in the universe that matters, his smile.

My heart thuds against my chest. I'm not sure which way is up or down. I can't mix things up. This is sex, no feelings besides desire.

I can't fall for him.

No matter how sweet he is under the don't give a damn exterior, I can't fall for Pete Steele.

My heart can't survive being torn in half again.

He scoops me into his lap. His expression shifts, back to desire. His hands go to my hips, adjusting our positions so I can feel his erection.

Damn, I'm actually considering mounting him right here, in the club, in front of all these people.

My thoughts go straight to my tongue, no stopover in the inhibition part of my brain.

"Can we go back to your place?" I ask.

"Yes." He pulls twenty dollars from his wallet and drops it on the table. "But I don't want to wait until we're back at my place."

⚜

HE ONLY WAITS A MINUTE AND A HALF, UNTIL WE'RE through the back door, in the empty alley.

His hands go to my hips. In one swift movement, he pins me to the wall. It's late, dark, not the best part of town.

None of that matters.

Tomorrow doesn't matter. Potential heartbreak doesn't matter. The only thing that matters is our bodies joining, Pete erasing every heavy thought in my brain.

He's not delicate this time. He nearly rips the zipper as he tugs my dress to my waist.

Immediately, his eyes go to my chest. "You have amazing tits."

"Really?"

"Uh-huh."

My cheeks flush. "I always thought they were a little small."

"No. They're perfect. And this." He slides his thumb into my bra and rubs my nipple until I'm groaning. "That's the best fucking music I've heard in a long time."

My thank you is messy grunt of vowels.

His hips press against mine. I can feel him, how hard he is, how big he is. I arch my hips so my clit rubs against his cock. His jeans and my dress are in the way, but the friction is enough to send shivers up my spine.

"This is a habit for you," I breathe. "Fucking in public."

"You're not going to convince me you don't like it." He drags his fingers over my sex. "You're still dripping."

Breath flees my body.

I gasp as he slips a finger inside me. God, it's such a tease. I need him filling me.

I need him. Period.

His voice is low, deep, in-control. "You want me to fuck you against the wall or from behind?"

"Against the wall."

My cheeks flush. I actually said that. I actually told him how I want him to fuck me.

I'm actually having sex in public.

He pulls a condom from his pocket and unzips his jeans. His eyes meet mine, this intense look that says *yes*.

He leans down to take my nipple into his mouth. His eyes stay on mine as he flicks his tongue against me.

Lust shoots straight to my core. I groan. When that's not enough, I let his name fall off my lips.

I do away with my bra. My chest is on display to him, to anyone who happens to walk by the alley for a smoke or a phone call.

God help me, the thought spurs me on.

"Please." I squeeze his shoulders. "Please fuck me."

He presses his palm against my hip, pinning me to the wall. "Not yet. Want to savor this."

He pushes his boxers to his feet. I watch with rapt attention as he unwraps the condom and slides it onto his cock.

He's huge.

His hands go to my ass. He holds me against the wall, the weight of his body sinking into mine. "Wrap your legs around me."

He shifts his hands under my thighs to help me. There. My thighs strain as I squeeze his waist, pulling him closer.

Pete's eyes stay glued to mine as he shifts our bodies

together. His cock nudges against my sex. I exhale deeply. It's a tease. It's not enough.

I stare back at him, pleading with my eyes.

He teases again.

Again.

Again.

I can't take it anymore. My need overpowers my shyness. "Please, Pete. I need you inside me."

His eyes go wide.

God, I love the look on his face. I take a deep breath. This time, it doesn't take much to get the words to my tongue. "Deep inside me. So deep I can barely bring myself to say your name."

He pins me to the wall. His eyes stay glued to mine as he slides inside me.

More, more, more. Then he's so damn deep I can barely breathe.

He slows, watching my reactions, waiting until my chest heaves with a steady inhale.

It's right, our bodies connected.

It's the most right thing in the history of the universe.

Still, I need him closer. One of my hands slides around his neck, to the back of his head. The other goes to his shoulder, under the soft fabric of his shirt.

His eyes stay glued to mine as he nudges deeper. Deeper. I squeeze him tighter, arching my back, spreading my legs.

My last hint of inhibition falls away.

He groans as he goes deeper. "Mmm. Jess." His nails are hard against the soft flesh of my ass. "You feel fucking good."

He presses me against the wall as he slides into me.

It's slow. I can feel my sex stretching to take him deeper, enveloping him. God, he feels good. I tug at his hair. No shyness. "You're huge."

He nods. No ego. Just an acknowledgment of facts.

His eyes are glued to mine. His voice is attentive. "Stop me if it's too much."

Slowly, he shifts out, so I can just barely feel him. He does it again. Again. Again.

Pete Steele is a hell of a tease.

My eyelids drift together. I'm dizzy with lust. I can't think. Can't do anything but feel his cock driving into me.

My body moves on its own. My thighs squeeze his hips. My hands go to his chest, tugging at the buttons of his shirt. There, one down. Then the next. The next. Three. Two. One.

I push the shirt to his shoulders, exploring every inch of his chest.

My sex clenches as he thrusts into me. It's hard. Deep. I feel full. Like our bodies are meant for each other.

I lose myself in the pleasure building between my legs. I arch my back so my clit presses against his pubic bone. The sounds of the street— the traffic, the conversations outside the club, the music—fade until all I can hear is his heavy exhale, our flesh connecting as he thrusts into me.

Again.

Again.

Again.

An orgasm rises up inside me. Almost. I bring my hands back to his shoulders, holding tight.

I've never come from penetration before.

But I'm almost there.

Like last time, my body knows what it wants better than I do. My fingers dig into his shoulders. My back curls, my shoulders pressing against the wall, my hips shifting towards his.

He's watches my reactions, moving in time with my grunts and moans. It's like he knows what I want before I do.

His hands stay tight around my hips, pinning me in place so he can work his magic.

Harder. Deeper.

Oh.

That's exactly where I need him. I dig my fingers into his skin, groaning his name.

"Don't stop," I breathe.

He grunts something totally incomprehensible. His lids are heavy. He's close. But he's still so fucking attentive.

My sex clenches. Almost. The bare skin of his chest presses against my mine. I soak in every inch of him I have.

It blurs together, like beautiful music, until my entire existence is pleasure. My eyes roll back in my head. My lips part.

"Pete," I groan. I see white. The entire world is this lovely shade of white, nothing but the blinding light of bliss as my sex clenches tighter and tighter and tighter.

One more thrust and all that tension unwinds. It spills through me. My sex pulses around him, pulling him closer.

"Pete," I groan it again. Again. Again.

He brings his hand to my chest and toys with my nipples.

Pleasure shoots to my core. He's playing me like an instrument, like he knows my body better than I do.

He rubs my nipple with his thumb. "Tell me when to stop."

I don't want him to stop. I'm sensitive enough this aches, but I don't want him to stop.

Words make it to my tongue without passing through my brain. "I want to come again. With you."

My chest feels light. Free.

It is exhilarating asking for what I want.

He plays me perfectly. I lose track of everything but the sounds of his groans. The way his chest shakes against mine. The weight of his body as he presses me against the wall.

He thrusts harder. Deeper. His cock pulses. His lips part with a heavy groan.

His pubic bone makes for the perfect amount of friction.

"Fuck, Jess." His hand goes to my hair, pulling me against him. His lips press into my neck. A soft kiss. Then harder. Harder.

Then his groans are sending vibrations down my chest.

My sex clenches. The sound of his pleasure is enough to push me to the edge. With his next thrust, I see all that perfect white light. I come again.

No holding back. I scream his name.

Then he's there, one hand knotting in my hair, the other holding my body against his.

"Jess." He lets out a low, heavy groan.

There. I can feel him come, even with the condom.

It does something to me, hearing my name on his tongue, feeling his pleasure.

It's different than with Nathan. Better. A million times better.

Pete holds me against the wall. He presses his lips against my neck and shoulder.

We stay tangled as our breath returns to normal.

Chapter Twelve

I'm still in a daze when we get to Pete's place. It's the picture of an expensive Southern California home—gated neighborhood, flat tile roof, front yard of pebbles and succulents. Damn, there must be two dozen cacti lining the walkway.

He parks in the driveway and leads me inside. The main room is a huge open space—there's a couch and a TV near the entrance. The kitchen and dining area are behind that. The sliding doors to the backyard glow from the aqua light of the pool. And there are even more plants in the backyard.

"You must have a hundred cacti here," I say.

He chuckles. "That's what you've noticed?"

"What am I supposed to notice?"

"Three thousand dollar flat screen TV."

"I watch TV on my laptop."

His lips curl into a smile. "Two thousand dollar couch."

"I don't even have a couch."

"All stainless steel appliances in the kitchen."

"Now, we're getting somewhere."

He nods to the backyard. "Pool is heated year round."

"Get bikini models in there at your loud rock star parties?"

"Throwing parties is Tom's thing." His voice softens. "It's dead quiet here without him."

Sadness flares in his expression. He blinks and the vulnerability in his eyes is gone.

He clears his throat. "You want the grand tour?"

I watch his expression, the way he looks around the massive room like it's empty.

He's lonely here all by himself.

I get lonely some nights at my apartment. Plenty of nights. It would be nice to have company. It would be especially nice to have the gorgeous, glowing pool as my nightly hangout spot. The stainless steel kitchen, the expensive looking leather couch, the spiraling staircase straight out of an old Hollywood movie—it's all amazing.

But not amazing enough to convince me to give up my space.

"Sure, give me the tour," I say.

Upstairs is just as nice. There are four bedrooms. One is nearly empty, another is cluttered with musical instruments and notebooks, the third is totally furnished. It's all out— disco ball on the ceiling, star and moon decals on the walls, bondage restraints tied to the headboard.

Bondage restraints plus me plus Pete... Beautiful images flash through my mind. I want him tying me up. The thought never occurred to me but now it's clear as day.

"Is this your room?" I ask.

Pete nods to the restraints. "Getting ideas?"

Uh...

He clears his throat. "Jess. You're imagining me again. I'm right here. If you want me, take me."

I want him very much, but I'm not sure I'm ready for

bondage restraints. I clear my throat. "After we finish the tour."

He nods and leads me to the balcony. It's beautiful—a perfect view of the backyard and beyond that the sprawling hills. I can already imagine a nice life here—lounging by the pool with my morning coffee, poring over my Kindle under the stars, sprawling out on the couch for a *Gilmore Girls* marathon.

But I imagine things I can't have—him joining me on the couch with a smile, pulling me onto his lap during the commercial break and whispering sweet promises about love and forever in my ears.

Damn. It *is* quiet. I can hear my heartbeat. I can hear his breath. I turn so I can get a good look at him. It's hard to make out Pete's expression in the starlight. There are still hints of sadness in his eyes.

"Mind if I use your shower before we... go again?" I ask.

His lips curl into a smile. "You're still shy."

"Compared to you, maybe."

"Try saying it."

"Saying what exactly?"

"Mind if I use your shower before you throw me on the bed, rip off my towel, and fuck me until I'm screaming your name."

A flutter builds below my belly. There's no way I'm saying that. Even half that.

"Not gonna try?" he asks.

"Later."

He nods and leads me back inside, to the bathroom in the hallway.

It's even more tempting than the pool. The faucets are shiny and clean. And the bathtub, goodness, that bathtub. It's big and deep with jets and a digital thermometer.

I point to the tub. "Can I?"

"California's in a drought," he teases.

"You could join me."

He cocks a brow. "To save water?"

I nod. It's a very plausible story.

"Don't like baths." He sits on the side of the tub and turns the faucet. He tests the temperature of the running water then looks back to me. "You can join me when you're done."

"Okay."

"You want anything else?"

I want too many things. It's confusing. I shake my head in the hopes of regaining some hint of sense.

His touch is gentle as he helps me out of my clothes. We don't talk, but still, I feel free and light. Like nothing else in the world can hurt me.

When the tub is full, I dip a toe to test the temperature. It's tolerably hot.

I slip inside. It's not like the tub I have back home. I can practically swim in this thing. I rest my chin on the side and stare back at Pete.

"Are you going to stand there and watch me?" I ask.

"You gonna touch yourself?"

My cheeks flush. "You'd want to watch that?"

His brow furrows with confusion. "Of course. You wouldn't?"

"Watch myself? No."

He nods to the mirror opposite the tub. "You should try it."

"Maybe."

He kneels on the tile next to me. His eyes meet mine. They're wide with enthusiasm. "Wouldn't you want to watch me?"

"Uh..." Delicious images fill my head. I nod frantically.

"Jess, if you want something, you should ask for it." He

pushes himself to his feet and takes a step backwards. "I'm gonna leave. Unless you want something."

I'm tongue tied.

He cocks a brow. "Last chance."

My lips refuse to part.

He takes another step backwards. His voice is a dare, his expression intense. "I'll be in my room. When you figure out what you want."

He steps into the hallway, leaving the door half-open. The bath is still perfectly luscious. The house is still gorgeous. The moon is still shining through the window.

But I don't feel light and free anymore.

I already miss his presence.

I know what I want. It's the one thing I can't have—his heart.

๑๑๑

THE BATH IS A MARVEL, REALLY. THE WATER STAYS WARM for all thirty minutes of my soak. My muscles relax but I'm still lacking the feeling of lightness I have around him.

When I'm finished, I towel dry and find Pete's room across the hall.

He's lying in bed, in his boxers, sound asleep.

Mmm. It's probably wrong, gawking at a man who isn't conscious, but the starlight falls over his chiseled torso just so. With him on his side, I get an amazing view of his shoulders, arms, stomach, back. I can even see the tattoo on his hip—roses in a mix of grey, black, and red.

My fingers brush the curving lines of the tattoo. His skin is soft, his muscles hard, his hipbone harder. I pull my hand back to my waist. It's definitely wrong, touching a man who isn't conscious.

CRYSTAL KASWELL

I find an extra toothbrush in the bathroom, an extra t-shirt and boxers in his dresser, and I climb into bed with him.

He stirs, murmuring something incomprehensible and pulling my body into his.

This isn't forever.

But, for now, it's really fucking nice.

۞

I WAKE UP COLD AND STIFF. I DON'T NEED TO OPEN MY EYES to know I'm alone. I can feel it all around me.

After I brush my teeth, I make my way downstairs. Worry threatens to overwhelm me—*why hasn't Dad returned any of my calls? Will Madison tell me if something is wrong?*—but it evaporates the moment I see Pete.

He's standing in the kitchen, one hand pressed against the counter, the other holding his cell to his ear. His posture is tense, strained. He taps his nails against the tile with an uncharacteristic franticness.

"Yeah, I know," he says into the phone.

His jaw clenches as he listens to the reply.

I take a few more steps towards the kitchen.

He looks at me. His voice softens some. "Hey. You want coffee?"

"Sure."

"Yeah, that's her. Give me a second." He sets his phone on the counter and turns to me. "How do you take it?"

"I can fix it. You should finish your phone call."

He nods to the full carafe in the coffee maker then picks up his phone. "Yeah." His shoulders tense. "Of course. You're right." He barely manages to keep his voice even. "It's a great idea. Don't know why I didn't think about it. But... I don't want this in the way of her life. I like her."

He's talking about me, telling someone—must be Aiden,

108

the awful manager—that he likes me. The way he says it, like it's an unarguable fact, makes my stomach flutter.

I pour myself a cup of coffee and fix it with plenty of milk and sugar. Pete steps aside to finish his phone call. When he's done, he drops his cell on the table. His hands curl into fists.

"Was that about me?" I ask.

He nods and turns towards me. "Aiden."

"He really gets under your skin, huh?"

Pete rolls his shoulders. Some of the frustration falls off his face as he takes a long sip of his coffee. "Yeah."

I move closer. There are still three feet between us. But I'm close enough I can make out every detail of his bare chest. "What does he want?" I drag my eyes up his torso until they connect with his.

"Wants us to land on a few gossip sites, so everyone knows I have a nice, blond girlfriend." His brow furrows. He shakes it off then takes another sip of coffee.

"Does the blond part matter?"

"To him, probably."

"Is it your type, blonde?" I ask.

"Can't say I've ever given it thought." His eyes pass over me. His voice shifts, teasing. "I like you blond. Looks natural. Even with the inch of roots."

His lips curl into the tiniest of smiles. Already, the room feels warmer and lighter.

"Are they really that noticeable?" I tease back.

"Need a view of the top of your head to answer that."

Oh. My cheeks flush.

His smile stretches over his cheeks. He takes another step towards me. "You fluster easy."

"You underestimate yourself." I take another step towards him.

He cocks a brow.

"The way you say things like that is really sexy. I can't

imagine anyone else pulling it off. Hell, if any other guy said that to me, I'd run the other direction."

"Other guys are suggesting you suck them off? Do I need to kick somebody's ass?" He slides his hand around my waist and pulls my body into his. "Fuck, you're making Aiden's idea seem reasonable."

"Would that really make you jealous?" I set my cup of coffee on the counter then do the same with his. It means I can move a little closer to him.

He nods. "Of course."

"But we're not really... I mean. We're not exactly together."

He stares back at me. "You're only with me. I'm only with you." His brow furrows. "That a problem all of a sudden?"

"No. Of course not."

"Good." His frown fades. He looks down at me, running his fingers through my messy hair. "You game for the gossip mission?"

"Depends what I have to do."

He plays with my hair as he thinks. He looks cute thinking, his brow knotted with concentration, his gaze drifting off some place.

"Fuck. Tom's good at this shit." His voice drops. "Wish I could ask him."

"Maybe you can."

Pete pulls his hands to his sides and takes a step backwards. He shakes his head. "I know a few places. You doing anything today?"

"Nope. Quit my job yesterday."

"Yeah?" His lips curl into a smile.

"Yeah." Which means I'm totally reliant on him. That's still scary.

"I'll transfer some spending cash into your account," he says.

Damn, he's a mind reader. I object out of habit. "You don't have to do that."

"Yeah. I do. Let's skip the part where you try to talk me out of it, cause it's not happening. I know you're gonna be a lawyer, so you need to practice arguing, but I'd rather save my energy for later." His eyes meet mine, his expression intensifying. "Deal?"

"I..."

"Jess, you're not taking advantage. I need you." He takes a step closer. "Agree."

I nod. "Okay, we have a deal."

His gaze turns to the backyard. Already, it's awash in bright light. The pool shimmers with reflections of the big yellow sun.

He keeps his gaze on the backyard. "That thing, yesterday, your friends emailing you. That's nothing. We go through with this, your life is gonna change in ways you can't imagine now. You sure you're in?"

Maybe. I think so. "Yes." My voice is far from confident.

"Need to know you aren't gonna back out." His voice wavers. "Need you to be sure."

"Can I sleep on it?"

"Yeah. But I need an answer soon." He shakes his head, shaking off his frustration. Finally, his eyes meet mine. "You have anything to wear?"

"At my place."

"Okay. Let's stop by your place on the way to brunch."

"You eat brunch?"

He laughs. "It's more about being seen at the right places." He bites his lip. "You sure you're okay with this?"

I nod. I'm as sure as I can be.

Chapter Thirteen

T he waitress giggles as she introduces herself. I barely manage to fight a glare. Who the hell does she think she is looking at Pete like she knows him?

I scoot my chair closer to his and slide my arm around his waist. This does nothing to wipe the flirty look off her face. No, apparently, it doesn't matter that he's my boyfriend.

Fake boyfriend, but she doesn't know that.

I order my vegetable omelet and latte through clenched teeth. She keeps her eyes on Pete the entire time, punctuating her questions with giggles.

When she goes on to her next table, he chuckles.

His lips curl into a smile. "You're jealous."

"No." Maybe. Absolutely. "A little."

"Didn't take much."

His smile goes ear to ear. He's enjoying teasing me. I don't take the bait. But I do scoot a little closer. In case any other woman has designs on taking him home.

I look at him. "How does this work, being seen?"

"Basically this. We'll spend the day hitting a few popular spots. Should get someone snapping pics—a fan or a paparazzi. Something will make its way to a gossip blog. Just have to give it time."

"People really take pictures of you eating brunch?"

He leans in closer. "Yeah. Most people are too shy to say hi. But they like having that story *once I saw this b-list celebrity at breakfast*. Picture helps sell it."

"Seeing a guy at breakfast is a pretty shitty story."

His lips curl into a smile. "What about, saw him causing a scene, making out with his girlfriend at breakfast?"

"Better."

He cocks a brow. "Saw him fingering his girlfriend under the table at breakfast?"

I swallow hard so I won't scream *yes, right now.* "You're going to get me into trouble."

He nods and motions *come here.*

I lean closer. Until I can smell his breath. A hint of coffee. And spearmint.

He presses his lips against mine.

Mmm. He tastes good. My lips part to make way for his tongue. Is this real or pretend? I don't know. I only know how much I like his lips on mine.

My hands slide into his hair. My hips shift, begging me to climb into his lap. Damn, I want to say yes.

We're in plain view of anyone who walks by.

His eyes bore into mine when he pulls back. His voice is clear and confident. "You want me to do it."

"Isn't that bad for your nice, blond girlfriend image?"

"Probably. Still do it if you ask."

"That's not a good idea." I take a long sip of my water then look back to him. "I still can't believe you go to brunch."

"Cause brunch is for girls? Expect better from you. That kinda thinking is retrograde." He shakes his head with mock outrage.

"What do you do most mornings?"

"Cereal." He takes a long sip of his coffee. "Can't cook to save my life."

"Really?" I'm so focused on his deep brown eyes that I stir extra sugar into my coffee.

He chuckles. "Set grilled cheese on fire once."

"You did not."

He nods.

"But you're good at everything."

"Not cooking."

I study his expression. He's actually sheepish. It's incredibly endearing.

"I can teach you," I offer. "At home, I always cooked for my sister and my dad."

His voice softens. "Your mom?"

"She left when I was about twelve." I cut myself off but the memory catches up to me—the way Mom looked at us like we were keeping her from what she really wanted, how casually she walked away and never looked back.

"Hey." His voice is deep and steady. "You're hurting."

I nod.

"Tell me about it."

Can I really do that? I've never talked about this with anyone. Not even Madison. We pretend like it never happened.

My entire extended family always toes the *everything is fine* party line.

I take a deep breath. I want to talk to Pete. I trust him.

I go on. "I didn't realize it then, but she never wanted to have kids. Never wanted to get married. My dad convinced her it was a good idea, that he'd stay home with us so she could put her career first. Never happened." My voice strains. "It was sudden. One night she came into my room and kissed me goodbye. In the morning she was gone. I had no clue where she went. I had no clue how to get in touch with her."

"I'm sorry you went through that."

"Thank you." My gaze goes to my thighs. "I thought it was my fault. That if I'd been less demanding or if I'd gotten better grades... if it hadn't been so hard for her to take care of us, then she would have stayed."

He squeezes my hand. "Your dad never picked up the slack?"

My stomach clenches. I'm not ready to talk about him yet. "No, he can barely take care of himself."

"Your sister the one who slept with your boyfriend?"

"She's my only sister."

"She did that after years of you taking care of her?"

"Sort of. She's only two years younger. She's been able to take care of herself for a while."

His fingertips find my chin. He tilts me so we're eye to eye. His expression is demanding. "Promise me something."

"What?"

"Promise you'll stop running from how much that hurts you." His eyes fill with affection. "You don't have to be her friend. Don't have to make up with her. Don't even have to talk to her again. But you have to stop pretending it doesn't hurt."

"Will you stop pretending it doesn't hurt that your ex cheated on you?"

"I'm not pretending. Just don't like talking about it." He scoots back. His eyes meet mine. "How long were you with your ex?"

"Almost three years."

"All due respect, but what the fuck were you doing with him for that long? Asshole doesn't even like *Hunger Games*."

I stare back at him. "I'll tell you if you tell me what you were doing with your ex for six years."

"I loved her."

"I loved Nathan. Or I thought I did. I'm not the one who said I didn't feel my ex in my soul."

"You ever feel something in your soul?"

The question disarms me. There are all sorts of things that hurt somewhere deep. Mom leaving, finding Dad drunk in a pile of his own vomit, that elation of getting into law school then the look on Nathan's face when he told me I had to choose between him and school.

"I don't know. Maybe." My breath breaks up the tension forming in my chest.

"You want to be assertive."

"Yeah."

"So tell me to fuck off or tell me why you were with your ex for three years."

I laugh. "You have a really strange way of wording things."

"Is that a *fuck off*?"

I shake my head. It's difficult to talk about Nathan. I can see, in hindsight, how awful our relationship was. But I missed every single sign.

His voice softens. "Not trying to judge you. Just want to know where you hurt."

A million feelings swirl inside me. He wants to know where I hurt? He might as well say *I love you and I want to take your pain away*. I feel light. I feel like I can fly. The thought of Pete loving me...

It's intoxicating.

But it's not true. I can't get ahead of myself. I roll my shoulders back to break up the tension taking hold of my shoulders. "Nathan was charming. And nobody ever really paid attention to me. He was popular, funny, smart. I didn't have a clue what relationships were supposed to be like, what love looked like. I thought it was normal, the way he'd convince me his way was best, the way he put his needs first.

I figured all guys were like that. Or else why would Mom leave?"

"Shit. I'm being an asshole. I'm sorry."

"Yeah, but you're right. I was with him for a long time because I thought that he loved me and that I loved him. I thought that he cared about me. But he didn't. How could I have been so blind to that? I was nineteen when we started dating. I was old enough to know better." My stomach clenches. It feels so pathetic looking back on it.

Will Pete think less of me for being spineless? I wouldn't tell anyone else. But I want him to know me, to know where I hurt.

And I want to know him. I want to know every single place he hurts. If he'll ever reveal them to me.

I take a deep breath. "When I got into law school, I thought he'd be happy for me. But he wasn't. I got into NYU. I would have stayed in New York for him. But he didn't want me to be a lawyer. He wanted me to be his wife, to stay home and take care of his kids, and always put him first."

"That's fucked up."

"You don't want that?"

His brow furrows. "Is that what you think of me?"

"No, I... I just thought. I don't know." I trip over my tongue. "I guess I don't know what adult relationships are supposed to look like. Not that it matters. We're... we're not together that way."

"Whatever you want to call this, we're equals. I always want to know what you want." His eyes turn down. "I'd never get in your way like that."

"Oh."

"Fuck, I'm glad I get to help you become a lawyer." He meets my gaze, his eyes brimming with affection. "You deserve the fucking world, Jess. Wish I could offer you more than this."

My heart sinks. He's being so sweet telling me he'll never really love me.

Everything is heavy. The air is colder, the sun is dimmer. He's never going to love me. He's never going to be my boyfriend.

How is that possible? The way he's staring at me, I'm sure he cares about me.

I try to push it out of my head but it won't go. How can he tell me I deserve the world in one breath then tell me he'll never love me in the next?

His arm slides around my shoulders. "You're like Katniss, trying to shoulder a whole fucking revolution."

"Are you talking *Hunger Games* with me?"

He nods.

"You can't do that, Pete. You're gonna make me fall in love with you."

"That's all it takes?"

"When it's you."

"Jess, I... I'm not gonna want a relationship."

"I know."

"And you're okay with that?"

I nod a yes, but I'm not sure I mean it.

❧

AFTER BRUNCH, WE SPEND AN HOUR WALKING AROUND THE outdoor shopping center. For the most part, people leave us alone. Either Pete is infinitely less recognizable in sunglasses or people really are used to seeing celebrities everywhere.

I forget all about what it is we're supposed to be doing and enjoy soaking in the afternoon with him. We browse the aisles of an independent bookstore. He picks books from the Young Adult shelf, skips to random passages, then asks me to deem the books as read-worthy or not. I do the same with the science fiction shelf. Despite my insistence that both of us read exclusively on our e-readers, he buys every book that makes it into our stack.

We sit at an outdoor cafe, sipping iced drinks and leafing through our new reading material.

I don't notice the day passing until my stomach grumbles. The sun is streaked with orange. It's already evening. Damn, it's easy being with him. I haven't thought about anything since brunch.

"You hungry?" he asks.

I nod.

"There's a great restaurant at this hotel in the hills. Don't usually go 'cause it's such a scene."

⚬❧⚬

PETE LEADS ME THROUGH THE LUSH LOBBY. THE restaurant is off to the left. Its gold signs make it look expensive.

He nods to a guarded pool to the right. "Should we crash?"

"We can't."

He slides his arm around my waist, pulling my body into his. "Want to bet?"

"No. I'm sure you can figure something out."

He leans in to whisper in my ear. "Too bad. Was gonna make my prize eating you out."

My cheeks flush. He really said those words. It shouldn't surprise me at this point, but I'm still tingly with anticipation.

He chuckles. "That a problem?"

"No. Just... is that really what you'd want for a prize?"

"Yeah."

"Uh..." It's impossible to think.

He presses his palm against my lower back. "Don't fucking tell me you don't like it. Been thinking about tasting your cunt for two days straight."

"Oh."

"Oh?"

I clear my throat. Okay. I need to get my senses back.

I pull back enough to look into his eyes. They're earnest. Hell, they're wide with desire.

"Jess, don't fucking tell me you don't like it." He stares back into my eyes. "I don't do oral with random hookups and I've been going fucking crazy thinking about feeling you come on my face."

"No. I like it."

"Good." His eyes pass over me. "What the fuck are we doing talking then? Let's go."

"Here?"

"Yeah." He nods to a single-stall bathroom in the corner of the lobby.

I'm not ready for public bathroom sex. I take a step backwards so I won't give into temptation. "You really want to do it?"

"What about *I've been going fucking crazy thinking about feeling you come on my face* was unclear?"

"Uh..."

He pulls me into a kiss. It's a hell of a kiss. When he releases me, my heart is thudding against my chest. I'm practically dizzy.

There's no way that's for show.

Enough talking. I can't ignore my body's demands any longer.

I want to come on his face.

I bring my lips to his ear. "I want to... I want you to go down on me."

His lips curl into a smile. He motions to the bathroom.

I'm not ready for that. Yet. I stare into his gorgeous brown eyes with as much confidence as I can muster. "This is a hotel, isn't it?"

He nods.

"We can get a room."

He chuckles. "And do what?"

"Don't tease me, Steele. You fell asleep on me last night."

His eyes meet mine. "I'll get a room, but I'm gonna tease you. Gonna tease you until you're begging."

Chapter Fourteen

I t takes much too long to register and ride the elevator
to our room. The entire time, Pete stays six inches from
me. His fingertips graze my wrist, my forearm, the back
of my hand. His fingertips are enough to undo me.

The ornate hallway is lit with tiny gold lamps. The carpet
and walls are beige. The door to our room is a thick oak
thing. Finally, Pete slides the key into the electronic lock. It
flashes green. He turns the handle, pulls me inside.

In one swift movement, he pushes me against the closed
door. His hand goes to the deadbolt. Locked.

His eyes stay on mine. There's always an intensity to his
gaze. Sometimes it's a mystery. Not right now. The desire in
his expression is clear as day. There's no pretending. No
trying to bend to someone else's will.

He wants me.

I want him.

Everything about it makes sense.

His eyelids flutter closed as he leans in to kiss me. Then
my eyes are closed and his lips are on my lips. Mmm. He
always tastes damn good.

Feelings rise up in my throat. This is more than want, more than sex. I don't want to fight it anymore. I have feelings for him. How could I not? He's amazing. Funny, sexy, intense, sweet in a strange way.

My thoughts fade away as his tongue slides into my throat. I'm not worried about our gossip mission. I'm not worried about my friends back home, about Madison, about Dad, about school.

When I'm with him, the rest of the world fades away.

His hands go to my hips. He pushes my panties to my knees. I kick them off my feet, spreading my legs to give him easier access.

His fingertips slide up my thigh. Closer, closer, closer. They skim my clit then they're on the other thigh.

The damn tease.

I follow his lead, arching to meet him, kissing back the way he's kissing me, dragging my hands up his arms until I'm at the sleeves of his t-shirt.

When our kiss breaks, I'm panting and desperate. Okay, I can ask for what I want.

"Can we go to the bed now?" That's not fast enough. I need to move things along, need him closer. I reach behind my back to unzip my dress.

Pete watches, transfixed. "Once you're naked."

Mmm. The desire in his eyes makes my sex clench. He makes me feel damn beautiful. I push the straps of my dress off my shoulders. In one swift motion, it falls to my feet. Only the bra left.

I stare back into his gorgeous brown eyes as I unhook it and slide it off my shoulders.

There. I'm naked in front of him. He's seen me plenty by now, but the way he looks at me makes me feel like it's the first time.

I've always been self-conscious about my figure. Even after a year with Nathan, I never felt sexy.

But the way Pete stares at me... I feel like I belong in a national lingerie ad. I feel like the sexiest girl in the whole fucking world.

His hands slide around my hips, settling on my ass. "Legs around me."

I wrap my legs around his hips as he lifts me off the ground. Damn. He's strong. There isn't a hint of strain in his expression.

Pete practically throws me on the bed. The mattress is firm with plenty of bounce. I settle onto the sleek white comforter.

It occurs to me that I should be concerned about the strength of my feelings for him. They go well beyond where they should given the boundaries of our relationship.

But I'm not concerned.

It feels good, letting my feelings flow through me. It feels good, knowing what I want. Sure, it might hurt more later. Odds are good that this will break my heart into a million little pieces. But, right now, I'm not worried. Right now, I'm flying.

His hands find my ankles. He pulls me to the edge of the bed and spreads my knees. I can feel his breath against my sex. Damn, he's close.

His lips press against my inner thigh. His groan reverberates against my skin. He kisses a trail up my thigh. Closer. Closer. Closer.

Almost.

Then he's on my other thigh. The fucking tease. He nips at the skin. His hand trails my stomach, to my breast. His fingertips circle my nipple. Pangs of desire shoot straight to my sex.

He groans against my thigh again and that hint of self-consciousness fades away. There's no doubt in my mind—he wants this as much as I do.

How the hell did I get so lucky?

Words refuse to make their way to my lips. Instead, I groan and sling my legs over his shoulders. It pulls him closer.

Closer still.

So fucking close I could scream.

Then his tongue slides over me, one long, slow lick, and everything in the world is right.

Then it's on my lips. My body cries with relief. His mouth is soft and warm. And it feels so intimate, his face buried between my legs.

I don't waste any time. I groan. I press my thighs into his cheeks.

He keeps one hand on my thigh, holding me in place as he works me with his tongue. There's something amazing about how soft his tongue is. The sensation is intense. I'm already halfway to an orgasm.

I relax into the bed, soaking in every moment of pleasure —the way his groans send shivers up my spine, his thumb brushing against my nipple, his tongue on my clit, the tension knotting inside me.

My fingers dig into the comforter. It's smooth and slick. I can barely get a grip.

We're in a hotel. We don't have to be quiet.

I scream his name. I press my thighs against his cheeks. For a second, I worry I'm cutting off his air supply. But he groans against my thigh again and again.

My body is nothing but pleasure. My entire world is nothing but pleasure.

With the next flick of his tongue, I go over the edge. The tension inside me knots to a fever pitch then everything releases. My sex clenches. Bliss spreads to every inch of my body.

My muscles go slack. Damn am I spent. I want to push myself up, to look at him, to touch him, but my body refuses to move.

He finishes the thought for me. His fingers trail up my thigh, over my stomach. The weight shifts on the bed. I turn. And there's Pete, lying next to me, the pride of accomplishment written all over his face.

I open my mouth to say something about how fucking amazing he is but all I manage is a murmured *thank you.*

He lies next to me, pulling my body onto his. His cotton shirt is soft and cool. His jeans are rough. My hands find his hair, his neck, his forearms.

He catches my lower lip with his thumb. "My pleasure."

I murmur my agreement. Press my lips against his digit.

He slides his thumb into my mouth. I suck hard. Anticipation courses through my veins. God, how I want him in my mouth, totally under my control.

I'm too on a cloud to feel self conscious. I blink my eyes open and stare into his. "Are you clean? I am. I got tested a few months ago. Haven't been with anyone but you since."

He nods. "I'm clean."

"Good. I'm on the pill. For later."

He cocks a brow. "Later?"

The words fall right off my lips. "I want to suck you off."

He takes my hand and drags it up his thigh. No waiting. I can't bear to wait another second.

I unzip his jeans. He shifts to his feet and pushes them to his hips. Then the boxers.

This is the first time I've gotten a perfect view of his body. The light streaming through the window casts him in a gorgeous glow. I take in every hard inch—from the desire in his deep brown eyes all the way down to his muscular thighs.

My sex clenches. He's ridiculously hot. And he's that hard for me.

I'm going to make this count. I'm going to have him at my mercy. I push myself to my feet.

Okay. I'm in control. I can do this. I motion to the wall. "Put your back against the wall."

His eyes cloud with desire. He takes a step backwards. Another. Until he's against the wall.

I study every inch of him. The way his lips part with a sigh of pleasure. The way the muscles of his stomach and thighs tense with anticipation.

He's desperate for me.

His eyes stay fixed on me as I take three steps towards him. There's that hint of vulnerability in his eyes. Right now, he needs me.

A rush of anticipation spreads through my stomach. I need him feeling as good as I do. I need him screaming *my* name as *he* comes.

I rise to my tip toes to kiss him. His hard cock presses against my stomach. Almost.

My tongue slides into his mouth. My hands slide into his hair. He's going to be panting and desperate.

Sucking on his tongue isn't enough. I pull back. I take his hand and bring his fingers to my lips. He pushes forward, sliding his fingers into my mouth.

I press my tongue flat against them. Mmm. Even his fingers taste good. My sex clenches as I suck on his soft skin. This is going too slow.

My hand finds his hip. Then it's curving around his thigh. I trace the lines of his tattoo. My fingers catch on something. A scar. But this isn't the time to ask questions.

Right now, I'm the one making him desperate.

I drag my fingers up his thighs, over that soft tuft of pubic hair, and I wrap my hand around his cock.

His pupils dilate. His lips part. There. He's where I want him.

He catches my lower lip with his thumb. The gesture is intimate, a reminder that this isn't just sex.

I suck on his thumb for good measure. Harder and harder until he's groaning. No more waiting. I'm getting back in control.

My hands go to his hips. I lower myself onto my knees. One hand slides to his firm ass. The other goes to his cock.

I watch his reactions as I rub his tip with my thumb. When he's groaning enough that I'm certain he's desperate, I brush my lips against him.

"Jess," he groans.

God damn, that's a beautiful sound.

I flick my tongue against his tip. His groan gets louder. I do it again and again, until he's groaning so loudly *I* can't take it anymore.

I wrap my lips around him, taking him into my mouth. He tastes good. Like soap and like Pete.

His hands go to my hair. They find the band holding my French braid together and do away with it.

My hair spills over my cheeks. He digs his hand into it, tugging just enough my sex clenches with desire.

I want his pleasure as much as I want my own.

I take him deeper. Until he's groaning. Until our bodies are the only things in the universe. His skin is soft but he's so fucking hard. I dig my fingers into his firm ass, using it for leverage to take him deeper. When I can't take anymore, I stroke him.

His hands knot in my hair. They nudge the back of my head.

Deeper.

I take him as deep as I can. Stroke him as hard as I can.

His moans blur together. It really is beautiful music. Much better than anything I've heard on the radio.

"Fuck, Jess," he groans as he tugs at my hair. "I'm going to come."

Hell yes.

His eyelids press together. A sigh escapes his lips.

He shudders. He's almost there. I watch the pleasure spread over his face as I suck on him.

He lets out another groan. His palm presses against the back of my head, holding me in place as he thrusts into my mouth.

"Fuck, Jess," he groans. "You're fucking amazing."

My body floods with desire. I feel amazing—powerful and sexy.

I swallow so I can take him deeper. I dig my fingers into the flesh of his ass. It's almost too much, but I can't do anything to stop the ecstasy in his expression.

It's the best thing I've ever seen.

With his next moan, he comes. His thighs shake. His hands tug at my hair. And he groans my name again and again.

He tastes good. Sweet. I hold him in my mouth until he's finished then I swallow hard.

He sighs with pleasure as he takes my hands and pulls me to my feet. Then his arms around me, his palms on my ass and between my shoulder blades.

He pulls my body into his. The embrace is so tight I can't breathe.

We collapse on the bed, tangled up in each other, everything in the world exactly where it should be.

෧෧

WE LINGER IN BED FOR THE BETTER PART OF AN HOUR. HIS arms are around me. My back is against his chest. I can feel his heart beat and hear his breath.

It's heaven.

I don't move until my stomach is grumbling. I push myself to a seated position and turn to face him. The moonlight casts highlights over the hard lines of his body.

My gaze is drawn to the tattoo on his thigh. I haven't had a chance to really look at it. My fingertips skim his knee. "May I?"

"You can touch me anytime you want."

I fight my blush. "You've got me all wrong, Steele, I'm only in it for the body art."

"Too bad. I wouldn't mind going again."

"Wouldn't mind?"

"Was planning to wait until after dinner."

"Oh. That's probably good. We need our strength."

He chuckles. Damn his eyes look even more beautiful in the moonlight. I want to drink them in.

My gaze rakes over his strong shoulders and chest, all the way down his torso and over his hip and thigh. His tattoo is huge—takes up most of his quad and some of his hip.

It's beautiful. Red and grey roses with strong, sweeping lines. Instead of thorns, the flowers are connected with barbed wire.

I trace the curving lines of the design. There's that scar again. I move past it but there's another scar. There are a lot of scars.

His voice is deep and steady. "You're gonna hurt my feelings not asking about my tattoos."

"You have more?"

He points to a tattoo that curves around his left hip and side.

"Nothing on your chest or shoulders?"

"Gotta save some skin."

"In case you feel something else in your soul?"

He nods.

"How many things have you felt in your soul?"

"A few."

"Are they all tattoos?"

"Yeah." His eyes meet mine. "But it's not one thing. There's a lot in this design."

"I wouldn't want anything I've felt that deep on my skin. It's too ugly."

"It helps, reminding yourself that you survived something ugly."

I swallow hard. "Did you get that to cover your scars?"

He takes my hand and brings it to his thigh. "The scars are part of the design."

I look closer. He's right. The scars are woven into the barbed wire.

My eyes meet his. "Why do you have scars on your thighs?"

"You really want to know?"

I nod.

"You sure? It's the kind of thing you can't take back."

"I'm sure."

"My dad hit me."

The words fall from his tongue like he's saying his dad was a mechanic. Like it's natural.

He stares back at me. "Once, he was drunk and miserable. He took the kitchen knife and started threatening to kill himself."

My stomach drops.

"I tried to stop him." He motions to the scars. "Got halfway there."

"Your dad did that?"

He nods.

My heart aches. "How old were you?"

"Young." His posture stiffens, a clear *we're not discussing this* message.

But I want to know him, know where he hurts. "Did that happen a lot?"

"Depends on your definition of 'a lot.'"

"Do you want to talk about it?"

"No. I don't like thinking about him. He's been gone a long time. Ten years since he died."

"I'm sorry you went through that."

He nods.

"What was it you felt in your soul?"

"Lot of things. It's complicated." His eyes meet mine. "You've never wanted ink?"

"Nothing has ever jumped out at me." Almost nothing. My cheeks flush. "You'll make fun of me."

"I won't." He holds up his hand. "Scout's honor."

"Were you a Boy Scout?"

"No. Tell me anyway."

"There's this couple's tattoo. If I ever really loved someone, I'd want to get it."

"What's there to make fun of?"

"It's from *The Hunger Games*. From *Mockingjay*."

His lips curl into a smile.

"See, you're going to make fun."

He shakes his head. "What from *Mockingjay*?"

"You've read it?"

"Of course."

"You know how Peeta gets brainwashed and he's not sure of his mind, so he asks Katniss if his memories are real or not real?"

Pete nods.

"At the end, he goes to her and says, 'you love me, real or not real.' And she says 'real.' I want that. One person gets 'real or not real' and the other gets 'real.' It could be with a mockingjay or an arrow or just the words."

My face is burning. I can barely bring myself to look him in the eyes.

There's no judgment in his expression. He's smiling. "That sounds sweet."

"You don't think it's lame I'm a super fan?"

"Fuck no. *Hunger Games* is good shit."

My fingers are drawn to the lines of his tattoo. "Will you explain it to me, what it is you felt in your soul? Why you got the tattoo?"

"It's not exact. If I could explain it exactly, I wouldn't need the ink."

"That's okay."

His voice drops. "My biological mom died giving birth. Dad never got over it. That's why he was always drinking. He never stopped blaming me for it." Pete's eyes go to the comforter. "Looked at me like I stole the sun from the sky."

He's been through an ocean of pain. I reach out to comfort him. My fingers find his cheek. He leans into the gesture for a moment then he turns away from me.

"Always knew I could lose anything at any moment," he says. "Wasn't till I landed with Ophelia that it mattered. She was the first person who thought I was worth something. Roses are her favorite flowers. Became mine too. Got the ink the day I turned 18. Can't explain better than that."

"I think I understand."

He moves closer. Pain slides off his face until his expression is all playful. Does he really feel better or has he just pushed it aside? I'm not sure.

All I know is how badly I want to be there next time he hurts, to do whatever I can to comfort him.

Chapter Fifteen

Dinner is a blur of good food and better conversation. We share two obscenely fancy seafood dishes—red snapper and scallops—and an array of amazing vegetable side dishes.

I don't snap out of the cloud until we're on our way back to my place. The drive takes too long. He has one hand planted on my thigh. My whole body sizzles from the touch.

This can't happen soon enough.

Pete parks on the street. I'm about to jump out of the car when he pulls me back.

"Hold on." His voice is rough. He's upset.

Oh. There's a stocky man standing outside my apartment, talking to one of my neighbors. There's a camera around his neck. He's a photographer.

"Let me handle this." Pete gets out of the car without waiting for my response.

His posture stiffens as he approaches the photographer. I can't hear anything from the car, but I can feel the anger all the way over here.

This is bad.

I'm not gonna sit and watch him get hurt. I open the car door and step onto the sidewalk.

"Let's go inside," I say.

"Be there in a minute." Pete glares at the photographer.

Okay. That's a threat. No way he's getting into trouble on account of me.

"No, come in with me." I try to keep my voice light. I point to the writing on my chest. "You did make me a promise."

That breaks up some of the frustration in his expression. He shoots the photographer one more glare then follows me into my apartment.

I lock the doorknob and the deadbolt. It's not enough security. My blinds don't work—they're stuck half open. Anyone across the street can see in here. Anyone can find me.

Is it really that interesting, Pete dating a random law student?

The air is stiff and tense. Something tells me this conversation isn't ending with him planted between my legs.

He presses his back against the wall. His eyes stay glued to me. "This should blow over in a few weeks."

I nod.

"Until then, you need to stay with me." His stare is demanding, intense. "I know you want your space. I respect that. You can take Tom's room and one of the empty rooms as an office."

I swallow hard. "This is my apartment."

"You can't stay here. It's not safe." He runs his hand through his hair. "I won't forgive myself if something happens to you." He moves closer, until he's only a foot away, then he pulls me into a hug. "Give it a few days. If you don't like it, we'll figure out something else."

"Okay."

I soak in the comfort of his arms for as long as I can.

Then I pack up everything I need for the next few weeks, get in his car, and say goodbye to everything I love about my apartment.

༖

HE GOES STRAIGHT TO HIS ROOM. NO DISCUSSION, NO concern, nothing but him locking me out again.

I try to soak in the atmosphere of the house—it *is* a beautiful place—but all I feel is the lack of his presence.

Did it mean that little to him, sharing how his father hurt him?

I try not to let it hurt. He isn't going to fall in love with me. He doesn't want a girlfriend. He doesn't even want to talk to me when it's not convenient for him.

I'll stay here for a while, but I'm not going to let him become a part of my life. Not if he's going to pull away like this.

Chapter Sixteen

It's fifty minutes and two transfers from Pete's place to the law school book store. Plenty of time for my confusion to settle in. Where the hell does Pete get off pulling away like that?

Damn. If only he'd been reasonable, we could have ended the night with fireworks and orgasms.

The five minute walk in the sweltering sun is enough to make me well aware of my body's other demands. It's well past lunch time. I'm tired. It's damn hot.

I need an iced coffee.

And I need him deep inside me.

Air conditioning pours over my skin as I step into the bookstore. Now, all I need is him deep inside me. It's wrong, thinking dirty thoughts in a law school bookstore. This place is practically a library.

I load my hands with required textbooks, trying hard to think of anything but the matter of fact text from Pete sitting on my phone. *I transferred some spending cash into your account.* What the hell is his problem? The guy closes off in a hot second then he transfers an obscene sum of money into my bank account.

Enough that I don't need to even think about getting a job for the next twelve months.

"Excuse me!" A student in slacks and an oxford shirt bumps into me. He looks at me like I'm out of place then nods to the bookshelf behind me. "You mind?"

"Yeah, sure." I step aside so he can grab his text book.

The guy scoffs. The look on his face says *shhh*. The volume of my breath displeases him. Or maybe the floral pattern of my skirt is too loud. Somehow, I don't fit his vision of law student to be.

Fuck him. Fuck Pete if he's gonna turn off his affection because some mean girls think I'm not hot enough to be a rock star's girlfriend. I'm not bending to what other people want anymore.

I ignore the rude guy as I collect the rest of my books. Damn. This is heavy. I make a pile of half a dozen books on the carpet.

A sound pierces the quiet. An Amy Winehouse song. Shit. That's my ring tone. I find my cell in my pocket. *Incoming call from Pete Steele.*

The rude guy stares at me like I'm evil. Asshole. I dig my fingers into the slick plastic of my phone case. Okay, I'm frustrated. But I'm not stooping to being an asshole.

I bring the phone to my ear. The irritation in my voice is more obvious than I intend it to be. "Yes?"

"Where did you go?" he asks.

"To get my books."

"Tell me next time."

"Fine."

"You okay?"

No, I'm not okay. I couldn't sleep a wink, because I couldn't stop thinking about how you locked me out. "About as good as a person can be getting textbooks." My stack is up to eight books. It's going to be miserable getting these home on the bus. "Why do you ask?"

"We're live."

"Oh. That's good, right?"

"Yeah." His voice is uncertain. "Pic's pretty racy."

"Send it to me."

My phone buzzes with a new picture message. It *is* racy. We're at the hotel, making out, his hands digging into my ass.

It wasn't a staged moment. It was real and raw. I can feel how much he wants me just looking at the picture.

A flutter builds below my belly. This isn't helping ease the ache between my legs.

I bring the phone back to my ear. "Looks great. And you can barely see my face. I doubt anyone recognizes me."

"It's only a matter of time."

I switch my phone to the other hand. I shift my weight between my legs. "I know what I signed up for."

"With all due respect, you don't know till it happens."

"I've been chased out of my apartment. I think I know."

"I didn't mean—"

"If you don't want a girlfriend, that's fine. Stop letting me in then pushing me away. I've got the point. You don't want intimacy with me. Right?"

He says nothing.

My chest heaves. How can he be so casual about this? Not my problem. My problem is school.

I do nothing to fight the frustration in my voice. "I should go. I need to figure out how to get these books home."

"Jess."

"Are you getting at something?" I ask.

"Don't play dumb. You can't pull off dumb."

"I know that you *can* pick me up, Pete. It's just that I

don't want to put myself through another round of you opening up to me then locking me out again."

"I'll be there in twenty." His voice softens. "If you need anything, call."

"Were you listening to me?"

"You don't have to talk to me."

"But, I—"

"Tell me to go fuck myself and I will."

I trip over my tongue. "You don't mean that you'd go touch yourself."

"Yeah. Sure. You want pictures?"

"Yes." My cheeks flush. I want a million pictures but he's not distracting me with sex. "But not right now."

"You want me to come or not?"

"Don't say it like that."

"You want me to pick you up or not?"

"Okay. You can pick me up. If you're going to stop jerking me around."

"Deal. See you soon."

I slide my phone into my pocket and offer the nosy asshole guy a weak smile.

My heart is still heavy. My stomach is still in knots. Okay, I can admit it. This is more than sexual frustration.

I have full blown feelings for him.

But I'm not letting that get in the way of law school. That's what happened to my mom. She met a guy, gave up her career to get married, had a few kids, then resented her family every minute of every day.

Not me. No way. I'm not letting anyone get in the way of what I want. Not anymore.

I collect my last few books, pay at the register, and find a cozy spot on the lawn.

I'm a law student.

No one is taking that happiness away from me.

For twenty minutes, I soak in the warmth of the sun, the soft breeze on my arms, the sharp aroma of fresh cut grass.

There are footsteps. Someone sits next to me. I don't need to look up to know it's Pete. I can feel his presence in the way my shoulders relax.

Even when he frustrates me, he makes me feel like I can float.

His fingers brush the back of my hand. "You excited?"

I take a long look around the quad, memorizing the shape of the tall trees, the red brick of the main building. "This is the next three years of my life."

He moves closer. Until our shoulders are touching.

Still, I keep my eyes on the school. Looking at him is too risky. I might mount him right here on the grass.

He drags his fingertips over my forearm. Damn musicians and their masterful hands. I'm already flushed and wanting.

"Any chance you're taking up entertainment law? Like you a lot more than our current lawyer," he teases.

"No. It pays well but it doesn't interest me."

"Atticus Finch doesn't argue royalty percentages."

My stomach flutters. He remembers what I said about *To Kill a Mockingbird*. "Am I that obvious, wanting to be a defense attorney?"

"You want to get murderers off. Cold. Exactly what I expect from you," he teases.

Finally, I look at him. Damn, the affection in his deep brown eyes takes my breath away. How can he have his guard down so quickly when it was up so high last night?

I run my fingertips over his chin. I can't help it. He's beautiful.

I make my voice as confident as I can. "Only person I want to get off is you."

His lips curl into a smile. "Only if I get you off first."

My cheeks flush. I want to. But I can't deal with him closing off again. "You bailed yesterday."

He says nothing.

Okay. That's not the best sign. I study his expression for a clue to his intentions, but the only thing I can place is confusion.

"Why did you do that?" I ask.

"I was thinking."

"About."

He moves closer. His eyes fix on mine. "You haven't told me why you want to be a defense attorney."

"I guess it started before *To Kill a Mockingbird*. My friend, Kathryn—"

"The one who sleeps around?"

I laugh. "That one. We've been friends since kindergarten. She got bullied a lot. One day, I think it was third grade, a few of the popular kids ganged up on her and started a fight. When the teachers broke it up, the popular kids all said Kathryn started it. Nobody listened to her. They barely gave her a chance to defend herself. It wasn't fair. Everyone deserves a defense."

"What about your ex?"

"It's not a crime, being a cheater or an asshole."

His brow knits. "But if it was?"

"I guess he'd deserve a defense. I always let him get his way, never challenged him. But I didn't offer much of myself. I didn't make an effort to get to know him. I didn't love him the way Tom loves Willow. Or, uh, what was it, Drew and Kara?"

"Yeah."

"It was nothing like that. Not even close." I swallow hard.

"Reasonable doubt is the cornerstone of our justice system." I sound like a textbook. I continue anyway. "The police can't just know what happened. They have to prove it. They need enough facts to convince twelve jurors."

He finds the tie holding together my French braid and pulls it out. "You're beaming."

"Really?"

"Yeah." He runs his fingers through my hair, undoing my braid. "Never thought a woman talking about the law could be so fucking sexy."

"Why did you run off last night?"

His eyes turn down. "Kept thinking that you're gonna back out of this."

"I won't. I swear."

He stares back with disbelief. "Can I get that in writing?"

There's all this vulnerability in his eyes. I want to wipe it away.

I nod. "Sure. You have a pen?"

He pulls a permanent marker from the front pocket of his skinny jeans and hands it to me.

"Hmm, where to write? No paper." I drag my fingers over the V of his v-neck. "This will have to do." I pull his t-shirt down and write my promise on his chest.

I won't back out of this. - Jess James

He looks down with a smile then takes the marker back. One hand goes to my shoulder, holding me in place. With the other, he scribbles on my chest.

"What's it say?" I ask.

He pulls back to admire his work. His lips curl into a smile. "I'll make you come every day."

"It does not."

He nods, pulls out his cell, and uses his camera to prove it. There it is, in black marker on my chest:

I'll make you come every day. - Pete Steele

Chapter Seventeen

✣

Pete's good mood slips when we get back to his place. He goes off to his room to work on a song. It must be true—there is music flowing from his door—but it's not exactly him being straight with me.

I want to talk to him. I want to pry his head open and look at all his thoughts. But I can't take him pushing back. Not right now.

After I unpack my books and organize my clothes, I say fuck it, and I give in to the allure of the glowing aqua pool.

There's some noise in the backyard. Mostly birds, breeze, a far away car driving through the neighborhood. I can see the hills for miles. I can see Downtown, the cluster of skyscrapers that makes up Century City, the white letters of the Hollywood sign.

I don't have a swimsuit. Pete's room has a view of the pool. The sun is setting. There's no reason why I need to be shy. I strip to nothing and dip my feet in the pool.

It takes me a minute to ease myself into the cool water. The chlorine will do awful things to my hair, I'm sure, but I don't care. I dive under the surface.

The water is refreshing, inviting. I swim in circles until the sun sets then I settle in the shallow end and turn my eyes towards the setting sun.

The backyard door pulls open. There are footsteps on the concrete. I don't have to turn to know they belong to Pete. No one else is here.

"Hey." His deep voice cuts through the backyard.

"Hey." My voice is not nearly as loud or confident.

I watch him strip out of his jeans, t-shirt, underwear. What is he doing—coming closer, pulling away, holding position? I don't know what to make of his reactions anymore.

My thoughts turn off as I watch him slide into the pool. The glow of the water casts highlights over his face. It makes his deep brown eyes look even more intense.

He moves closer. Closer. Then he's a foot away, close enough to touch.

"Been thinking," he says. "I'm asking too much of you. Fucking up your life."

"You're not."

"Listen to this before you argue with me."

I stare back at him. I know he's wrong, but I'm willing to listen. I nod an okay.

"It's only gonna get worse, this fame bullshit. I don't want that for you." He moves closer. "I'm giving you an out. If you can't do this anymore, you can walk. Keep the money. No hard feelings."

"What about your manager, Aiden?"

"I can deal with him." His fingertips brush my chin. "This is it. If you stay, you have to be in. You have to be sure."

I drag my fingers over the promise I scribbled on his chest. "I was sure this afternoon and I'm sure now." My chest and shoulders feel light. It's obvious. I need him. I can't walk away.

"Don't like that I'm fucking up your life."

"I've dealt with worse." I rise to my tip toes and run my fingers through his dark hair. It's still dry. I'll have to change that. "All I've done since I moved to L.A. is work and read. I was too tired to do anything else. Now, I'm going to law school, I'm getting a hell of a tour around town, and I... I've never had sex like this before."

Some of the doubt in his eyes fades away.

"I like hanging out with you. Like that I can be myself. I trust you." I press my body against his. "I know we aren't together, but we are friends, right?"

"Yeah."

"You're the closest friend I've had in a long time. I won't throw that away."

He's still far away. I don't like it. I want him here, with me, in this amazing moment. We're naked in a pool. The air is warm. The water is just right. Other parts of my life are still fucked, but this is paradise.

I point to the writing on my chest. "You made a promise."

There. He's back. His lips curl into a smile. His eyes fix on mine.

"You have a one track mind, Jess."

I shake my head. "We can talk. Do you want to talk?"

"Not at the moment." His hands go to my ass. He pulls my body into his.

His eyelids press together. I rise to my tip toes. Then our lips are connecting. It's a hell of a kiss. All the frustration of the day fades away until the only thing I can feel is the affection pouring between us.

He cares about me. It's there in his kiss.

I dunk him under the water. He gets revenge by splashing me.

A smile spreads over his face. It does things to me, that smile.

I can't wait anymore. I need all the intimacy I can get with him.

I wrap my arms around his shoulders and pull my body into his. I kiss him deeply.

He doesn't waste any time. One hand slides between my legs to stroke my clit. The other goes to my chest, playing with my nipples. It's different in the water—smoother. I arch my back to push my chest into his hands.

When he breaks our kiss, his eyes find mine. The mystery is gone. He's here and there's nothing in his gaze but desire.

"Hold on." He pins me to the side of the pool with his hips, reaching for something on the concrete. His jeans.

He reaches into the pocket and pulls out a bottle of lube.

"Were you planning this?" I ask.

"Not exactly." He drags his fingertips over my chest, stopping to play with a nipple. "More that I saw you in the pool and I couldn't stop thinking about how fucking good it would feel to have you come on my cock."

I'm not shy today. I know what I want and I'm asking for it. "I need you inside me. Now."

"Mmm." His lips press into mine. He squeezes lube over his fingers then brings his hand between my legs.

No teasing. He slips two fingers inside me. There's no resistance from my body. The lube makes it easy.

Thinking time is over. I kiss him harder. My body melts around his. He works me with his fingers, stroking my clit with his thumb. I dig my nails into the soft, wet skin of his back. Damn, that feels good.

Pleasure knots in my core. I'm already close. But I don't want to come on his hands today.

I pull back from the kiss. "I want you inside me." I drag my hand up his neck and play with his hair until his lips part with a sigh of pleasure. It feels good, saying what I want. "I need you inside me. Now. Don't make me ask again."

He shifts my hips so our bodies are aligned. Anticipation builds in my chest. It feels like it's been ages since we've been here.

There. His cock strains against me. No teasing. In one slow, sweet movement, he slides deep inside me. I can feel my sex stretching around him.

Damn, he feels good.

I dig my fingers into his skin. My lips go to his neck. He tastes like chlorine, and soap, and Pete. I plant kisses on his skin until I find the spot that makes him groan. It's the crook of his neck, right next to his collarbone. I work it every way I can—sucking, kissing, biting gently.

He drives deep into me, one slow stroke after another. There's such an intimacy to it. I can feel his heartbeat against my chest. I can hear his breath in my ear. This isn't fucking. It's making love.

I don't care that it's cheesy. It's true.

I get lost in the pleasure building in my body. His skin is soft and slick. I explore every inch of it I can. Until I can't take the knot of tension in my core any longer. Until I have to dig my hands into his hair and rock my hips against his.

"Fuck, Pete." I tug at his hair. "You feel so good."

He slides his hand behind my neck, cupping the back of my head. He tilts me so we're eye to eye.

I stare into his gorgeous eyes for as long as I can. The way pleasure spreads over his expression—his pupils dilate, his lips part, his eyes roll back in his head—is enough to send me over the edge. But, God, the intimacy of it. I can barely breathe.

My eyes close of their own accord. With his next thrust, I come. My fingers dig into his skin. I groan his name again and again. My body goes slack.

Damn, that's intense.

He slows, waiting for me to catch my breath. His eyes are heavy with lust but he stays attentive.

My hands go to his shoulders. I nod an *okay*. Better than okay. Amazing.

He stays slow, thrusting deep enough I forget to breathe. All my attention is on him. I love the way his shoulders shake. The way his lips part, and his voice gets deep and low, and my name falls off his tongue.

We stay pressed together against the pool wall until we catch our breath.

The rest of the night is perfect. We swim under the stars until we're exhausted. Then it's takeout on the couch and a crime procedural TV marathon. I fall asleep on the couch, in his arms.

⚜

FOR DAYS, LIFE IS PERFECT. I HIKE IN THE HILLS ALL morning, spend the day studying, join Pete on the couch every night. We take turns making dinner—I cook, he orders takeout—and picking movies. Mine are soapy teen dramas. His are sci-fi thrillers.

Everything is perfect until I wake up to a missed call from Madison.

There's no voicemail. Only a short text message.

Madison: We have to talk.

Chapter Eighteen

I press my cell between my palms.

It's been radio silence between me and my sister for months. There hasn't been a hint of contact. Not even anything as innocuous as a comment on a social media post.

Now we need to talk.

What the hell does she want to say?

My head is swimming. I brush my teeth, wash my face, and stare back at my reflection. What does the girl in the mirror want? There's no clarity in her expression. Only confusion.

I squeeze the phone as I make my way downstairs. My knuckles turn white. I lose all feeling in my hands.

Is she calling to apologize or to deliver bad news about Dad?

I'm not sure I can stomach either.

"Hey." Pete's voice cuts through the quiet room. He's sitting at the kitchen table with a cup of coffee and a bowl of cereal.

I nod a hello back to him. I want to tell him about the call. I want to share the weight of this with someone. If it is bad news, if something has happened to Dad... I can't deal with that on my own.

Words refuse to find my lips. My mouth is sticky. Okay. I need more time to think. I take a seat on the couch. It's no good. The couch was comfortable last night. Right now, it feels like I'm sitting on a pile of rocks. Crossing my legs does nothing to help.

There are footsteps as he comes closer. I keep my eyes on the hardwood floor. I keep my fingers curled around my phone.

The weight on the couch shifts as he sits next to me. I can feel all the warmth of his body. I can feel his breath on my shoulder.

"You don't like me pushing you away," he says.

I nod.

"Don't like you locking me out either." He drags his fingertips over my shoulder and down my arm. "What's wrong?"

I open my mouth to speak but the words stay trapped in my throat. How do I explain my feelings towards Madison? I hate her and I love her. I never want to see her again and I miss her more than anything.

His hand finds mine. He peels my fingers from my phone.

"Hey, that's mine." I reach for my cell but he's already hiding it above my head. "Pete. Don't!"

"Don't what?"

"Give it back."

"If you tell me what it is that's upsetting you."

"You're pushy." I reach for his arm but I get distracted by how good it feels to touch him.

"Hey." He pulls me into his lap and hands my phone back. "Talk to me. You look miserable."

"My sister called."

He runs his fingertips over my chin. "What did she say?"

"That we need to talk."

"You need to talk to her."

"Excuse me?" I stare back into his eyes, but the affection in them disarms me. "You don't tell me what to do."

"I'll get you some coffee." He slides me off his lap and pushes himself to his feet.

I play with my phone, staring at Madison's text. It's matter of fact. She's not a matter of fact kind of person. She's expressive, loud, joyful. Is she treading lightly or is it bad news?

Pete's footsteps come closer. He kneels in front of me and hands over my coffee.

I get lost staring into his deep brown eyes. He doesn't like me locking him out. He wants in my heart. I want in his.

How can this be casual?

I bury my thoughts in my coffee. It's sweet and creamy. Incredibly sweet and creamy. "You must think I'm a kid putting this much sugar in the coffee."

"Comfort food." He runs his fingertips over my knee. "Not gonna force you to do shit, Jess, but I'm gonna make sure your sister knows she hurt you."

"I don't like the sound of that."

"Madison, right?"

"Yeah."

"If you don't call her, I'm gonna release a bonus song called *Fuck you Madison. You better apologize to Jess for Hurting Her.*"

"That's a disgustingly long title."

"Eleven words? That's nothing. I can name twenty songs that are longer."

"I believe you." I down half my coffee in one sip. It's so sweet my teeth hurt, but the sugar *is* comforting.

"Look me in the eyes."

I do.

"Tell me the truth. Do you want to make up with her?"

"Yes. I miss her."

"Tell her that."

"But I... I'm still mad. And she hasn't apologized."

"Tell her that too." He slides onto the couch next to me. His fingers trail over my bare thighs. "I'll be right here the whole time."

"What if it's bad news?"

"You have reason to believe that?"

"Yeah... my dad. It could be something about him." I take a deep breath. "He has health problems." There. That's the truth even if it is lacking the critical detail of his health problems being ten years of enabled binge drinking.

Can I even talk to my family without falling back into those patterns? The second I hear their voices, I lose my spine. I want to do whatever it takes to make them feel better.

I've been protecting Dad and Madison for the last ten years. I don't know how to talk to them as equals.

"Don't want to stoop to bribing you with sex, but I will." He traces the outline of my phone, his eyes on mine. "Call her."

"What about the sex bribe?"

"Jess, if you want me, ask for me."

"Can we have sex after this phone call?"

"Fuck yeah."

"Okay." That eases some of the tension in my chest. I have something to look forward to. I unlock my phone screen and stare at the *call back* button. Okay. I can do this.

I dial and hold the phone to my ear.

She answers right away. "Jessie, is that really you?"

Her voice is excited and needy. She misses me too.

A million feelings rise up inside me. I'm angry, sad, nostalgic. I miss her but it still hurts.

I keep my voice even. "It's me."

"I miss you. I know that isn't any consolation, but I do."

Deep breath. I have to stay strong, to tell her she hurt me. "Why did you call?"

"To explain about Nathan." Her voice drops. "And to apologize. I know you hate me right now. I deserve it. I'm so sorry, Jessie. It was a bitch move sleeping with Nathan, but I really thought it was over. He told me you'd ended it."

Oh. That sounds like Nathan. But that's not enough to absolve her. "You didn't just sleep with him. You two are dating. You've been together for six months."

"I know. I'm sorry. There's no excuse. But you know how he is. He made me feel smart and special. And he had that way of explaining things that convinced me his ideas were right."

"Had that way?"

"We broke up a few days ago. When those pictures of you and... is that really you with Pete Steele?"

"Yes. But I'm not willing to discuss that with you."

"Oh. Sure."

I can hear her heart breaking through the speaker. I take a deep breath. She wants me to forgive her. And I want to forgive her. But I can't do it yet... it still hurts.

I rest my head on Pete's chest. He's warm and he smells good.

He runs his hand through my hair. "Want me to take over? I have some choice words for her."

I can't help but laugh. I shake my head and turn my attention back to the call. "I don't want to hate you forever, Maddie. But I'm not ready to forgive you."

Her voice is meek. "Please, Jessie. I'm so sorry. He got all jealous when those pictures came out and started going off about how he wanted to hurt you, how he only slept with me to hurt you. It made everything clear. I never should have been with him. I never should have let you go to California. I think about calling you every night. I miss you so much. I even read the *Hunger Games* books to feel closer to you."

"You make it sound like it was a chore."

"No. I liked them. And you're right, Peeta is way better than Gale." She takes a deep breath. "I... I understand that I hurt you. Let me do something to make it up to you. Please."

"Eventually. I need more time first."

"How much time?"

I hold strong. "I don't know. A few more weeks at least."

"Uh... Well, you did trade up. Pete Steele is a lot hotter than Nathan."

Pete chuckles. I guess he can hear the phone. Madison is loud. I throw him a *shhh* look.

"My sexy librarian." He smiles. "Should I make my mouth useful?"

As soon as I'm done with this.

"Is that him?" Madison squeals.

"Yes, but I'm not going to discuss him with you."

"No. I'm not looking for gossip. I just... I hope you're happy. That you finally have someone who deserves you."

"Thank you." This is about as much of this conversation as I can take. But I can't let her go without discussing Dad. "Do you know how Dad is doing? He's been dodging my calls."

"I'm not sure. You know Dad. He could be drowning and he'd insist he's going out for a nice dip."

Sounds about right.

"I'll find out," she says. "I'm going to make this up to you. I'll call about Dad next week. Okay?"

"Okay."

"I love you."

"I love you too." I hang up the phone and drop it in my

lap. It's the first time I've said I love you to anyone in ages. But it feels natural.

The tension in my shoulders relaxes. I'm angry at my sister, but we'll get past it. She's still my best friend.

Pete pulls me into his lap. His arms slide around my chest. His mouth hovers over my ear.

"I'm proud of you," he whispers.

"Thanks."

"She's right. About Peeta being better than Gale."

"Glad you agree."

"And about me being hotter than your ex."

"How do you know?"

"Saw pictures on your Facebook." His cheek brushes against my neck. "You have any energy left?"

"I could use another coffee."

"Tom's throwing a party tomorrow. I'd skip it, but it sounds important. He wants us to have dinner with Ophelia and Ellie first."

"Ellie?"

"Mom's girlfriend."

"Oh. Your mom is gay?"

"Yeah. You didn't know?"

"Never looked you up."

He plays with the bottom of my tank top. "You shoulda. I've been all over your Facebook."

"Really?"

"You look hot in those pictures on the beach."

"When did you look at those?"

"After we met. Had to see what I was dealing with. You should change your privacy settings. Want me to do it?"

"Well, if any pervert can see pictures of me in a bikini, yeah."

He chuckles. "I will. But I have something else to do first."

"What's that?"

"You ever watch yourself come?"

"No."

He pulls me off the couch. "Then I have to pop your cherry."

⚜

PETE LEADS ME TO THE DOWNSTAIRS BATHROOM. HE'S aggressive and hungry as he pins me to the wall and presses his lips to mine.

We're moving quickly from conversation to kissing, but it feels right. There are so many things I can't articulate. That he can't say. But the feelings are there in our kiss. They pour between us.

He plants his body behind mine, his chest against my back, his crotch against my ass. Mmm. He's hard.

"Palms against the wall." His voice is deep, commanding. He pulls his t-shirt over his head. Pushes his boxers to his feet. "Look at the mirror, Jess."

My gaze goes right to the reflection of his eyes. There's so much desire in his expression.

"Watch how fucking sexy you are." He digs his hand through my hair, pulling my body onto his.

My cheeks flush. Can I really watch myself? I have a side view of us, from our knees all the way to the tops of our heads.

He pulls off my t-shirt. Pushes my shorts to my ankles. He has my body pinned to his.

I'm at his mercy.

I can't do anything but watch. I can see my chest, my stomach, my ass, my thighs. My glasses. I'm still in my glasses. I go to take them off but Pete stops me.

"Keep them on." He brings his hands to my hips. "This might be fast. Was thinking about you all night."

My sex clenches as I watch him position our bodies. As I watch him slide inside me.

Mmm. He always feels so good.

He kisses his way from my lips to his ear. Then he's sucking on my earlobe. One hand stays in my hair. The other stays on my hips, pinning me in place as he works his magic thrusting into me.

Pleasure knots inside me quickly. It's intense. I want to close my eyes. But I don't. I keep watching us, watching our bodies join, watching the way his thighs tense and his fingers dig into my skin.

He pulls away from my ear, watching the reflection the way I am. Damn, the way he's watching me. It makes me dizzy.

I'm almost there.

Every thrust is intense. I arch my back, rocking my hips against his. It pushes him deeper. Deeper.

"Harder," I breathe. "I want to feel you come."

He groans into my neck.

Then he's going harder. Deeper.

"Fuck." He groans. He tugs at my hair. "Fuck, Jess."

My last hint of shyness fades away. I stare at our reflection, taking in everything. None of my usual insecurities—the not quite flat stomach, the fleshy thighs, the round ass—pop out. Right now, I'm perfect.

Hell, I'm a sex goddess.

My lips part with a groan. My sex clenches. With his next thrust, I go over the edge. I scream his name again and again as I come.

I keep my gaze on the mirror, watching my muscles clench and relax, watching my teeth sink into my lips, and especially watching the pleasure spread over his face.

Damn, what an orgasm. It's not enough. I need his.

"Fuck me harder, Pete. I want to feel you come." My inhibitions are gone. My words go straight to my tongue.

He groans something incomprehensible. His grip tightens on my hips. He shifts forward, pinning me to the wall, sinking his lips into my neck.

His groans reverberate over my skin. His hand goes to my chest, playing with my nipples. Harder and harder, like he can't contain himself.

There.

His breath goes wild. His nails sink into my skin. I can feel his thighs shaking again mine, his cock pulsing inside me as he comes.

I watch his reflection—the way his eyelids squeeze together as he groans my name. Everything about his reflection is bliss. His orgasm is the best thing I've ever seen.

He keeps me pressed against the wall until he catches his breath. Then his lips are on my neck, making their way to my ear, my jaw, my cheek.

Pete turns me around. Pins me to the wall again. His eyes meet mine. He runs his fingertips along my cheek.

The expression on his face is pure affection.

I open my mouth to speak but my tongue is sticky. Screw words. I rise to my tip toes and kiss him hard. That same affection pours between us. It's still hot as hell, but it's sweeter than before.

Chapter Nineteen

❦

The Italian restaurant is across from the marina in the aptly named city of Marina Del Rey. We're in a private room upstairs. It's much too big for our small group but it's gorgeous—exposed brick walls, thick white table clothes, sheer curtains letting in the soft glow of sunset.

My stomach is in knots. I'm meeting Pete's mom. I know we aren't really together, that there's no risk of pissing off my future mother-in-law, but I want her to like me.

She's the second most important person in his life, after Tom. First even. I'll be crushed if she doesn't like me.

Thankfully, Pete and I are the first to arrive. We wait by the window, our hands tightly interlocked. His touch is comforting. Intimate.

There are footsteps then the door opens. That must be his mom. I struggle to take a deep breath.

"Peter, you look great." A woman's deep voice echoes through the room. "This must be Jess."

I turn towards the door. There's a woman in her late 50s

with short hair in the same ombre style as Willow's, only hers is teal instead of pink. It brings out her blue eyes.

I nod a yes and shake her hand.

"Ophelia." She looks to Pete. "She's lovely. How did you find someone so nice so quickly?"

He cocks a brow. "The usual way."

Ophelia lets out a low, throaty chuckle. "You really do take after your brother."

Are they making sex jokes? With the way they're smiling, they must be. I know he's adopted, but still. I can't imagine making a sex joke to anyone in my family.

A tall, curvy woman in a wrap dress steps into the room. She pulls Ophelia into a tight hug and plants a kiss on her lips.

They look happy. Not as happy as Tom and Willow but that's a high bar.

The woman turns to me. "I'm Ellie. You must be Jess."

We shake.

She turns to Pete. "It's nice to see you again, Peter."

He shoots Ophelia a look.

Ophelia chuckles. She has the same low, deep chuckle that he does. "Honey, don't call him Peter. He hates it." She looks at me. "Everyone called him Peter Parker in high school."

"The emo glasses," I say. "I still haven't seen them."

"He looked very studious in them." Ophelia smiles. "You can't imagine how many calls I got from his teachers, wondering why he wasn't doing better in school."

"Really?" I ask

She nods. "He wasn't like Tom. He did his homework. But if he didn't care for a class, he didn't pay it any attention."

I look back to Pete. "Is that right?"

He protests. "I aced physics and chemistry."

"And history?" she asks.

He shrugs.

"You should have seen his Spanish teacher." She laughs. "She called me in tears, wondering why he wouldn't apply himself."

"She was hitting on you, Mom," Pete says.

Ophelia laughs. "She was barely twenty-five."

"You were a MILF," Ellie says. "I knew it."

"Was?" Ophelia teases her girlfriend. "Don't make me kick you to the couch. I have plans for tonight."

Pete turns bright red. Ophelia shakes her head at his sudden shyness.

She throws her hand over her mouth like she's whispering. "Peter and Tom never got over me talking about how I eat pussy."

Somehow, Pete turns even more red.

"Jess doesn't need to hear that," he says.

"Sweetheart, women love talking about cunnilingus. Or they should." She turns to me. "You have to demand what you want."

And now I'm bright red.

Ellie shakes her head. "Poor kids. She was probably worried about accidentally cursing in front of you."

"Curse all you want sweetheart. Especially the c-word. We have to take it back," she says.

"We do?"

"Mom! Jesus!" Pete gets high pitched. He's in full on embarrassed teenager mode.

They share a look.

Ophelia laughs. "Okay. I'll stop torturing you." She smiles at me. "Your frames are lovely."

"Thank you."

"Spider-Man had a blond girlfriend, didn't he Peter?" she asks.

"I don't know," he says.

"Sure you do."

He nods. "Gwen Stacey. But she gets murdered and he ends up with Mary Jane. She's a red head."

"But you don't know." Ophelia laughs.

Pete runs his hand through his hair. "Yeah. Course not."

Ophelia turns to me. "Do you like Spider-Man? I'm always trying to tell Peter that Spider-Man is one of the better super-heroes. He lives with his grandparents, he's a photographer, and he really respects women."

Pete shakes his head. He turns to me with a smile. "I hear this every week."

I stare back at him, trying to picture him as Peter Parker/Spider-Man. I can't say that I know enough about comics to decide one way or another. I do like the mental image of him in a tight bodysuit.

And I like Ophelia already. She's a bad ass.

Ellie jumps in. "I'm doing a week on comic books in my 101 class this semester."

"What do you teach?" I ask.

"Sociology." She nudges Ophelia. "She teaches Anthropology. We're not supposed to date within the department."

Ophelia points to her hair. "And I'll have to dye over this before the semester starts."

She motions to the table and everyone takes a seat.

Ellie continues. "Spider-Man's power, slinging webs from his hands, is a metaphor for ejaculation."

I bite my lip. "What?"

Ophelia laughs. "Let's not scare the poor girl off any more than we have."

"No, I'm interested," I say.

"Most fiction aimed at men has phallic imagery—a man with a machine gun, spraying bullets. Or he's using this huge sword to destroy his enemies. All his power comes from his metaphorical penis." Ellie laughs. She turns to Pete. "He's quite virile, Spider-Man."

Again, Pete blushes. My heart melts. He looks adorable with his cheeks flushed.

I barely have time to consider how adorable he looks with his cheeks flushed. The door opens and a loud, excited voice booms through the room.

"We're here," Tom says. "You can finally enjoy yourselves."

He's dressed the same as Pete, only his button up shirt is white and his slacks are grey while Pete is in all black. It's strange seeing the rock star brothers dressed up like the nice boys next door.

Willow looks beautiful, as usual. Her pink tipped hair contrasts against her flowing ivory dress.

After a round of hellos, Tom turns to Willow and whispers something in her ear.

"Are you sure?" she asks.

"Go for it, kid," he says.

She turns to the table. "We set a date. In two weeks. In Maui. Everything is booked. It's going to be small, family and a few friends."

Tom slides his arm around her. Both of them are beaming.

"Wow, sweetheart, that's fast," Ophelia says. "Are you sure you don't want more time to plan?"

"Yeah. I don't want a big wedding. I don't want to fuss about the colors or the dress." She turns to Tom. "I just want to be with Tom forever."

It's sweet enough to make me sick. But the feeling of dread in my stomach isn't from the syrupy display. Tom and Willow are adorable and in love.

And honest.

They're practically transparent.

You're a liar, a big fat liar. They're sharing their happiness with you and you're a liar. My thoughts scream at me. I shouldn't be here. I shouldn't be sharing their happiness when I'm lying to their faces.

I bite my tongue and take a deep breath. My gaze goes to Pete. There's frustration in his brow. I know he's happy for them. I know he loves his brother.

So what is all that frustration doing in his brow?

He shakes it off, stands, and hugs them, one at a time.

Then everyone is hugging. Tom squeezes me. Then Willow. She hugs me so tightly I can barely breathe.

"I'm so glad you're here," she whispers." And that you and Pete are happy."

He addresses the table. "She's not pregnant."

Willow turns red. She barely manages to take a seat next to him. "Tom, they weren't thinking that." She studies expressions, one by one. "Okay, I guess I'd jump to that conclusion."

Ophelia laughs. "I'm surprised you two didn't fly to Vegas the night you got engaged."

"I pitched the idea," Tom says. "She wouldn't budge."

"We can't get married without you, Ophelia. Or Pete. Or Drew. Or Kara. Okay, I'm going to stop listing people in case I leave someone out." She takes a deep breath. "We checked flight prices. They're reasonable. The ceremony is on a Saturday and Monday is a holiday, so it will be a nice chance for everyone to get away."

"You have a dress, sweetheart?" Ophelia asks.

"I think so," Willow says. "I... uh... I'm asking Drew to be my maid of honor." She turns to Pete. "Will you be the best man?"

"Of course," he says.

Her face fills with relief. "Okay. Good. I know it's really sudden. We should have done it in Malibu. It would have been easier for everyone."

"Sweetheart, it's your wedding. Hopefully, the only one.

You're allowed to have it in paradise," Ophelia says. "It will be perfect. I promise."

Willow smiles. She turns to me. "Of course, you have to come too, Jess. Will that be okay with school? Tom told me you're starting USC Law. I'm sure that's a lot of work. I understand if you can't get away."

"No, I'd love to be there." My stomach clenches. She's inviting me because she thinks I'm Pete's girlfriend, because she thinks I make him happy.

It's all based on a lie.

These people are accepting me openly and honestly and I'm lying to their faces.

I get lost in the conversation. Tom and Willow are taking two weeks off for their honeymoon. They're going to see half the Hawaiian Islands. Somehow, we get back to the topic of superheroes and their various powers. Ellie is something of an expert on phallic imagery. Ophelia teases her about the choice—it's, in Ophelia's words, a strange focus for a woman who prefers pussy.

Tom and Pete turn every shade of red every time their mother mentions the female anatomy. It's amazing to watch her make them fluster. She's funny, bold, in control of the conversation but giving at the same time.

She's amazing and real and I'm a liar.

❦

I DRIFT IN AND OUT OF CONVERSATION. THE FOOD IS FRESH and beautifully arranged—caprese salad, pasta primavera, flourless chocolate cake—but it barely makes an impression on my taste buds.

All through dinner, Pete tries to cover his frustration with a smile. He doesn't get quite there.

After dessert, we exchange long goodbyes. Ophelia whispers something about how glad she is that Pete is finally done fucking everything that moves. Apparently, he seems much happier with me.

Of course he does. That's the idea behind the lie. I should be on board with this. I know the drill. We keep up appearances so no one asks questions.

I'm good at keeping up appearances. So why do I feel like I'm going to throw up every bite of the rich chocolate cake?

I stay quiet on the drive to Tom and Willow's place. There are only three feet between me and Pete but it feels like a million miles.

I don't like it.

He pulls into a spot on the street, right between two equally expensive cars. This is where he belongs. Of course, three blocks from the beach isn't a bad place to belong.

His deep brown eyes focus on me but he says nothing. I'm tempted to make an excuse for my mood, to find a place to hide at the *OMG we're getting married in two weeks* party. The other guys in the band are due any moment. Then there are all sorts of friends and peers and people who should be focused on the bride and groom to be.

There are a million reasons to ignore the frustration in his eyes and the knot in my stomach.

But I can't do it.

"You're not supposed to lock me out," I say.

He stares back at me. "And what is it you were doing all through dinner?"

"Trying to play by the terms of our agreement. You?"

"I'm not gonna upstage my brother and his fiancée."

"Why are you miserable?" I ask.

"I'm not."

"You look like you got punched in the gut." I go to grab his wrist but he's too fast about pulling it to his lap. "I know you aren't jealous. You don't look at Willow like that."

"Don't look at anyone but you like that."

"You are upset. It's written all over your face."

His eyes go to the steering wheel.

"Because you're losing your best friend?" I ask. "That has to be hard, him moving on so quickly. He moved out a month ago, right?"

"Just about."

"How long did you live together?"

"Since I was twelve." He turns back to me. "You gonna talk to me?"

"I'm trying to do what you want, to play your sweet, demure girlfriend." My stomach clenches. "But I don't like lying to your family. They're honest and open and they clearly love you. Why won't you let them in, let them help you?"

"This is what I want."

"But—"

"Are you backing out?"

I take a deep breath. Words find my lips without passing through my brain. "Do you care about me?"

"What? That's not relevant."

"But do you?"

His brow furrows as he gets out of the car. I can't stay here. I get out and follow him to the sidewalk.

It's hard to make out the details of his expression in the dark, but his posture gives enough away.

"Do you?" I ask. "Tell me the truth. It won't break me if you say no." In theory.

"Are you backing out or not, Jess?"

"I'm not."

"Then let's go."

"But—"

"I'm not discussing this any more." He takes three steps forward then he turns back to me. "Are you coming or not?"

Chapter Twenty

Tom's place is right on the beach. It's an enviable house with a huge living room and a bigger upstairs. Everything about it is sleek and modern, even the wide glass windows. I can see the ocean from the couch. I can see the waves crashing into the beach, pounding the sand into even smaller particles.

Pete talks with Tom in the kitchen. They speak with hushed voices, serious looks on their faces. It's some kind of family secret. I'm not invited.

"How is everything with Pete?" Willow asks. "You looked a little frustrated at dinner."

I offer her my best smile. What can I say that isn't a total lie? "It's been difficult with the press paying attention to us."

"Oh. I'm sorry. It should pass quickly. A happy couple isn't the most exciting news."

"There was a reporter at my apartment a few days ago, so I've been staying with him."

"How do you like it? That house is nice. And it's so big for the two of you." Her voice wavers. "Empty."

"A little."

"I'm glad you're there. Sometimes I worry about Pete being alone in that house. I feel like I stole his best friend."

Do I lie to her or tell her she's right? I clear my throat. "Change is hard." I can't take any more of this conversion. "Excuse me. I'm waiting to hear back from my sister." I pull out my phone and pretend to answer a text.

Willow nods a goodbye. Finally, I'm alone. My thoughts sink in.

Pete doesn't care about me enough to say anything beyond *that's not relevant*. At least I know where things stand. I mean nothing to him. I'm a means to an end. He gave me plenty of chances to back out. He held up his side of the bargain. That means I need to hold up mine.

I press my eyelids together. If I focus on the prize, on getting through law school without crushing loans, maybe my stomach will finally settle.

The door swings open. Drew and Kara step inside. He looks totally casual in jeans and a t-shirt. She looks totally gorgeous in a clingy dress and fuck me heels.

Even though they're among friends, his grip around her waist is protective.

Thankfully, they go right to the kitchen, right to the conversation. I stay planted on the couch by myself until Meg and Miles arrive.

Tom calls everyone to attention and he announces the wedding date. There's gushing and hugging and laughter and another promise that Willow isn't pregnant.

Everyone is happy and honest and real.

I'm still a liar.

⚜

MY RESIDENCE AS THE WOMAN OF THE COUCH IS SHORT lived. It only takes twenty minutes for the party to fill. There are two dozen people here and the room is loud with laughter and conversation.

Drew joins me on the couch with a nod hello. Tom takes the armchair kitty corner to us.

He looks at me. "I'm hogging your boyfriend."

"He was your brother first." I offer a weak smile. "He looks like he's having fun."

It's not quite a lie. Pete is talking to Willow and Kara in the kitchen. They're joking, laughing.

Miles walks up to us. "Jess, right?"

I nod and shake his hand. He plops on the couch next to me. I'm sandwiched between the dark haired guitarist and the blue-eyed singer. I should be in heaven.

But I feel like hell.

Miles leans towards Tom. "Come on. Admit you slipped one past the goalie."

Tom motions to Drew. "Do I look like I have a death wish?"

"Our secret." Miles winks.

Drew turns to me. "Miles likes to get a rise out of people. He thinks he can get me to hit Tom—"

"You've done it before," Miles says.

"I saw my life flash before my eyes." Tom laughs.

"You kissed his girl. What did you expect?" Miles asks.

"If she'd already been his girl, I wouldn't have had to kiss her." Tom turns to Drew. "Worked out, didn't it?"

Drew shrugs a whatever. "You're not gonna piss me off. My sister is happy. That means I'm happy. And I'm glad we're in a community property state where she'll get half your shit if she gets tired of your ass."

Tom laughs. "She can have all my shit if she gets tired of me. I don't want anything but her."

"Damn, when did you get soft, Sticks?" Miles asks.

"Please. You're way mushier with Meg when you're alone," Tom says.

"How do you know if they're alone?" Drew asks.

Tom cocks a brow. "Wish I didn't know. They were going at it all tour."

Drew laughs. "Was funny watching you get more and more pissed the worse your blue balls got."

"You were almost as moody as Guitar Prince," Miles teases.

Drew flips him off but he's smiling.

Tom turns to me. "How are you, Jess? Feel like we barely know each other."

"An enigmatic woman for an enigmatic man," Miles says. "You're going to law school, right?"

"Yes. USC." I offer a smile. Is there any way I can convince them to go back to bantering like I'm not here? I guess discussing law school is as neutral as it gets. "I'm good. Tired but good. I've been doing a lot of summer coursework and—"

"Fucking Pete every place in that giant house?" Miles offers.

My cheeks flush. They're trying, hard, to be friendly, but I can't escape the voice in my head screaming *you're a liar*.

The front door opens. There's a flash of bright blue. A balding man in an ugly suit. Aiden.

The temperature must drop by ten degrees. Drew, Miles, and Tom exchange frustrated looks.

Tom leans in to whisper to me. "You know what he and Pete have been talking about?"

Yes. I bite my lip.

"Who the fuck invited him?" Drew scowls. "Want me to tell him to get lost?"

"No. We need your hands for the studio," Tom says.

"Don't need my hands." Miles cracks his fist. "Have to admit, it's been a while. Kinda miss the thrill of it."

"No way. Meg still hasn't forgiven me for telling her to get lost," Tom says.

"Who'd think she'd hold a grudge about a little thing like that?" Miles says.

"Fuck off. You were the one doing coke with him in the bathroom." Tom frowns.

"Yeah, but I barely liked coke," Miles says.

Okay, I have to laugh. "Did you really say that?"

Miles shrugs. "It's true."

I clear my throat. "There isn't much to say about me. I'm going to law school. I'm from Long Island. I love *The Hunger Games*." I push myself to my feet. "And I need to get some air. It was nice talking to you guys."

Pete is still in the kitchen. His gaze flits between me and Aiden. I point to the outside patio. A nice quiet place to think. Hopefully.

It takes great effort to move through the party. I spot Ethan with a model on his arm. She has a platinum pixie cut and a very short dress. She claws at him like she's already ready to take him home.

He nods hello. "You okay, Jess?"

Damn, am I that transparent? "Just getting some air." I nod to his date. "Have fun... later."

He laughs. "Let me know if I need to kick his ass for you."

I play dumb. "I'm not sure what you mean."

"Yes, you are." He nods to Pete, still in the kitchen, still staring at us. "I'd help you make him jealous if I wasn't busy."

"That's okay. I... uh, I guess I'll see you later."

"Dangerous Noise is opening for Sinful Serenade on their US tour next year. Should be interesting, me being Drew's replacement's replacement." He nods goodbye. "You'll be sick of me soon."

He thinks I'll still be around by the time the band is on tour again. I'm not sure if it's sweet or pathetic that everyone is assuming I'll be around for good.

Finally, I find the patio. It curves all the way around the house, to a small side yard. There isn't much room—a tall, wooden fence housing the next door neighbor's side yard is four feet in front of me—but there's a patio table.

I collapse in the plastic chair.

Ah, quiet. Sort of.

It only makes my thoughts feel more jumbled.

I need to keep my eye on the prize. School comes first. Whatever is happening with Pete is secondary. Even if the strength of my feelings for him is going to swallow me whole. Even if I feel sick over lying to all these people.

A nasally voice grabs my concentration. "Miss James, is it?"

Aiden is standing by the fence. The sight of him does nothing to help in the holding down my dinner front.

Still, I smile. "Yes. How are you?"

"I can see why he went with you." His gaze fixes on my chest. "You're prettier than you seemed at first."

What the hell? From the polite expression on his face, this is his idea of a compliment.

He continues. "It's working. His fans are going crazy, wishing they were the normal girl he'd fallen for. Girls love him. Especially the teenagers. That's why marketing wants him with someone nice."

"Okay."

His eyes narrow. "He really believes you care about him."

"I do."

He stares back, incredulous. "You think I was born yesterday, honey?"

I push out of my chair. I don't like where this conversation is going. "Excuse me. I should get back to the party. I'm sure Pete is looking for me."

He grabs my arm. Hard. "We need to have a conversation."

"I don't think Pete would like that."

"I don't care what he'd like." His grip tightens on my arm. "I know your type. I've seen it happen before. You pretend to be a nice girl, convince him you love him and not his money. Thought he'd see you for the gold digger you are but the kid is too sweet for that."

"I'm not. I do care about him. I'm not trying to convince him of anything."

He leans closer. "I know how much he paid you. You really expect me to believe you're in this for something besides your bank balance?" His hand goes to my hip. "You belong to the band. And I control everything that belongs to the band."

My blood goes cold.

"Don't fuck with me. I know what that kind of money buys. You want the world to know you're a whore?" He moves even closer. "My car's around the corner. It won't take long."

I can barely breathe. Okay. Stay calm. Think. The best way to deal with it is a smile. "I'm sorry, but you're misunderstanding the situation, Aiden. Pete and I are exclusive. It's very important to him." I swallow hard. "It's part of what he's paying for."

He glares at me. "I've seen bitches like you before. Think you're too good for a regular john now that you have your claws in a rich guy."

He pushes me against the wall. Okay, no more polite smiles. I kick him in the shin. It doesn't help the situation any, so I aim a little higher.

But I miss. He's not there at all. He's against the wooden fence opposite us. The thing is shaking.

Pete has his arms around Aiden's collar. He doesn't give the asshole a chance to explain.

His punch lands with a thud. Then another. Another. Another.

I turn away, checking if the coast is clear. There's no view of the side yard from downstairs. We're not upstaging the party.

We're not at risk of someone calling the cops.

Pete isn't going to end up in jail.

It should be okay.

Maybe.

It's possible.

Finally, the sound of fist pounding into flesh stops. I turn back. Pete still has Aiden pinned to the fence.

Pete's voice is low and angry. "I'm done with you."

"Mr. Steele—"

"Don't bother. I heard enough that you can't bullshit your way out of this. I don't want to see you unless we're meeting with the label."

"Don't you think Tony—"

"I *know* your uncle will be interested in what you did to Alice. She's like a daughter to him."

I blink my eyes open. Pete still has Aiden pinned. The coward is shriveling. And Pete is fuming.

My stomach flip-flops. I have to protect him. "Let's go. Please."

Pete turns to me. "You okay?"

"I will be."

"Good. I'd like you to stay there, but if you want to go, do it." He turns back to Aiden. "This is something I should have said a long time ago."

"Pete, come on. We're friends. We're good."

"One more word and I'm going to knock you unconscious. Don't care if you press charges for assault. Don't care if you make good on your threats to have the label bury our album. You do anything but exactly what I say, and the entire world is gonna know you're a rapist."

"I didn't..."

"Maybe she won't admit it. But she's not the only one, is she?"

Aiden swallows hard.

"You're gonna stay out of our fucking way until the record's done. Then, the second I say, you're gonna resign as our manager and retire from music."

"I can't—"

"You will."

"How do you think Tom is gonna react to the album getting buried? And right before his wedding? That will break his heart."

"Threaten my brother again and it will be the last thing you ever do."

"Pete. Come on. This is a misunderstanding."

Pete drops Aiden on the ground. "If you touch Jess again, I'll fucking ruin you."

Aiden steps backwards. He mumbles a yeah.

"Get the fuck out of here. Now."

The manager does as he's told.

Pete goes to me. He runs his fingers over my cheek. "Did he hurt you?"

I shake my head.

"Did he touch you?"

"What if he did? Will you kill him?"

"Might." His eyes fill with concern. "Good thing you're not allowed to lie to me."

The intensity of his stare makes my knees weak. Or maybe I'm still terrified.

I nod. "Only my arm. I'm okay. I can handle myself."

"Yeah. But you don't have to." His arms slide around my

waist. He pulls me into a tight hug. "He's not gonna bother you again. I promise."

I dig my hands into his shoulders. "Isn't this whole thing for your reputation?"

"Still have my reputation. Just Aiden isn't a part of that." He pulls me to my feet. "Come on. I want to take you home."

"But then..." I look up at him. "What are we?"

"I need you to stay with me through Tom's wedding."

"Okay." I want to tell him how I feel about him, but my mouth is too sticky.

Instead, I slide my arm around his waist and let him lead me to the car.

The ride passes quickly. Then we're home, going inside, in his room, in his bed.

He peels off my glasses and sets them aside. Then my shoes. My dress. My bra and panties.

I watch him strip to his boxers. The moonlight falls over his body in such a flattering way, but lust isn't what's stirring inside me.

He climbs into bed next to me. Again, he pulls my body into his, my back against his chest. It's so intimate, the skin on skin contact.

His fingertips trail over my hips. "I still owe you one today."

I shake my head. "Just hold me. Please."

"You sure?"

"Positive." I nestle into his body. "I... I'm not pretending anymore. I really do care about you."

He undoes my French braid and runs his fingers through my hair. "I know."

I don't ask how much he cares about me. I know he does. The way he acted with Aiden, the way he's holding me now—that's not pretend.

Chapter Twenty-One

I wake up alone. The house is quiet. Pete's car isn't in the driveway. There's no sign of him anywhere.

Shit.

I go for my usual morning hike, get home, and shower. There's still no sign of him.

No sense in putting off my day. In the kitchen, I put a pan on the burner, break eggs into a plastic bowl and whisk. Now coffee.

The carafe is already full. And there's a note next to it, black marker on torn piece of paper.

Making sure everything is taken care of with the label. Should be back by lunch.

He left me a note. It's domestic as hell, like our relationship is normal instead of complicated.

After cooking, I sit down with breakfast, coffee, and my latest YA novel. It's no *Hunger Games* but it's still quite the page-turner. I get caught up in the book until the door swings open and slams shut.

Pete is wearing a frown. His brows knit. He runs a hand through his dark hair and lets out a sigh.

I put down my book and push out of my chair. "Hey. Thanks for the coffee."

He looks back at me with surprise. "Hey."

"How was it? Is everything taken care of?"

"Should be." The frustration falls off his face as he moves closer. Then he's six inches away and he's smiling.

He's smiling because I'm here.

Because we're together.

"Should I make lunch?" I ask.

"Later." He slides his hands around my waist and pulls me into a soft, slow kiss. When it breaks, he runs his fingers through my messy hair, his eyes filled with affection. "You busy today?"

"I have a lot of reading to do."

"I'm gonna practice." He motions to his room. "Stop by if you need a *break*."

⚬⚬⚬

AFTER AN HOUR OF READING, I'M MORE THAN READY FOR A break.

I go to knock on Pete's door but it's already open. There's music flowing into the hallway. It gets louder as I step inside.

He's sitting on his bed, his bass in his lap. The instrument is plugged in to an electric amp and there are headphones over his ears.

"You don't have to use headphones," I say. "I'd like to listen."

He pulls his headphones off as he turns to me. "Nobody listens to a bass on its own."

"What about house music at clubs? Isn't that nothing but a bass line?"

His lips curl into a smile. "You gonna put on a tight dress and dance?"

Dammit, it's hot. I shake my head. "I'm just going to listen."

He unplugs his headphone and pats his bed.

Tempting. Incredibly tempting. I take a step backwards. School first. Then sex. "I have to get my book."

Pete nods then his attention turns back to his bass. Music fills the hallway. It's familiar. Something off one of the Sinful Serenade albums.

I close my eyes and try to place the song. It's not one of the singles. I listen to enough alternative rock radio to recognize those.

The answer doesn't come. My eyes open and catch his. There's all this affection in his deep brown eyes.

Last night, I told him I cared about him. He hasn't said anything. Hasn't responded.

My heart aches. How the hell am I supposed to stomach all these feelings? I want to talk, to tell him how much Dad's non-response is weighing on me.

But not if he's going to keep running off.

His eyes turn towards me. He cocks a brow. "You okay?"

Yes, great. The lie forms on my tongue. I swallow it down. I like being honest with him.

I shake my head.

He slides out of his shoulder strap, sets his instrument in its stand, and kneels in front of me.

Pete pulls me out of the chair so I'm kneeling next to him. His fingers brush my chin and jaw. He brushes stray hairs behind my ears, his eyes fixed on mine.

"Please don't pretend you care about me," I say.

"Do you really think I'm pretending?" He pulls me into his lap as he sits cross-legged.

I shift so I'm straddling him. I stare into his eyes. Run my fingers through his short hair. He smells good. Like soap and shampoo.

The expression in his deep, brown eyes is earnest. He does care about me.

That makes this harder.

My chest heaves as I inhale. I can't tell him how I have feelings for him. Not yet.

"You're going to explode, keeping everything bottled up." He pulls me closer. "Talk to me."

"Don't you do the same thing?"

"I have music. You don't have anything."

He looks up at me, brushes my hair from my eyes. "I want to know you. The person you want to be."

The words jump into my throat. He's warm. He's comforting. I really do believe he cares about me.

I squeeze my inner thighs against his hips, settling onto his body. "Even the ugly things?"

"We all have ugly things in our past."

"Yeah, but you turned yours into something beautiful." I point to his tattoo, though it's covered by his jeans. "And your music too. You make your pain so beautiful."

"No." He stares back at me. "The pain is ugly. Dealing with it is the beautiful thing."

"You sound like a self-help book."

He pulls me closer. "Tell me anyway."

I want to tell him. I really do. It's not just that I want this off my chest. I want Pete knowing me. The ugly parts too.

I swallow hard. I have to find out. "My dad is an alcoholic. He went to rehab last year, but there's no telling if he's really sober. He's high-functioning. He's good at hiding. My whole family, we're great at hiding things."

His voice is steady. "His whole life or after your mom left?"

I nod. "It got worse when Mom left. He'd fall asleep drunk on the couch. He'd miss work."

He rubs my shoulder. It puts me at ease. My self-preservation instincts don't kick in.

I stare back at him. "When it started, I was a kid, and I didn't know better. But after a while, I could tell he had a problem. I knew I had to do something or he'd drink himself to death, but I didn't. I lied for him a million times. I lied to teachers, to my aunt. I even lied to Madison, so she wouldn't know how bad it was."

"He's not your responsibility. He's an adult."

"Maybe when I was a kid. But, by high school, I was old enough to know better. Madison is the one who got him help. I don't know if I'd have ever stopped lying. I woke up one morning to him passed out in a pool of vomit. Madison had already called 911. They said he was a few minutes from dying. Would have been my fault."

"It wouldn't have been your fault, Jess. You can't fix someone else. No matter how badly you want to."

"Yeah." I press my fingers against Pete's cheeks. It does something to me, his skin against my hands. It makes me feel safe. Like I can take the pressure of this. "I'm sure it's nothing compared to your father hitting you."

"You can't win at having a fucked up childhood." He slides his hands to my waist. "Don't make it a competition."

"You're mature for a guy who became famous at 19."

"I know." He slides his hand into my hair and pulls me into a tight hug.

My body floods with relief. It feels good getting this off my chest.

There's no running from my feelings this time. I'm falling hard and fast. There's no way to avoid it.

I whisper in his ear. "I lied so much, Pete. I thought it was for the best, that I was protecting my family. But all it did was make him sicker and grind me to nothing. I barely know who

I am now, what I want. That's why I had to leave New York. So I could figure it out."

"Have you?"

"Getting there." I press my hands together. "But... I don't think he's doing well. He keeps dodging my calls. The way Dad lies... I won't know what it is that's wrong until the doctor calls me to tell me he's gone."

"Come here." He pulls me closer, his chin nestling into the crook of my shoulder.

My eyelids press together. I squeeze him tightly, then I release everything. When a sob rises up in my throat, I do nothing to choke it back.

Within moments, I can't keep my eyes closed. I'm crying. Ugly crying. Instead of wiping my eyes, I dig my fingers into his t-shirt.

"Hey." He slides his hand to my cheek and wipes a tear with his thumb. "It's okay, Jess. You're gonna be okay."

"You promise?"

He nods. "It's not your fault. But I know it feels like that sometimes."

I choke back another sob. "I'm sorry. I shouldn't unload on you like this."

"You walk around like you're carrying the world on your shoulders."

"No." I press my lips together. He has a point. "Maybe."

"Maybe just North America?"

I laugh. He's the only person who could make me laugh at a time like this.

My heart flutters. I let my eyes close. I let my muscles relax as I sink into him. "I'm sorry."

"What for?"

"I'm crying."

"So?" The pad of his thumb presses against my cheek. "Was it hard for you, telling me this?"

"You know it was."

He nods. "That's strength, not weakness. Most people spend their lives running from intimacy."

Intimacy. It's a beautiful word.

"Most people run from all the ugliness in their lives."

"How did you get so perceptive?"

"Emo music." He smiles.

"Are you kidding?"

He nods. "It was metal."

I laugh. "That's not funny."

"Okay, you got me. It was hip-hop."

I swat him playfully. Another laugh rises to my throat. It helps dissolve the pain.

I look back into his eyes. I run my hands through his hair. "Tell me the truth."

"I tried running from my feelings. For a long time. First, my dad, the way he took out all his misery on me. Then some of my particularly bad foster homes. Then everything with Ophelia."

"The cancer?"

He nods. "She was sick when I was in high school. Breast cancer. It tore me up here—" He places his hand over his chest. "But I managed to keep calm, for her, to be strong for her. That's something I'm good at."

"Is that why you're lying to your family about us being together?"

"Guess I'm a hypocrite, lying to protect my family but telling you that you shouldn't." He brushes my hair behind my ears. "It was more than that. I needed space to think. Been touring since I was a teenager. This is the first time I've been alone in forever."

I let my body sink into his. It feels good getting all this off my chest. It feels honest. Intimate.

I've never wanted to share my feelings with anyone but

Madison. Even with Nathan... there was always this space between us. Something missing.

I slide my arm around his neck, soaking in the softness of his skin. "So where do your feelings go?"

He nods to his bass in the corner. "And if that's not enough, I've got a keyboard and a guitar in Drew's old room."

All the tension in my body eases as I pull back and stare into his eyes. "Does it really work?"

"Yeah. Try it." He takes my hands and pulls me to my feet.

"I can't sing or play an instrument."

"I'll teach you." He grabs his bass with one hand. The other slides around my waist. He sits on the bed, pulls me onto his lap, then positions my hands on the bass guitar.

His touch is gentle as he shows me how to pluck and how to fret. The strings are thick and heavy. I'll have callouses tomorrow.

"I have no musical talent," I whisper.

"That's okay." He slides his hands over mine. "You have a great teacher."

I actually giggle. I want him so much. I want every single piece of him.

I close my eyes and soak in the warmth of his breath on my neck, the hardness of his chest against my back, the comfort of him guiding me through playing the instrument.

"You have a favorite song?" he asks.

"You can teach me the bass line to any song?"

"If you give me fifteen minutes to look it up."

"Really?"

He nods. "You like pop music. The bass parts are pretty simple. Can't teach you to play *Hysteria* or *YYZ*."

"What about one of your songs?"

He nips at my ear. "Pick your favorite."

"I don't have one."

"Jess, that hurts. My ego is shattering."

"It is not."

"No, it's not." He presses his lips against my neck.

Again, I'm floating. It's like I've been let out of a cage.

I ignore my inhibitions completely. "How about the one you're working on?"

"Your wish is my command."

He takes me through the bass riff, one note at a time. I'm a hopelessly slow learner, but Pete is endlessly patient. We go through the riff a dozen times before he pulls his hands away.

"Try it," he whispers in my ears.

"I've already forgotten it."

"Try anyway."

His voice is steady and reassuring. Okay. I'll try anyway. I close my eyes and let my fingers do the thinking for me.

The deep sound of the bass fills the room. I'm actually playing the riff. It's a crawl compared to the tempo of the song, but I'm doing it.

I squeal with glee when I get to the end. "It worked." I shift off his lap so I can look him in the eyes. "I can't believe it."

He smiles. "You're a natural."

"Will you teach me the whole song?"

"It gets tricky. I'll teach you something easier. You like The Beatles?"

"I guess they're okay."

He chuckles. "Okay. We'll go for something a little more grunge. How about *Smells Like Teen Spirit*?"

I bite my lip. "Okay."

He smiles the widest smile in the history of the world. "Ready to drop out of school and drive around in a van playing gigs?"

I shake my head.

"Then you can't hack it as a rock star."

"Maybe I'll fall in love with guitar or drums."

"Or piano?"

"Yeah. Maybe." Or I'll fall in love with Pete. That's a lot more likely.

He moves closer. "Did you feel it when you played?"

"A little."

"Come here." He pulls me onto his lap. His voice is dripping with enthusiasm. He's passionate about this. "You will feel it."

"Okay." I melt.

Chapter Twenty-Two

✦❧✦

I t takes Pete an hour and a half to teach me the three minute song. By the end, I can play the entire thing by myself.

He pushes me off his lap and directs me to turn. His lips curl into a smile. "Play for me."

God, that smile. It makes me warm all over. Okay. I can do this.

I sling the instrument's strap over my shoulder. Pete's eyes are locked on mine. His gaze makes me blush.

My eyelids press together. I position my hands on the bass and I play. Damn, that's loud. The deep, rich sound flows through the room. I'm the one making that noise.

I'm the one playing the song.

It's a rush. I try to let my fingers find their memory. I stumble, but I pick it back up. I make through all three minutes of the song. Okay, more like five minutes at the speed I'm playing, but I still feel victorious.

My eyes connect with his. He's beaming.

"Was I okay?" I ask.

He nods and pushes himself to his feet. "Amazing." He

presses his lips to mine then takes the instrument and sets it back in its stand. "Did you feel it?"

I nod. "I can see why you're addicted."

He wraps his arms around me and pulls me closer. His palm presses against the back of my neck, his touch soft and tender.

This is so much more than sex.

My eyelids press together as he pulls me into a kiss. Mmm. I part my lips to make way for his tongue. I bring my hands to his waist and I hold his body against mine.

When the kiss breaks, I'm floating.

He looks down at me. "You hungry?"

Now that he mentions it, yeah. "Starving. What time is it?"

He turns to look at his alarm clock. "Well past lunch. You done with your reading?"

"Someone distracted me."

"You shouldn't come in here wearing those." He taps my glasses. "Can't help myself."

"You like my glasses that much?"

"Want you to wear them next time you suck my cock."

My sex clenches. "What were we talking about?"

He smiles. "I'll make lunch. Finish your reading."

Oh food. Yes, I should eat food. My mind refuses to switch gears. He wants me to wear my glasses the next time I suck him off. He was thinking about that.

It's so hot in here.

I shake my head. Come on, Jess, focus. I only barely manage to look him in the eyes. "You'll cook?"

"Use my credit card. You prefer Thai or Indian?"

"Surprise me." I don't want to untangle our bodies, so I stay pressed against him.

"Jess."

"Yeah?"

"You still have to read?"

"About an hour's worth, yeah."

"Then you should go." He slides his hands to my hips. "If you're here in one minute, I'm going to throw you on the bed and have my way with you."

"You're not making your case well."

He smiles. "I'm not the future lawyer." He presses his lips to mine. "School's important to you."

Damn, he's right.

"Jess, you have ten seconds."

"Give me an hour." I step into the hallway before I get any ideas about prioritizing him over school.

⚭

I'M AN HOUR INTO MY READING WHEN PETE KNOCKS ON MY door with the announcement that lunch is ready.

It smells amazing downstairs. Red curry paste, ginger, garlic, and shrimp waft into the air. Thai again. I take a seat at the table and pile my plate with a heaping scoop of each of three dishes—spicy chili green beans, red curry shrimp, and basil eggplant.

Two of the dishes are all vegetables.

He ordered what I like.

My heart melts. I'm not used to people taking care of me.

He pours two glasses of ice water and slides into the seat next to mine. His eyes meet mine as he motions to my drink. "Excited about school?"

I nod. "A little scared. It's already hard, all the reading I have to do."

"You'll ace it."

"How do you know?"

"You don't half ass things." He scoops rice onto his plate then tops it with half the curry shrimp. "We have a corporate gig Thursday in Chicago. Gonna miss your first day. It's a last minute thing."

I chew and swallow a slice of eggplant. It tastes of oil, lime, and Thai basil. "Was that part of you making sure everything is taken care of?"

He nods.

"I understand. This kind of thing must happen all that time."

"Yeah. Thought I was used to it but I'm pissed I can't celebrate with you." His gaze goes to his plate then goes back to me. "I'll make it up to you. Do owe you one from yesterday."

There's something I can't place in his expression, a frustration. He shakes his head and it's gone.

That's better. But there's still something off about his posture. A stiffness to his shoulders.

I don't like it. I want him here, with me, now.

"How about, after lunch, you start making it up to me?" I ask.

His lips curl into a smile. "Done."

⚜

IT'S BEFORE DAWN ON MY FIRST DAY WHEN PETE stops by my room to wish me luck. He climbs into my bed, pulls me into a hug, and presses his lips to my forehead. It occurs to me that we could be sleeping in the same bed then I fall back asleep.

When I wake, he's gone, already off to his corporate gig.

I let myself get caught up in fantasies of a real adult life, here, with Pete, as I get ready and drive to school.

Once I'm on campus, my other thoughts drift away. The day passes in a breeze—two classes, lunch at a place off campus, two more classes, checking out articles in the library, the drive home. I love every second of it, even though it leaves me without a moment to think.

There's a lush bouquet of roses on the kitchen table.

Dinner's in the fridge. I'll call at ten. Check your room. And mine.

I'm proud of you.

- Pete

Sure enough, there's a container of takeout in the fridge. Thai food. Chicken and vegetable curry with brown rice. I heat it up in the microwave and eat in the backyard. It's a new habit of mine—dining poolside, under the moon and stars.

I'm on a cloud as I clean up and make my way upstairs. I'm a law student and Pete bought me flowers and dinner.

And there's a wrapped present on my bed.

I tear open the card.

I'd rather watch these with you but I'll forgive you if you can't wait. I have something special reserved for tomorrow night.

I tear the paper off. It's the four *Hunger Games* movies.

My heart melts.

There's a post it note on the back of one of the movies.

Check my room.

It takes great effort to push myself off my bed, turn the knob, pull open the door, and step inside Pete's room.

There's a gift bag on his bed. It's crimson red with gold paper. USC colors. It's in my school's colors.

I toss the tissue paper on the ground and reach into the bag. My fingers brush something soft. Fabric. But nothing I normally wear.

It's a lace bra and panty set in a soft shade of pastel pink.

I change and go right to the mirror in my bathroom. Checking myself out in my underwear is not part of my usual routine. But, in this gift from him, I feel beautiful and sexy.

He always makes me feel like I'm the sexiest woman in the universe.

Like I'm light enough to float.

My ringtone bounces off the walls. I practically jump to find my phone. There it is on my desk. *Incoming call from Pete Steele*. Thank God.

I answer and bring the device to my ear. "Hey."

"Hey." His voice is deep and even.

"You bought me all of the *Hunger Games* movies."

"I did."

"I warned you about doing that." I fall back on my bed, my head resting comfortably on a soft pillow. "I'm going to fall in love with you if you keep it up."

"Thought that was talking *Hunger Games*."

"No. Anything *Hunger Games*." I run my fingertips over my comforter. It does nothing to ground me. I'm still floating.

"How was your first day?"

I launch into the longest story in the history of the world. I include every boring detail, from the honey mustard dressing on my salad bar lunch to the last names of my new professors. Pete listens with rapt attention the entire time.

His voice is light. Happy. "Fuck, wish I was there. Bet you're beaming."

"I am. I miss you." That's too much too fast, but it can't bring me down from my cloud. "This would be our life if we really were boyfriend/girlfriend, huh?"

"Close to it."

"How much of the year are you on the road?" I ask.

"About a third. Sometimes more."

"That's not so bad." Not that I'm entertaining a million ideas about being with him forever.

"You change your mind about picking up a bass?"

"No, I just mean, if we—"

"I know."

"Was it hard, with your ex, being away?"

"She went to school in New York. Columbia. Didn't make much of a difference whether I was touring or staying home."

"Oh."

He lowers his voice. "Gotta tell you something before I ask what you're wearing."

My cheeks flush. I like where this is going. "What's that?"

"I had an issue today. Took care of it. But it means you're gonna see something tomorrow that's gonna surprise you."

"You're speaking in riddles."

He chuckles. "Guess I am."

"Is it bad?"

"It's taken care of." He clears his throat. "Want you to know that I wasn't under duress. I weighed my options, thought about the potential consequences, and made my decision."

I'm not coming close to following. "What?"

"It's not a big deal. You'll see tomorrow."

"Promise it's nothing bad and I'll drop it until tomorrow."

"I promise."

"We're not allowed to lie to each other."

"I know."

I trust him. If he says it's okay, I believe him. "Then we can go on to the next part."

"Which part is that?" His voice is light, teasing.

I take a deep breath. I'm sexy, confident, in control. "Phone sex. How does it work?"

He laughs. "I love that." He imitated my confident voice. "We're having phone sex." Then he feigns cluelessness. "How does it work?"

"Enough teasing, Steele. I demand an explanation."

"Way I like to do it, is I describe what I want to do to you while we both get off."

"Yes. Let's do that. How do we start?"

"What *are* you wearing?"

"That lingerie you bought me. It's gorgeous."

He groans.

"You want a picture?"

"No." There's frustration in his voice. When he exhales, it's gone. "It'll be better if I wait till I can see you tomorrow."

I'm not sure I believe him.

"Fuck. I'm already hard thinking about it." His sigh is heavy with desire. "Put the phone on speaker."

Thoughts flee from my brain at an alarming rate. I put the phone on speaker. "Done. What are you wearing?"

"T-shirt and boxers."

Mmm. "What color?"

"Black."

"Damn, I like you in black."

"I know. Take off your bra."

I reach behind my back to unhook the bra and peel if off my shoulders. There's something sexy about stripping for him, even if he can't see me.

"You don't have to try with this, Jess. Just let the words wash over you."

"Okay." I run my fingertips over my stomach. I'm already flushed and wanting, knowing he's waiting to listen to me. "Take off your t-shirt."

There's a sound on his side of the phone. Then his breath is heavy in my ears.

"Gone," he says. "How do you want me?"

For a second, I feel shy. I push it away. "In the bed. With me. On top of me."

"I'm there. I take your hands and bring them to my hips. You can feel my cock over my boxers. I'm that hard just thinking of you. You push the boxers to my knees then wrap your hands around me."

I push my panties to my knees and bring my hand between my legs.

"I've got my lips on your neck. Kiss my way to your tits. Then I'm sucking on your nipple. Biting it. Hard enough you have to scream my name. Take my hand between your legs. You're already wet."

His breath hitches. He's getting close.

It spurs me on. I stroke my clit. Harder. Harder. There. Just enough pressure. I let out a low moan.

"Mmm. Where do you want my cock?"

"Inside me."

"Want to split you wide open."

I groan a yes.

"I pin your knees to the bed. Drive deep inside you. You feel like heaven. Like you were made to take my cock."

My sex clenches. I groan. "I'm gonna come."

"Come on my cock."

There isn't any shyness left. I stroke myself harder and harder, moaning and screaming so loudly that I can't make out any of his words.

Then there are no words. Just his breath and a low, deep groan. He's almost there too.

It's better than words, his groan. It echoes around the room, filling me in a way nothing else can. A few more brushes of my fingers and I'm at the edge. Pleasure spills to my fingers and toes as I come.

I scream his name.

It's not enough. With the way he's groaning, he's close. I want to be there with him.

"Louder," I breathe. "No more words. Just fuck yourself. I want to hear you come."

His groan is deep and animal. It's the most beautiful music I've ever heard.

I wait until his breath is hitching, until I'm sure he's

almost there, and I stroke myself again. Within moments, I'm at the edge.

"Jess," he groans.

With my next stroke, I come again. It's more intense. Tighter, heavier, better. He's there too. His voice gets higher. Then he's groaning my name again and again.

Then he's letting out this delicious sigh of satisfaction.

For a few minutes, we listen to each other breathe.

He breaks the silence. "How was that?"

"I like listening to you."

"Me too."

"I like touching you better though." I let out my own sigh of satisfaction. "When do you get back tomorrow?"

"By dinner. Don't start without me." He chuckles. "It's late and it's a school night. You should go to bed."

"I'm in a bed."

"Go to sleep."

"Okay. I... I miss you."

"I miss you too."

Chapter Twenty-Three

✦✦✦

Friday is another blur of class and sunshine. I already love law school. Even if I have a mountain of work to finish this weekend.

The house is still quiet when I arrive. I go to check my phone for word from Pete but something else catches my attention.

A text from my old friend back home. The only person I can still stand.

Kathryn: Isn't this your boyfriend?

There's a shortened link attached. I open it without asking for clarification.

It's a gossip site with the headline: *Not So Leaked Nude Photos of Bassist Pete Steele.*

I clean my glasses and read again. The headline remains the same.

What?

I try to skim the text of the article but my brain refuses to cooperate. Not so leaked nude photos. What does that mean?

I have to see them.

Now.

There's one at the bottom of the page. It's not a cell phone picture. It's a real portrait, artsy, black and white, and hot as hell. Tragically, it's chest up.

But it's still fucking sexy.

There's a link to more of these. On some photographer's website. Hazel Alexander.

Well, if it's not leaked, there's no reason for me not to look.

I click away. There are a solid two dozen pictures. The first few are chest up. Then they go lower. Lower. Lower.

Holy shit.

That's Pete, standing there, totally naked and totally yummy.

I spend far too long studying the photographs. By the time I put my phone down, I'm completely desperate to have him.

These are there, on the internet, for anyone to see.

I'm sure gossip sites, Twitter, and Facebook are ablaze with commentary. Thankfully, I gave up all of them when my friends starting reaching out with *wow, you know a famous person* messages.

What was it he said—he made a decision knowing the consequences? I get lost trying to figure out what that means. I'm so deep in thought I don't notice the door open until he's three feet away.

His eyes fix on mine. "Take it you saw the pictures?"

I nod and push myself to my feet. "What was that?"

"Explain in a minute. Come here first." He slides his arms around my waist and pulls me into a slow, deep kiss.

Mmm. He tastes good. His body feels right against mine. I don't want him to explain. I don't want to talk at all.

When our kiss breaks, he stares into my eyes.

Okay. This seems important.

"Need you tomorrow," he says. "Meeting with the label. Everybody wants you there."

"Really?"

"Yeah."

"Why are you meeting on a Saturday?"

"Has to be right away. The usual ego BS." He runs his fingertips over my chin. "But it's handled. Aiden isn't gonna bother you."

I nod to my cell—it's still displaying one of the pictures of him. "The explanation."

"Had an offer from an old friend I had to take up. Hazel's our photographer on tour. She was in Chicago."

"She offered to take nude photos of you?"

He nods, but there's guilt in his expression. He's hiding something.

"We promised honesty," I say.

"Yeah." He runs his hand through his hair. "Sit down."

"What happened?"

"Sit." His eyes cloud with frustration.

This is serious. I sit.

He kneels in front of me and takes my hand. His eyes find mine. "Somebody leaked a topless picture of you."

"Oh." No... it's not as devastating as it used to be, getting caught naked on the internet. But it could tear my career chances in half. Lawyers are still held to certain standards of behavior.

Who would do that to me?

My stomach is in knots. I sent Nathan pictures a few times. And there might be some left in one of the accounts Madison has access to. I know my trust meant nothing to them, but this is a new low.

This is my future. Someone is trying to destroy it. Or they're willing to trade it for a quick buck.

"Hey. It's gonna be okay." He runs his hand through my

hair. "I know it's scary, but Tom's got his eye out. Anything else comes up, we'll convince the site to change their story."

"But... this could destroy my career before it starts."

"I know." He pulls me into a tight hug. "I won't let it."

"What if you can't stop it?"

"I'll die trying."

"But what if you don't catch it in time?"

He meets my gaze. "There a lot of pics of you floating around?"

"No. Three or four maybe."

"Same person has them?"

"Yeah."

"Then they probably sold them all in one go. If something does get through, I'll do everything it takes to shut the site down."

"But... who would do this to me?"

"Your ex had the pictures?"

I nod. "I didn't think he'd... did he really think that little of me?"

"Want me to take care of him?"

"What would you do?"

"Know people who can fuck with his future."

I shake my head. "No... that's okay." I stare into Pete's deep brown eyes. "Are you sure this won't get out?"

"Yeah."

"You promise?"

"Anybody who wants to hurt you is gonna die trying."

I take a deep breath. The certainty in his expression eases some of the tension in my shoulders. "Okay."

He runs his fingertips over my chin. "You want to talk about it?"

"No. I want to... not feel so vulnerable."

"Fuck, Jess. I'm so sorry. This is my fault."

"Stop saying that. I knew what I was getting into agreeing

to do this. I made my choice and I don't regret it." My eyes meet his. "You leaked those pictures so the site would bury mine."

"Yeah. That a problem?"

"No. It's sweet. Weird but sweet."

The fear in my stomach melts. He's willing to go to great lengths to protect me. I trust him that there won't be any more leaks.

I trust him with my heart.

I... I'm falling in love with him.

His lips curl into a smile. "I have better ones for your eyes only."

"Better how?"

He pulls out his cell, taps the screen a few times, and hands it to me.

Oh my. These are better. He isn't just naked. He's touching himself.

I think I'm going to faint.

"Wait. Did this Hazel person shoot this?" I stare back at him.

He chuckles. "You're jealous?"

"Did she?"

"No. Tripod."

"Good."

He plants a kiss on my lips. "I like you jealous."

৩৶৵৹

AFTER A DINNER OF THAI DELIVERY AND A VIEWING OF THE ultimate legal thriller *The Firm*, we settle in the backyard. I sit on the cool concrete and dip my feet in the pool.

Pete sits next to me, his hands planted behind him, his eyes on the sky. It's dark enough in the hills that the black night is dotted with shining stars.

They're beautiful. They have nothing on him, but they're beautiful nonetheless.

Between the pool, the stars, and the warm breeze, the mood is disgustingly romantic. If I didn't know better, I'd be tempted to pin him to the concrete and confess my feelings.

I nudge him playfully. "Is this your usual seduction style?"

He smiles. "Not without a bottle of whiskey."

"Really?"

Pete cocks a brow. "You tell me."

I shake my head, trying not to get lost in the light flickering over his eyes. "I don't buy it."

"Don't think I need to try that hard to seduce you."

My cheeks flush. It's true. Judging from the proud expression on his face, he knows it too.

Still... "I confess nothing."

"So I need to present evidence to prove my case?"

I nod.

He slides his hand under my skirt.

It skims my thigh. Closer. Closer. Closer. Then his palm is pressed against me, over my panties.

His fingers slip inside my panties. They skim my sex. I gasp, clutching at his muscular bicep so I'll maintain some hint of control.

He leans in to whisper in my ear. "You're wet."

I groan.

He continues his cruel teasing, taking my earlobe between his lips and sucking hard, rubbing my clit with a feather light touch.

I groan. "Pete. Please. If you keep teasing me, I'm going to report you to the authorities for mistreatment of a contractor."

He pulls away instantly. His expression hardens. "That's not what you think of our relationship."

"How do you know?"

"I know." His voice gets rough. "Why say that?"

Because I can't say what I'm actually feeling. I take a deep breath. "Because I'm scared of the truth."

He doesn't acknowledge my statement. Instead, he slips back to teasing. "Might allow you to make it up to me."

"Generous of you."

A smile breaks up the frustration on his face. He moves close enough to kiss me. He slides his hand around my neck with a gentle touch.

He looks at me like he's going to kiss me.

But he doesn't kiss me. He just stares into my eyes with that penetrating gaze. The one that sees through me.

His voice softens. "Are you gonna make me guess at the truth?"

"No. You know what it is." My eyes meet his. A look of understanding passes between us.

"You have feelings for me."

I nod. "I'm sorry. You've been clear. I can't help it."

"Promise me something, Jess."

"Yeah?" I finally manage to look him in the eyes. All the affection in his expression flows through me. I forget how to breathe.

"Promise you won't apologize for your feelings ever again."

"Why should I promise you anything?"

"Cause you want to get in my pants."

"Do I have to work that hard?"

He nods.

His lips curl into a smile. It does things to me, that smile. He takes my hands, his fingertips skimming my palms.

His gaze is fixed on me. I can feel it, even with my gaze on my thighs.

He has feelings for me too. I know he does. But does he realize it?

He slides his hands around my waist and pulls me into his lap. I squeal, clutching at his shoulders. No way am I falling into that pool.

In one swift motion, he lies on his back and pulls my body on top of his.

The way he's looking at me with affection, the way he finds the tie holding together my French braid, pulls it out, and digs his hands through my hair—he must know what he's doing.

I take a deep breath. I have to ask. "Do you have feelings for me?"

"You really want to know?"

I nod.

"Yeah. I do." He brings his palm to my cheek, running his thumb over my chin with all the affection in the world. "But this isn't going to turn into something forever. Don't want a relationship."

"I know," I whisper.

"And you're okay with that?"

No. Yes. It's confusing.

What the hell am I supposed to do with all these feelings?

I care about him.

He cares about me.

We're sharing things we've never shared with anyone else.

But somehow, this can't be forever.

It doesn't add up. For a second, I wish I'd majored in math instead of literature. There's always an answer with math. Two plus two is four. With literature, everything is open to interpretation.

But then Pete isn't an algebra equation. He's fucking *Heart Of Darkness*—impossible to understand without careful scrutiny.

I want to tell him the truth. "I don't know." My eyes find

his. I'm hot and cold at once. Every part of me wants every part of him.

Which is worse—my heart breaking now or later?

"I don't want to hurt you," he says. "I care about you."

"I..." I take a deep breath. It's better to get him now, whatever that means later. "I'm okay with it." I think. Mostly.

My stomach clenches. It's close to a lie.

He stares back at me, picking me apart. Can he tell it's close to a lie?

I'm not sure.

"I had something planned for tonight. Still want to do it." His eyes bore into mine. "If you're sure."

I nod. "I'm sure."

"Haven't told you what it was yet."

"I trust you."

His lips curl into a half smile. "I want to tie you up."

Instantly, my body is buzzing. I'm not sure which way is up or which way is down. I want him every way I can have him.

If this is the only way, it's better than nothing.

It's better than most things.

He stares back at me. "Talk to me, Jess."

"Yes. Now."

He takes my hands and pulls me up with him.

Chapter Twenty-Four

By the time we're in my bedroom, I'm buzzing. Pete is going to tie me up.

Holy fucking hell.

He's seamless about sliding his arms around my waist and throwing me on the bed. I bounce from the impact. I'm hungry. I'm desperate.

I let my legs splay open. I arch my back. I toss my glasses on the bedside table.

He's on top of me in an instant. The weight of his body sinks into mine, pins me against the mattress. This one is springs, not foam. It has little give.

I get every inch of him. Not the mattress. Me. I'm greedy enough that it matters.

His lips press against mine. He's just as hungry. Just as desperate to be out of his head.

He drags his teeth over my lower lip. It draws all my attention back to the moment.

He does it again, harder. I gasp into his mouth. My hands go to his hair. God damn, how I love that thick hair of his.

Just enough to grab. I hold his head against mine, parting my lips for him, sliding my tongue around his.

Is it possible to get off from a kiss? It must be with the way my sex is pulsing.

This isn't going to turn into something forever.

The words echo in my brain. I have to prove him wrong.

Is it even possible to prove him wrong?

I have to make him realize it.

Somehow.

The decision eases the tension in my back. No more thinking. I need to go back to light and free, the way I felt before, the way I only feel with him.

I kiss him harder. Bring my hands to his shoulders then down his back.

He groans into my mouth. I groan back. It's not enough of him. I need all of him. I wrap my legs around his waist and pull his body onto mine. Better. I can feel his hard-on. Only the thinnest layers of cotton between us.

Pete breaks the kiss. His eyes meet mine. Right now, I know exactly what he's thinking.

He wants me.

He wraps his hands around my wrists and pins them over my head. "You sure about this?"

A shiver runs down my spine. I can't remember ever being more sure of anything. I nod. "I want to try everything with you."

He straddles me then reaches for the restraints. "You can tell Tom about this tomorrow. He'll flip."

"You've got me in used restraints?" I tease.

He nods. "I think they're clean."

"Think?"

"You want to back out?"

"God no."

Despite his insistence that he hasn't done this before, he

cinches the leather restraint in seconds. Then he's onto my other wrist.

"Why are you so good at this?" I ask.

"You know what they say about bassists."

I shake my head. "What's that?"

"Great with their hands. But they're not showy about it." He reaches under my back and unhooks my bra.

I groan as he pulls one cup down. He teases my nipple with his thumb. The whole time his eyes are fixed on mine.

It's intense, the way he's looking at me like he wants to consume me. I understand him here. I'm going to understand him everywhere.

But we are here. And I like here. I take a deep breath as my eyelids press together. I'm in this moment. Only this moment. Tomorrow doesn't exist. The end of this, whenever that is, doesn't exist.

He presses his lips against mine. It's a hard kiss. My wrists tug against the restraints as I go for his hair. There's a pressure but it doesn't hurt.

It's different kissing him without being able to touch him. I can feel more subtleties in the movements of his mouth— the way he sucks on my bottom lip then scrapes his teeth against it. The way his tongue slides into my mouth. The vibrations of his groans against my skin.

I kiss back and wrap my legs around his waist. I get lost in the movements of our mouths.

His lips break with mine. They plant on my jaw, soft and wet. Then they're on my neck. My collarbone. My shoulder. The top of my chest.

Lower. Lower. There. His mouth closes around my nipple. My instincts scream that I want to grab him, hold him, do something to react. Instead, I groan his name.

"Pete. Please. Stop teasing."

He flicks his tongue against me. "This is nothing."

He smiles a truly evil smile that screams *I'm going to tease you until you're begging.* My sex clenches at the thought. God damn, I love what a tease he is.

He spends minutes sucking on my nipple. Harder and harder until I'm groaning and squirming. I wrap my legs around him, my thighs against his hips. I buck my hips in hopes of some contact for my aching sex but get none.

"Please," I groan. "Please touch me."

"Soon."

He moves to my other nipple and teases it just as mercilessly. He's sucking hard when he finally brings his hands to my hips. He pulls our bodies together, so his cock presses against my clit. God damn underwear is in the way. It's still enough to send a wave of pleasure through my body.

Now.

I need him now.

My groans run together as he scrapes his teeth against my nipple. It's light enough it doesn't hurt, but the difference in sensation sends shock after shock of pleasure to my sex.

Mmm.

"Please, Pete. Are you really going to make me beg?"

"Make you beg? No." He rocks against me. "This is what you want. I'm not gonna make you do anything."

Pleasure shoots to my fingers and toes as he rocks against me again.

He shifts. In one smooth movement, he nudges my legs apart and pulls my underwear to my knees.

There. It's at my feet. It's gone.

"I want you to come on my face." He scrapes his teeth against my inner thigh. "Is there a problem?"

"No," I groan.

His lips trail up my thigh. Almost. Almost.

His tongue flicks against my clit. With my hands bound, I

can't hold him against me. Can't tug at his hair or claw at his back. All I can do is groan and move my lower body.

He teases with another feather light flick. Again. Again. Again.

I'm at his mercy. Completely under his control. But then, that's always been true. It's just a little more technical this time.

Anticipation courses through me as he teases and teases and teases.

His tongue slides over me, flat and wet and just the right amount of pressure. I sigh with relief. A thank you rises up in my throat but it comes out as a mumble of vowels.

No more teasing, he licks me up and down. I gasp as his tongue plunges inside me. Holy fucking hell. This is the most intense sex I've ever had. Period.

Tension knots in my core. Closer. Closer. He works his way back to my clit, replacing his tongue with one finger. Then two.

I feel full, whole. Everything is right in the universe. Within moments, the pressure of my orgasm is unbearable. It's enough it hurts.

Almost.

With his next lick, I go over the edge. My sex pulses as I come. I groan. Still, I can't tug at his hair. Instead, I dig my heels into his back.

He grabs my thighs and pins them to the bed. The roughness of the gesture makes me needier. He's even sexier in control. It shouldn't be possible, but it is.

Pete looks up at me. He wipes his mouth with his hand then sucks on his wet fingers. "You want another?"

Yes. But I want him more. "I want you inside me."

He groans.

That, I understand.

He brings his body onto mine. His hands slide behind my ass, holding me in place.

Almost.

Our eyes lock. The intensity of his expression is enough to leave me breathless. Those deep brown eyes of his are filled with an ocean of desire. He wants me as much as I want him, needs me as much as I need him.

His tip strains against me. Every molecule of my body cries out for more. I need all of him and I need it now.

Pete remains a merciless tease. Again and again, he teases me. I'm full up with anticipation. Every tease is agony. I focus on his expression. The way his eyes roll back in his head. It's killing him too, waiting.

I'm not above begging when he looks at me like that. "Please," I groan. "Fuck me, Pete."

His eyes lock with mine. He nods. His fingers curl into my flesh.

There. He thrusts into me with a quick motion. I'm wet. There's no resistance. I can feel myself spreading around him as I take him deeper and deeper.

I'm full but it doesn't hurt. Only feels good. Only feels right.

He's got me. He's going to give me what I want.

He thrusts into me again and again. Each time it's with full force—hard and deep. My legs shake. I cry out from the intensity of it.

Still, it doesn't hurt.

His hands plant outside my shoulders. My legs wrap around his hips. I use them for leverage, pulling our bodies together as he thrusts into me. It takes him a little deeper. It's not enough.

I curl my back. Deeper.

Again. Again. Again.

Pleasure wells up inside me. There's no way to contain it.

I lose any last hint of shyness. I scream his name. I rock back into him.

"You feel so good," I breathe. My eyes meet his. "Can you go deeper?"

He groans a yes and shifts off me enough to bring my legs to his chest. My ankles hit his shoulders.

He takes his time filling me. It's a tighter fit. Ow. It's too intense. I stop breathing.

"I've got you." He pulls out.

My body cries from the feeling of emptiness.

He adjusts our positions. Slowly, he slides inside me. Slowly, he brings the full weight of his body against mine. His hands dig into my hair. His eyes connect with mine. I remember to breathe.

It's still intense, but it's just enough.

I'm pinned. I can barely move. My eyelids press together. My lips press together. Then his thumb is on my bottom lip. In my mouth. I suck greedily. I want to touch him. But I want to finish this experiment.

A few more thrusts and I'm at the edge. I groan against his hand. My sex clenches. He slows.

His eyes meet mine. "I want you to come on my cock."

God yes.

I watch the pleasure spread over his face. A few more thrusts and his eyes are rolling back in his head. His lips part.

"Jess," he groans. "Fuck, Jess, you're so fucking wet."

Pleasure knots inside me. With his next thrust, I'm coming. My sex pulses around him, pulling him closer. Then he's shaking, biting his lip, groaning these perfect low groans.

I can feel his orgasm in the way his cock pulses inside me. In the way he fills me.

"Jess," he groans my name as he comes.

He sets my legs down and wraps his arms around me. He's

still inside me. The entire universe still feels like it's exactly where it needs to be.

Pete undoes my restraints then shifts to the spot next to me. My hands go to his skin instantly. I press them against his chest, his shoulders, his stomach. God, I need his skin on my hands.

His hair between my fingers.

I slide my hand around his neck as I pull him into a long, deep kiss.

"New favorite?" He asks.

My cheeks flush. "I need to touch you next time." I soak in every inch of his skin against my fingers.

He catches my lower lip with his thumb. "I like you at my mercy."

"Me too." Of course, I'm always at his mercy.

There's this beautiful look of satisfaction on his face. Like he's never felt an ounce of pain before. Like he's exactly where he needs to be.

He brings his mouth to my ear. "I teased you ruthlessly."

I nod.

"I have to make it up to you."

"For once, you're making sense."

"Turn around."

I do. My back presses against his chest.

He presses his palm against my stomach and pulls my body into his. "Two orgasms isn't enough."

"A lot of sense. You must have taken a seminar or something."

"I must have." He chuckles. "You want to go for three or four?"

"Three."

His hand slides between my legs. "Too bad. I want four."

I can't exactly object to that. My body is still putty. I melt into his touch. My eyelids press together. The room fills with our breath, our heartbeats, the moans escaping my lips as he strokes me to another orgasm.

I groan his name as I come.

He gives me a second to rest, then he's stroking me again. The pressure is intense. I'm not sure I have anything left.

His groan against my ear convinces me.

Within moments, I'm coming again. I dig my nails into his thighs to contain the pleasure that spills through my body.

When I'm finally finished, I nestle into his body.

"You're going to kill me at this rate," I groan.

"Is that a complaint?"

"No." Death by orgasm isn't a bad way to go.

"Didn't think so." He pulls me closer.

My eyelids press together. I should get up, brush my teeth, wash up.

But I can't. Right now, the world is perfect.

I fall asleep in Pete's arms.

Chapter Twenty-Five

The morning is perfect. We drive to Pete's fancy Hollywood gym. It's a huge room but it's mostly empty. There are two dozen people here, half civilians, half B or C-list celebrities. Nobody makes a fuss or introduces themselves.

Big glass windows let in the soft glow of morning and offer a 360 view of the city. It can't convince me to stare at anything other than Pete.

He's working out shirtless.

It becomes clear how he maintains such a brilliant, work of art of a body. The man is focused when it comes to lifting. He focuses with the same concentration he brings to his playing.

Between sets, he shoots me flirtatious glances.

Usually, I hate the cardio machines at the gym. I feel like a hamster on a wheel running on the treadmill's endless belt. Not today. Today, I'm ready to go for hours.

No one notices me—no one notices the girl with glasses, a messy ponytail, and an ample ass—until Pete checks on me.

He tugs at my loose tank top. "Seems unfair that you're wearing a shirt."

"Convince me to take it off."

His smile lights up his face. "I will." He leans in close and lowers his voice. "Don't want you dripping till you're in the shower with me."

Yes please. I nod an okay.

"How much longer you want to stay?"

"None."

He chuckles. "Let's say fifteen minutes."

"Let's say fifteen seconds," I counter.

Pete winks and takes a step backwards. "I'll make it worth the wait."

۞

THE DRIVE HOME IS PAINFULLY SLOW, BUT BEING PRESSED against Pete in the tile shower is more than enough to make up for it. Warm water makes us slick and slippery. I only barely manage to hold him close as I kiss him.

Everything stays above the waist. He's such a damn tease.

Still, I stay on a cloud all the way through breakfast and the drive to the Santa Monica building.

Pete parks his Tesla in a VIP area. He carries my bag around his shoulder, his arm around my waist protectively.

He even presses me against the elevator wall, kissing me until I'm groaning and clawing at his hair. He's hard. He does nothing to hide that fact as we step onto the floor.

This isn't the behavior of a man who doesn't want forever.

It's the behavior of a man who is fucking crazy about me.

How the hell do I make him see it that way?

Miles, Tom, and Drew are already here. They're hanging out on the couches that line the giant lobby. The label's logo is plastered on the wall with shiny silver letters.

Tom shakes his head. "Jesus, you're gonna put an eye out walking around like that." He looks at me. "Which one of you is the tease?"

"You really have to ask?" Miles jumps in. "She's panting. He's cool as a cucumber."

"You guys need hobbies." Drew pushes off the couch and turns his attention to his cell.

"I need a hobby? I'm not the one who texts my girl every three minutes," Tom says.

"'Cause she's working." Miles laughs. "Willow won't take your shit." He motions come here and pats the spot on the couch next to him. "Come on. Lay the gossip on me, Jess. I know Pete is a filthy pervert."

Miles shoots Pete a playfully accusatory look. Pete nods *it's all true*. His expression is the picture of confidence.

I'm the center of attention. But I can handle teasing. I cross my legs and look Miles in the eyes. He has gorgeous blue eyes and a devilish grin. Anyone's definition of the word handsome.

But it does nothing to make my heart race or my stomach flutter.

Not even the thought of his sexy voice can make me nervous. I much prefer Pete's groans in my ears.

Miles chuckles. "Jess, you've got something juicy. It's not nice to hold back."

"He is the tease." I look to Pete to make sure he's fine with this line of conversation.

He's smiling, proud, practically beaming.

I turn back to Miles. "He's a merciless tease, actually."

"Better hope you make that up to her." Miles winks at Pete. He turns back to me. "I was hoping Pete would pick up my manwhore mantle but he looks a lot happier with you than he did fucking his way through every girl who licked her lips like she wanted to suck him off."

Tom clears his throat. "Jesus."

"Even for you, Miles." Drew shakes his head.

Miles shrugs. "Can either of you deny it?"

The guys nod with acceptance.

Miles smiles in victory. "Not like I asked Jess how often she sucks him off."

Tom facepalms. "How am I still the asshole?"

"Don't know. You'd think it would be Drew with how many times he's punched somebody in the face," Miles says.

Drew flips him off. His eyes stay on his phone.

Tom shifts out of teasing. He beams. "I'll be back in ten." He winks at me on his way out the door. "Keep an eye on these three."

Miles chuckles. "Settle a bet for me, Jess."

"Um. With who?" I ask.

"Me and Drew made it a while back."

Drew groans. "You're not—"

"I am." Miles's lips curl into a mega-watt smile. "You met Pete a few months ago?"

I nod.

"And you were aware of Sinful Serenade before that?"

"I have a radio," I say. "You're inescapable."

"You'd seen us live?" he asks.

"Yeah. My sister dragged me to a few shows."

"Dragged? Jess, that hurts. Was it really that awful, watching us live?" Miles teases.

My cheeks flush. "No. It was fun. But back then, I didn't have time for fun. I think you stripped."

"He always strips," Drew says. "It's the only reason why we keep him in the band."

"Love you too, buddy." Miles blows Drew a kiss. He turns to me. "Who did you think was the sexiest guy in the band? Before you laid eyes on Pete's monster cock?"

"What's the point of this?" Drew asks.

"Curiosity isn't a crime." Miles looks at me. "Ex-future lawyers have to stick with current future lawyers."

"You're right. Curiosity isn't a crime." Truth be told, I never really thought about Sinful Serenade beyond them being Madison's favorite band. It seemed like her thing. But I did spend a lot of time in her room. I did do a lot of staring at those posters. "You're all very handsome, very sexy in your own ways. I could never choose."

"None of that political bullshit." Miles raises a brow. "It can be our secret. I won't tell."

"Who did you bet it was?" I ask.

"Can't influence your decision." He throws Pete a *watch this* look then turns back to me. "It wasn't Tom, was it? That would be cold to your boy."

"No, it wasn't Tom. I'm not into blonds." I point to my hair. "We'd look like brother and sister."

"Was it Drew?" Miles nods to the guarded guitarist.

Drew rolls his eyes.

I shake my head. "No. Sorry, Drew. You're very attractive but a little standoffish for my tastes."

Drew shrugs, unmoved. "You should ignore Miles. He invents ways to entertain himself since he can't drink."

"I enjoy conversing with my friends," Miles says. "I know it's a strange concept for you, Guitar Prince, what with you despising everyone."

Drew smiles as he flips Miles off. His voice is light, teasing. "Fuck. You are a bigger asshole than Tom is. Why don't you tease Pete for once?"

"Cause he doesn't react. It's no fun. You and Tom rile up in a hot second," Miles says.

"Why'd you stop carrying *Star Wars* novels? You only started shit every ten minutes back then," Drew says.

"You really want me to get into *Star Wars*? Got a lot to say about the new one." Miles teases.

"Fuck, that would be worse. Save it for your Princess." Drew laughs.

Miles looks at Pete and raises a brow. Then he looks at me. "Pete that cool and collected when he's naked?"

"We know he's not," Drew says. "We've all heard."

Pete grins with pride.

My cheeks flush. "He was always my favorite. Sorry, Miles. You're very handsome but I like a man with a little more mystery."

Miles chuckles. "Forgot what the fuck that bet was for. Or what the hell I bet." He winks at Pete. "You know I'd never bet against you."

"I know. Sexiest guys goes me, you, Drew, Tom." Pete laughs.

"Put your brother last? That's cold." Miles shakes his head. "And he can't still be last now that he has that piercing."

Pete cocks a brow.

"I've asked Tom if the two of them ever shared. He says no," Miles.

"I can hear you." Drew shakes his head. "I wouldn't even think about having a threesome with Tom." He rubs his forehead. "God damn. Thanks for those mental images. You do realize he's about to marry my sister?"

Miles shrugs, feigning innocence. "If you had to pick somebody?"

"You and Meg looking?" Drew asks.

"No." Miles smiles. "Just entertaining myself. Like you said."

"One of you three?" Drew asks.

Miles nods.

"To join me and Kara or in a parallel universe before that?" Drew asks.

"Before," Miles says. "You wouldn't share Kara in a million years."

Drew nods. "Pete. No question."

Pete laughs. "Told you." He locks eyes with Miles and motions to Drew. "He need a cool down before this?"

Drew's eyes stay on his phone. "No, I'm fine."

"Kara work out all your energy this morning?" Miles asks.

Drew doesn't bat an eye. He just nods.

I smooth my sundress. The air conditioning is on full blast. Even with all the thoughts of Pete naked and groaning in my head, I'm cold.

I push myself off the couch and join Pete leaning against the wall. He slides his arm around my waist, pulls my body into his, presses his lips to my forehead. Is it for show or because he wants to hold me? His friends are still teasing each other. They aren't even looking at us.

My eyelids flutter closed. I allow myself a few moments to soak in the comfort of his body. I'm not sure what it means, but I love having his arms around me.

God, Pete smells so good. Like soap and shampoo and like him. I'm tempted to drag him to an empty office and have my way with him.

"Hello, Miles. Mr. Denton, Mr. Steele." Aiden steps into the room.

Instantly, I'm cold. Even his voice is slimy.

Pete pulls me closer. He holds me so tightly I can barely breathe. Or maybe that's how disgusting Aiden is.

"That's a nice dress, Ms. James. Do you need me to turn the air conditioning down?"

His eyes go to my chest. I look down. Sure enough, the high beams are on.

Aiden is looking at my nipples. Gross.

"No, I'm fine."

His eyes lock with mine. They're threatening.

Miles jumps in. He motions *I've got this* to Pete. "How's Bruce? Still fucking his assistant?"

"No. His assistant moved to another label."

"That's a shame. Rehab take this time?" Miles asks.

"How many tries did it take you? I forget." Aiden glares. "Where is Tom?"

Everybody tenses.

Pete presses his lips against my forehead. He leans in to whisper in my ear. "Give me a minute."

I nod.

He shifts off the wall. His eyes meet Aiden's with a threatening glare. "Let's speak privately."

"No need. I understand. It won't be a problem." Aiden shrinks back. "Main conference room. Ten minutes. The executives have notes on the new single."

Damn. Even rock stars have to deal with obnoxious bosses. Nobody gets a break.

Miles clears his throat. He's quick to change the subject. "You coming over after this, Jess?"

"Am I invited?" I ask.

He throws Pete a *work on your game* look. "I insist. Your boy is the only guy in the band who can play the piano. We're writing a new song together."

"Really?" I nearly squeal. I'm being invited to sit and listen to Pete play the piano. I might die of happiness.

Pete shakes off a frown.

Or not.

"You should go home, finish your schoolwork." Pete's eyes meet mine. "School *comes* first."

"I'll finish here."

"Jess—"

"I appreciate your concern for my studying, but I've got it under control."

There's displeasure all over Pete's face, but I don't know

why. Does it really mean that much to him, keeping me out of his jam session?

I take my bag from him and sling it around my shoulders. Still, Miles and Drew are looking at us. The room is silent. Must be they're concerned.

I pull Pete into a deep kiss. For show, I guess. His lips are soft. He tastes good. But there's all this resistance in his body. Even as he plays up the gesture.

My stomach twists. What happened to our sweet morning together? He's pushing me away again.

I take a step backwards with my best smile. I still don't know him, don't know anything about him. "I'll be at the coffee shop down the street if you need me."

But something tells me he won't.

Chapter Twenty-Six

The inside of the mansion is just as beautiful. The ground level has an open floor plan. The kitchen, dining table, and glass door are on one side. The glass door that leads to the balcony lets in soft, white light. The other side of the room is dimmer, yellow and fluorescent. It houses two couches, a TV, a coffee table, and a piano.

Miles and Pete are sitting on the piano's bench. They're lost in their own world. They don't notice me come in.

I pour a glass of water. They seem busy. I hate to interrupt, but I'm starving.

"Do you mind if I raid your fridge?" I yell to the other side of the room.

"Help yourself to anything," Miles calls back. His voice echoes around the room.

I stay busy fixing a snack. There's plenty of food in the fridge. Actually, there's a ridiculous variety of food in the fridge. Everything from fresh pasta to Thai curry paste to vegetables I barely recognize. A water chestnut, maybe?

"Are you guys hungry?" I call back. "I can make something."

There's murmuring on their side of the room. Finally, Miles replies.

"Make enough for four. Meg is studying upstairs." His voice softens. "Thanks, Jess. Nice to have someone who can cook around. My girl is hopeless at it, and she's never gonna learn if I keep making her breakfast and dinner."

"Does she live with you?" It's strange yelling the conversation across the cavernous room, but it's nice focusing on something besides my thoughts.

"Some of the time. She's going to med school in Irvine. It's about an hour and a half south without traffic. With traffic, could take three or four hours. She stays with her parents during the week."

"You miss her?"

"Mhmm." He chuckles. "Course she'd never get anything done if she lived here all week. She looks damn cute when she's studying. Can't resist distracting her."

"Pete's the same way with me." Sort of.

Miles tsk tsks. "Can't get in the way of an ambitious woman. Thought you had better game than that, Steele. Her career's gonna come first."

I can't quite make out Pete's reply. But it must be something clever, because Miles's chuckle fills the room.

"No wonder I don't let you write any songs," Miles says. "It'd be pure filth." He sings. "*Baby you always come first, dripping on my face as I plunge my tongue into your cunt.*"

My cheeks flush. Did Pete actually say that?

Uhhh. Need to focus on anything else. "Do you have any dietary restrictions?"

They whisper something else and chuckle. Finally, someone calls out a no. I scan the fridge for my options. The thing is full of exotic ingredients—gangal, snapper, scallops. How the hell do you cook a scallop? I'm determined to find out.

I settle in the kitchen and browse recipes on my phone.

Miles and Pete shift back into working. By the time I've decided on a spicy stir fry dish, they're playing around with piano riffs. It sounds like they're having fun. Every few minutes, one of them bursts into laughter.

It's strange—the sad piano ballad mixed with their infectious laughter—but it's fitting. Like my mood the last few weeks.

The food cooks quickly. Everyone breaks to eat. Even Meg comes down from her room. I let her and Miles lead the conversation. They joke about little things—*Star Wars*, Tom's face when he's pissed, a neighbor with a ridiculous yellow SUV.

They don't press me or Pete for details about our relationship. They aren't the snooping type. That, or our lie is more seamless than I think it is.

After lunch, I set up shop on the couch with my required reading. The guys go back to work.

This time, I'm close enough to listen.

I know how to use my hands
my mouth, my hips
I know every single place that
you want my lips

BABY, I KNOW THIS HURTS
but it could hurt worse
fallin' head over heels
baby, that's a curse

I KNOW HOW TO LOCK YOU OUT
no screams, no lies
the anguished frown as I convince

you not to try

BABY, I KNOW THIS HURTS
  but it could hurt worse
  fallin' head over heels
  baby, that's a curse

I KNOW HOW TO MAKE YOU LEAVE
  can't let you stay
  but do I believe myself when I beg you
  to run away?

BABY, I KNOW THIS HURTS
  but it could hurt worse
  fallin' head over heels
  baby, that's a curse

Miles sings them with that gorgeous tortured voice of his. He never phones it in. Not even on the tenth or twentieth reading of a line. Every word flows from his lips with a wealth of passion.

After an hour, I give up on my work and listen to them piece together the song. Pete plays a few bars of piano. Miles sings. They go back and forth for a while then put it together.

"That's the chorus. That's it," Miles says.

"No. More like—" Pete sings.

baby, I know this hurts
but it could hurt worse
fallin' head over heels
baby, that's a curse

My heart rises up in my throat. Pete's not nearly as good a singer as Miles is, but there's a certain rawness to it. His feelings pour in through my ears and fill me everywhere.

The words are in my soul.

His voice is in my soul.

He's hurt. I replay the words again.

baby, I know this hurts
but it could hurt worse
fallin' head over heels
baby, that's a curse

Finally, I have some insight into his heart. It's not enough. I need more.

I turn around, peeking my head over the back of the couch, and I watch them play.

Miles takes his turn singing the chorus. He embellishes the pitch, sells the ache in the words, but it's not the same.

"Will you sing it again?" I ask.

Pete's eyes meet mine. "Thought you were studying."

Miles swats him. "Damn. It's like you don't want to get laid."

"Don't need your help with that."

Miles shakes his head. "Your girl wants to hear you sing. You know what happens after you sing?"

"Something about how she'll be convinced I'm great with my mouth." Pete makes eye contact and raises a brow. "Do I need to convince you of that, Jess?"

"Yes. Convince me." I press my fingers into the soft leather couch.

"Not gonna do it by singing." Pete smiles.

"Singing first," I say.

"You've got no game, Steele," Miles says. "I expect better."

"Don't need game." He cocks a brow. "If I ask, Jess will slide her panties to her feet right now."

"With me here?" Miles asks.

Pete nods. "I'd put a hundred bucks on it."

"Make it worth my while. Make it a thousand."

"You guys know I can hear you," I say.

"What do you say, baby?" Pete locks eyes with me. "Want to split the winnings?"

Baby. He called me baby. My heart thuds against my chest. My body refuses to contemplate whether or not this is pretend.

This isn't fair. If he's going to tease me, I'm going to tease back.

I smile back at him. "Why stop with panties? I'll take off everything. Except my glasses. You did want me to keep them on next time."

His pupils dilate. There. He's under my thumb.

Miles cocks a brow.

Pete nods a yes.

I nod back. "If you sing me the song. Please."

"Sexual blackmail. That's low, Jess. I expected better." Miles winks then nudges Pete. "Should I stay in the middle of this flirtation or you want to put the poor girl out of her misery?"

"She knows what she's doing. She enjoys the misery." Pete turns back to the piano.

Despite his protests, Pete plays what they have of the song. He sings the whole time. When he's finished, I'm equal parts turned on and torn up. It's just like his tattoo—the pain is clear but it's damn beautiful.

Miles pushes himself off the bench. "Give me fifteen minutes." He throws me a stern look. "Keep your clothes on. Keep your leverage."

He makes his way up the stairs.

Pete holds my gaze. "Was that for my benefit or his?"

"Mine." I smooth my skirt. I can do confidence too. "Unless you have a problem."

"No, I want your gorgeous pink lips wrapped around my cock." He stares back at me. "I want you aching from how badly you want to be filled as I come in your mouth."

My sex clenches. I've already lost all the power. I'm quickly losing interest in keeping it. I'm quickly losing interest in anything except our bodies connecting.

He copies my tone. "Unless you have a problem."

"No. No problem."

"You're going to come on my hand, baby. You're going to come hard enough you forget your name."

My heart pangs. It pulls me away from the ache in my core. "You called me baby again."

He cocks a brow.

"We're alone." *We don't lie when we're alone*. I adjust my glasses and rack my brain for some way to explain it. "Don't call me that unless you mean it."

He pushes himself off the bench and makes his way to the couch.

Then he's next to me. He pulls me into his lap, so I'm straddling him.

His hand slides under my skirt.

"What are you doing?" I ask.

"Feeling how wet you are." He presses his palm against my sex, over my panties. "You want me to stop?"

I shake my head.

His fingers skim my sex. "You like thinking about sucking me off."

"Yes."

He brings his mouth to my ear. "What else, baby?"

"Why are you calling me that?"

"Cause it makes you whimper." He pushes my underwear aside and teases my sex with his finger.

"I don't care. Stop calling me that."

He just barely nods. It's not much of an agreement but it's something. It's enough.

Pete slides a finger inside me and takes my earlobe between my teeth. "Where else do you want my cock?"

My tongue is sticky. I can barely draw a breath through my nose. "Miles is coming back."

"I don't care if Miles sees. Do you?"

At the moment, no. Not even a little. In fact, I like the idea of getting caught. It makes me feel dirty.

I shake my head.

"Where do you want my cock?" He slides his finger further inside me. "Here?"

I whimper a yes.

He takes his other hand and brings it to my ass, over my panties. "Here?"

The cotton fabric presses against my entrance.

My body shudders. I do. I never thought I would, but I do. I nod. "Later."

"You think I'm a tease now?" He nips at my ear. "You have no fucking idea how badly I can tease you."

"What are you trying to prove?" I groan as he slides a finger inside me.

"This isn't about proving shit." He stares into my eyes. "I want to watch you come."

"But..."

But he's so much more aggressive than usual. He must be proving something.

I have no idea what it is. But he does. It's there, in the determined expression in his deep brown eyes.

"You want to come, baby?" he asks.

"Pete, why do you keep calling me that?"

"Didn't think about it."

"Well, stop it. Please. If you say it again, I'm done. I don't want to hear the word baby, unless it's followed by *I love you and not just pretend*."

"You want to come, Jess?" he corrects himself.

My heart pangs. I don't feel any better. I only crave the word in my ears again. It doesn't have to be *baby*. Any term of endearment will do.

He slides another finger inside me.

I dig my hands into his shoulder. "Yes."

Right now, this is the only way I can have him.

He's not gentle today. He fucks me with his fingers. His other hand goes to the back of my head and he pulls me into a deep kiss.

His tongue slides around mine. He tastes fucking good.

His hand goes to my dress. He pushes the straps off my shoulders. A few flicks of his wrist and my bra is on the couch.

"Miles is gonna see," I groan. But I'm not really objecting. It makes me hotter, knowing we might get caught.

He presses his thumb against my clit. "You want me to stop, baby?"

Again, my heart pangs. No, no, no. I can't take this anymore. Even if it means I'll be achy and desperate all day. "I asked you not to call me that. Take it back or get the fuck off me."

"You're on me." He pulls his hand to his side.

"Take it back or tell me you mean it, that you really want me to be yours."

His brow knits. His eyes fill with confusion.

For once, he's tongue tied.

I push myself off Pete. It's not fair, having your heart and your body at war. I'm still aching with desire. He's on the couch, hard, his hand wet from me.

I take a step backwards. "Stop teasing, Pete. You know how I feel about you. You're being cruel."

His expression darkens as he turns to the other side of the room. "Yeah."

Yeah?

That's it?

He pushes himself off the couch.

What the fuck? That's not a response.

I take a deep breath. "Why? Why do you keep calling me that?"

He shakes his head and marches off towards the bathroom.

I search the ground floor for another bathroom. There—it's opposite the kitchen. I lock myself in it and I stay busy washing my hands.

This is a whole new level of mixed messages.

He was right. I had no fucking idea how badly he could tease me.

Chapter Twenty-Seven

Wen I return to the main room, Miles and Pete
are back at the bench.

Miles shakes his head. "That was embarrass-
ingly fast. You're better than that. I've heard you go for half
an hour. A whole hour once." He looks at me. "Was a sight,
well, a sound to behold."

I clear my throat. "The way you're phrasing that suggests
that you were trying to catch us."

"Why would I do something like that?" Miles feigns
innocence.

Pete can't muster up the enthusiasm to banter back. He
shrugs.

Miles looks between us. His expression shifts, an
acknowledgment of the tension in the room. He doesn't
mention it. Just pulls his guitar into his lap.

"How about *No Way in Hell*?" he asks.

"That the only song you know acoustic?" Pete teases, but
his heart isn't in it.

"When you have a voice this beautiful, you don't need to
know anything." He slides a guitar pick between his teeth and

spends a moment tuning. "You doing it Pete Steele style or Miles Webb style?"

"I'm a poor imitation," Pete says.

"It's a pretty good imitation."

Pete chuckles, shifting out of his bad mood. "You pretend you hate it."

"At first, I did hate it. But after Drew punched Tom... that warmed my heart."

"First time he punched someone besides you."

"Someone in the band, yeah." Miles laughs. "You really did instigate that one. All that shit about love being worth it and you wanting him to be happy."

"Getting at something?" Pete asks.

"No. Like Drew says, gotta entertain myself somehow when my girl is working." He pulls his shirt down his chest. "You can't pull off the imitation without the hot tattoos. You can admit you're jealous." Miles points to a tattoo of a rose covered in thorns. "Can't beat this."

I nod my agreement. "You can't." Pete's is better, but I'm still pissed and needy. I'm not admitting anything. And I am making this difficult. "Though I am fond of Pete's thigh tattoo. I'm lucky I get some insight into what he's been through."

"Jess—" Pete's eyes narrow.

"Plus, I get an up close and personal view when I suck him off."

Miles clears his throat. "As much as I prefer you dirty talking to Pete dirty talking, I'm gonna clear the room next time either of you goes there."

"You jealous?" Pete asks.

"No offense, Jess—you're a beautiful woman. Back in the day, I would have thrown you on the bed and made you come three times. But, no, I can't even think about other women anymore. Not even if I try."

"Think that counts as dirty talk," Pete says. "Gonna clear the floor?"

Miles looks from Pete to me. "If you guys need another fifteen minutes."

"No. It's fine." Pete's gaze goes to the piano.

"Whatever it is, I won't tell Tom." Miles pushes himself off the bench. "It's not my place but—"

Pete scowls. "You're right. It's not."

"You can be pissed if you want. Anybody would be pissed three months after their girlfriend of six years betrayed their trust. Would ask himself how he didn't see the fucking signs."

"Can we get on with this?"

The aloofness falls off Miles's face. "You're not yourself lately."

Pete huffs. "Play the God damn song."

Miles looks to me as if he's asking my permission. It's sweet that he's concerned about my well being. At least someone is.

My body and heart are still at war. As pissed as I am about Pete's mixed signals, I really, really want to hear him sing.

I nod. "Please play the song."

Miles shakes his head like he finds this a bad idea. Still, he positions his limbs. "Show must go on." He strums the guitar.

The acoustic version of the song fills the room. I press my hands into my thighs as I watch Miles's hands move.

Then Pete starts singing and I can't feel anything but his voice.

I've heard this song a million times. It played on the radio, every single hour, for months. It was inescapable.

But I never heard it like this.

Three am and I can't sleep
A common refrain, I know
As a sentiment, it's cheap
Someone to call To hold

To love no way that word-
She smiles and I drift away—
Oh hell no
This can't be
No way I, no way she
anyone else, maybe
but not me
I don't do this kind of thing.

The words sound so different on Pete's lips. There's a certain relief to them when Miles sings it, like he's embracing falling in love even though he's scared of it. But Pete sings with pure resistance.

Morning now and I can't think
of anything but her laugh, he cries
the sound she makes when I sink
my teeth/oh wow, those details
are mine to keep/ but she's not
And suddenly I want-

OH HELL NO

This can't be
No way I, no way she
anyone else, maybe
but not me
I don't do this kind of thing

My heart pounds against my chest. His voice is dripping with pain. No wonder he's running at the speed of light. He doesn't want to fall in love again.

He's not being cruel on purpose.

But that doesn't make it any more excusable.

When they're finished I offer a small clap. "That was beautiful. Thank you." I scoop my books into my hands and keep my eyes anywhere but Pete's. "But I really should finish this assignment."

"There's a desk in the guest room." Miles sets the guitar down. "I'll show you."

"Thanks."

I can feel Pete staring at us as Miles leads me up the stairs. He takes me to a large room with colorful decoration and a wide desk and explains all the bits and pieces of it.

He lingers in the door for a minute. "Want me to talk to him?"

"You strike me as the kind of guy who will do whatever you feel like doing, no matter what I say."

"Fair point. Do you?"

"You think it's a good idea?"

Miles nods. "Something is wrong. Pete's always been the steadiest guy in the band. I keep pretty cool. Not so much back in the day. But now, I can take shit in stride. Tom and Drew—they fly off the handle like that." Miles snaps.

"You push their buttons."

He smiles. "Me? No."

"You enjoy it."

He nods. "Teasing is great when everyone is on board. When they're not—" He cocks a brow. "What the hell happened? You still look needy."

"I barely know you," I say. "I'm not about to share my relationship problems with you." That's already too much.

"I can give him a verbal lashing about being a cunt-tease."

"No. I'm the one who stopped him." I bite my lip. "It's complicated."

"He does care about you. Whatever is going on. He does."

"What do you mean?"

"Details don't add up. I don't care. Whatever you're trying to prove, whoever you're trying to prove it to, it's not my place to get in the way."

Miles knows we're full of shit.

I swallow hard. I'm not going to convince him otherwise. The best I can hope for is a poker face.

"I'm not gonna let him fuck this up. He cares about you. Make him realize that."

"How do you know?" I ask.

"Known the man since he was thirteen. I can see past the bullshit. Tom... he's gonna see that you're pretending. Pete's real good at convincing everyone he doesn't need help. I get it cause I'm the same way."

"Is it that obvious?" I ask.

"No. Aiden said something. Doubt anyone else picked up on it. Especially given how Drew and Tom were bickering." Miles shifts his weight. "I remember how it felt, losing the only family I had left. I never thought I'd breathe again." He pulls down his shirt and points to a tattoo that says *be brave, live*. "My uncle. He was a great guy. I spiraled out of control a lot worse than Pete did. Was lucky I had people who cared about me when I hit bottom."

"I'm sorry. I'm not following."

"He told you about his tattoo?"

I nod.

"He's never told anyone about that."

"How do you know?"

"Heard him and Cindy screaming enough times to know. They fought like cats and dogs. But I get it. Sometimes, you hold onto something so long that you don't know how to let go."

The sun pokes through the window. It casts orange light over the room. It's almost evening. Already.

I can't stomach talking about this anymore. I set my laptop on the desk. "I'm going to study now. Are you going to talk to him?"

"Only about the song."

"Oh. Good."

"Mmm." He steps into the hallway. "Maybe a word about being a tease. That's no good."

My laugh diffuses the tension in my back.

Miles nods a goodbye. I settle into the desk with my assignment. But once the piano music floats into my ears, I can't concentrate for shit.

❋

IT TAKES HOURS TO GET THROUGH MY ASSIGNMENT. WHEN I finish, I hide under the pink comforter with my Kindle and a soapy YA romance. Ah, life really was so much simpler before sex complicated everything.

It wasn't better, but writing off boys made it simpler.

High school was awful. Between acing my classes, serving as editor of the school paper, and taking care of Dad and Madison, I had no free time. College offered a little more freedom, a little more time, but mostly I filled it with worry. And with Nathan.

It's late when someone finally knocks on the door. The handle turns and Pete steps into the room. The light from the moon casts highlights over his face. It's not fair how beautiful he is. It makes it harder to resist him.

"We should go," he says.

No apology. Not even a word about his ruthless teasing.

I turn my back to him. "I don't want to go."

"We're overstaying our welcome."

"Then you go." I hug my chest. It takes great effort to keep my voice strong and steady. "I'll ask Miles if he minds me spending the night."

Pete takes steps towards me. The weight on the bed shifts as he sits next to me.

His fingers graze my neck then they're back at his sides. "I'm not leaving you here alone."

His voice is heavy. Is he worried about me or about himself?

I keep my eyes on the pastel bedspread. "I'm not alone. Miles and Meg are here."

"You know what I mean."

I try to wait him out. Nothing. For a full minute, the room is filled only with the sound of our breath.

Finally, I break the silence. "Are you going to apologize?"

"I got carried away."

"That's not an apology."

"Come on, Jess." Frustration breaks through his calm voice. "We'll talk at home."

"At your home."

"It's our place."

"No, it's your place. I have a corner of a room. It's not even decorated with my stuff. It's still Tom's because you'll kick me out as soon as I stop being useful to you."

"If you want another room, you can have it. Decorate however you want. I don't care about that house."

"It's easy to offer things if you don't care about them." I pull the blanket tighter around my chest.

Pete leans closer. He brushes my hair behind my ears. "What do you want?"

I turn, so we're eye to eye. There's all this intention in his deep brown eyes, but I've got no clue what it is he's intending.

I swallow hard. My voice is a whisper. "You knew what you were doing."

His gaze goes to the blue light falling through the window. "I'm sorry if I led you on."

"There's no if."

"I'm sorry. I wasn't thinking."

"Is that what you do when you forget your inhibitions— you call me baby?"

"It was dirty talk." His posture stiffens. "Didn't mean anything."

I push myself to a seated position. I need some semblance of power here. Even if being inches from him is doing things to my concentration. Damn body is fighting with my heart again. It doesn't need to respect itself in the morning. It doesn't care about anything but getting its satisfaction.

I allow myself a second to consider it. If it's all physical, if I use him to get *my* pleasure and give him nothing—

No. Even that won't work. I can't separate love and sex. Not with Pete. Not right now.

"You said you'd never lie to me." I stare into his eyes. "Don't start now."

"What do you want to hear?"

"Explain why you're playing with my feelings."

"I don't want to lead you on." He shifts off the bed.

"Do you love me?"

"No."

His voice is utterly to the point. He didn't even have to think about it.

"Are you falling in love with me?"

"This isn't going to be a relationship."

"That's not an answer."

"I'm not answering. It doesn't matter." His stoic facade breaks. For a second, his expression fills with vulnerability. He runs his hand through his hair. It's like the words are on the tip of his tongue. Like he's desperate to tell me how he feels. "This isn't going to be a relationship."

"Why can't it be a relationship?" I swallow hard. "You tell me things you don't tell anyone. You get carried away calling me baby. You have feelings for me too. Give me one good reason why you can't throw away that idea and let yourself fall in love with me."

"I can't."

That's it. He can't.

No. I shake my head. "Bullshit. You don't want to."

"Fine. I don't want to." He takes a step backwards.

"That's a choice you're making."

"Yeah."

"I can make choices too."

He stares back at me.

"I'm not going home with you tonight. That's my choice. I..." I thought I could trust him. I was wrong.

Pete holds strong. "They're gonna—"

"Miles already knows. He more or less told me." I smooth my skirt, but the gesture doesn't soothe me. "If they don't want me here, I'll take a cab somewhere. I'm not going home with you. Not tonight."

"You said you could handle this."

"You didn't mention that you'd lead me on." He certainly didn't mention that he'd be fucking perfect in every fucking way. "How do you expect me to feel when you hold me and whisper *you'll be okay* in my ear, with that sexy, reassuring voice?"

His expression hardens. "Fine. I'll see you tomorrow. What do you want me to tell them?"

"I don't care. You think of something."

He takes a step backwards. "I'm not trying to hurt you."

Yeah, but he's succeeding. "It's only another week until your brother's wedding. I'll be fine as long as you stop pretending."

"Pretending what?"

"That you care about me."

"Jess. I do—" He runs a hand through his hair. "Okay. You're right. It's better if we don't hang out for a while."

My stomach rises up in my throat. He's barely fighting this.

I manage to nod. Manage a poker face. "Glad we're on the same page. Have a safe drive."

"Call me if you need anything."

"I won't."

"But if you do. Promise." His expression is demanding.

I hate how much I want to reassure him. "Fine. Goodnight."

"You too."

His eyes cloud with frustration.

Still, he steps into the hallway. I can hear him at Miles's door, talking about something, then he's making his way down the stairs.

Then the front door slams shut.

And he's gone.

Chapter Twenty-Eight

Meg and Miles go out of their way to convince me I'm not a third wheel. I claim a need to do homework away from my overwhelming attraction to Pete. Neither of them buys it, but they still leave me alone for most of the day.

I hang out in the guest room, getting ahead on my coursework. The wedding is in two weeks. I need to stay ahead of things if I want to keep the three day trip to Hawaii from derailing my studies.

I don't mind massive homework. Actually, I enjoy it. Not just because school makes sense, but because it's exciting. I already love law school. I love studying precedent. I love rearranging and twisting rules to fit my argument. And God how I love making arguments.

Sometime after sunset, Miles knocks on the door and steps into the guest room.

"As much as I'm impressed with you for getting a *rise* out of Pete, you should head home if you want to make your morning classes." He nods to the hallway. "We picked up dinner. You like sashimi?"

"I've never had it."

He smiles and calls downstairs. "Jess has never had sashimi."

Meg's shriek of delight pierces my ears. Damn, the girl is loud. She should be the singer.

Ugh. Singing. I try, hard, to push the memory away, but my brain refuses to cooperate. Instead, it replays Pete singing again and again and again.

My stomach tenses.

You're right. It's better if we don't hang out for a while.

Maybe some food will convince my stomach to shut up.

I power down my computer and follow Miles to the kitchen. He's a tall guy, but he only has an inch or two on Meg. She looks like a model—long legs, slim frame, dramatic features. If I didn't know better, I'd assume he was another celebrity who only cared about appearances and she was another wannabe actress who was using her sexuality to curry fame.

There's nothing fake about them. They're clearly in love.

He slides his arm around her waist and pushes her against the counter. His mouth goes to her neck. A moment later, she's groaning.

Okay, they're clearly in lust too.

"Miles, don't you think Pete teased her enough?" She can barely get the words out.

"Mhmm." He squeezes her then takes a step backwards. Miles turns to me with an apologetic look. "Always figured he was a tease."

I'm not entertaining this line of conversation. The two of them talk. A lot. I go with the first subject I remember. "So how about the new *Star Wars* movie?"

Meg screws her face in distaste. She shakes her head.

Miles chuckles. "She's still upset about Han and Leia getting divorced."

"They're the perfect couple." She sets the table and unboxes the takeout. "You should appreciate it. You're a scoundrel."

He smiles. "You're my princess, babe."

"Am I your princess or your babe?" she teases.

"Princess, you're a total babe." He presses his lips to hers.

It would be tacky to ask them to can the affection. I'm at their house. I'm enjoying their hospitality.

Still, I'm considering it.

Meg catches me watching and clears her throat. She takes a seat, motions for Miles to do the same.

He does.

Meg takes me through the different dining options—red-purple ahi tuna, soft coral salmon, firm ono, glassy fish eggs, octopus. I take one of everything. I'm about to drench a piece of salmon in soy sauce when she grabs my hand.

"Try it plain first. That way you can taste the flavor of the fish," she says.

"You're religious about this," Miles teases.

She shoots him an accusatory glance. "Every single server at Nobu knows your regular order."

"Only because you want to go every Saturday night."

"Nuh-uh."

He smiles and nods. His eyes fill with affection.

It's funny. I've never had a peek into what love really looks like. My parents never even liked each other. My high school friends were casual with their relationships—having fun, screwing around. Even our friendships were casual, surface level. I liked it better that way. I didn't have to worry about revealing too much.

I didn't know how deep love could go, how much another person could free you or tie you up in knots.

Again, my stomach clenches. I sample the salmon sashimi. It's a little soft but it's good. Fresh. I try dipping it in soy sauce, but I like it better plain. There's nothing hiding the flavor.

Then I think of Pete, and my stomach is in knots again.

I'll deal with my feelings later. Once I've held down dinner for an hour. I fill my plate with salmon sashimi, turn to Meg and Miles, and bring up science fiction films until I stumble on something that makes one of them gush.

Turns out it's *Jurassic Park*. Pete's favorite book. Exactly the topic that will help me not think about him.

⚫

AFTER A LONG, PAINFUL GOODBYE—MEG AND MILES WILL be apart until Thursday evening—Meg gives me a ride back to Pete's place.

Mercifully, we converse only about local radio stations.

The drive goes quickly. She pulls into the driveway of the Hollywood place with a wistful sigh.

"There's a lot of memories here. It's a shame the label is finally kicking Sinful Serenade out," she says.

They are? I try not to let my surprise register. "Oh?"

She nods. "After Thanksgiving. Miles said it has something to do with that asshole manager. Aiden." She turns to me. "Are you and Pete looking for another place?"

"Uh..." Thanksgiving is well past our expiration date. No reason why he needed to tell me. I keep up my poker face. "I can't decide if I want to get an apartment close to school or if I want to find a place on the beach."

"Do the beach. Downtown is dead on the weekends and it's nearly as expensive as Santa Monica." Her gaze goes to the house. "You're from Long Island, right?"

I nod. "That means I have to love the beach and Billy Joel."

She laughs. "The guy who does *Piano Man?*"

"Exactly."

"Then definitely do the beach."

I allow myself a moment to fantasize about living on the beach with Pete, at some luxurious place like the one Miles has. The house doesn't matter to me. Just his arms, the sun, the sand, the crashing waves, his voice in my ear as he whispers *baby, I love you.*

I clear my throat. "I should get going. Early class."

She groans. "My first class is at eight." Her dramatic features soften as her expression fills with concern. "I'm terrible with relationship problems. The worst. But. Um. Pete's really hot."

I laugh. "So is Miles."

"Yes, but if you try to sleep with Miles, I'll have to kill you."

"Would you really?"

"In a hot second." She laughs with evil glee. "But I don't think you would. The way you look at the quiet bassist... You're smitten."

"I can't help it."

"Same thing happened to me." Her voice gets serious. "Pete... he really keeps things to himself. He and Miles, they're pretty close. I've gotten to know him. And he's... he's a really great guy. A great brother to Tom. A great friend to everybody. Whatever is happening, I'm sure he wouldn't hurt you on purpose."

"I know."

"Okay. Fuck guys. They're the worst." She turns to me. "And clothes—just as bad. Your dress is cute. You might not need help, but Kara and I are shopping next Sunday. For dresses for the wedding. We have our shit together, getting our dresses five days before we fly to Hawaii."

"We're grad students. We don't need to have our shit together."

"I like the way you think." She laughs. "You should come. On Sunday."

"Sure." Anything that will get me out of the house and away from Pete.

She claps her hands together. "Awesome. I'm sure, uh... Well, I don't think we'll need to worry about coordinating or anything. Since Drew is the maid of honor."

"He is?"

She laughs. "Yeah. He's cute about it." The joy falls off her expression. "I'm happy for Tom and Willow. Really. But... Not your problem. Nevermind."

"No. It's okay. I don't have any friends out here." I curse the desperation in my voice, but maybe it's okay to sound desperate if I'm being earnest. I want to stop bullshitting everyone all the time. "You're more than welcome to talk to me."

For a minute, Meg is silent. When she speaks, her voice is barely more than a whisper. "It can be hard, seeing all these close siblings who care about each other."

"My sister cheated with my ex-boyfriend."

"So you know the feeling."

"Yeah." I play with the strings of my backpack. "What about you?"

Her voice drops. "My sister overdosed last year. She's... gone."

"Oh. I—"

"You didn't know. You can't top an overdose. I always have the saddest sibling story."

I laugh. She has a really dark sense of humor. "I'm sorry—"

"Don't be. Laughing helps."

"You must miss her a lot."

"Yeah... and I worry. Miles alone by himself all week."

"He's in recovery, right?"

She nods. "I don't think I'd ever breathe again if something happened to him." She offers a weak smile. "I know it's hard... dealing with the Sinful Serenade guys. Their heads are so dense sometimes. If you want to talk, give me a call. Even if you want to spend an hour complaining about how he doesn't wash the dishes. Anything. All I do, all week, is study and watch TV. I'd love a distraction."

"Thanks." I offer her a smile as I step out of the car. "Same for you. If you're worried about Miles. Or anything. I know what it's like, loving someone who had those problems."

My hand goes to my mouth. I almost told her about my dad. I never tell anyone, but the words left my tongue before I had a chance to stop them.

But it feels good, being honest. I want to stay honest.

She waves goodbye. "Good luck." She winks. "Let him earn his forgiveness with his mouth."

My laugh surprises me even more this time. Meg seems genuine, but there's no way to know if she's befriending me because she thinks we'll get along or if it's because I'm supposedly Pete's girlfriend.

I push it out of mind as I unlock the door.

The energy changes the second I step inside. There are two magnets pulling me apart. One tells me to stay and talk to him. One warns me to run far, far away.

Pete is watching a movie on the couch in boxers and a T-shirt. He's wearing thick black glasses. Somehow, he looks even sexier in the dark frames. They highlight his eyes.

I say the first thing that makes it to my tongue. "You look sexy in your glasses."

He meets my gaze. There's all this intensity in his eyes, like there's something on the tip of his tongue. Then he blinks and it's gone.

He turns back to the TV. "I'm sending our housekeeper the grocery list tonight. You need anything specific?"

"No." I sling my bag over my shoulder and take a step towards the stairs. "Enjoy your movie. I'll see you later."

I hide out in my room, but I don't feel any better.

Only colder.

Only more pulled apart.

Chapter Twenty-Nine

In the morning, the living room is filled with the smell of coffee, but there's no sign of Pete.

I drink a cup, eat a quick breakfast, dress in my best not quite business casual outfit, and drive to school.

Class grabs my concentration all day. I get dinner off campus and stay late in the library. When I get home, Pete is locked in his room.

I consider knocking. Asking for an apology. Asking for an emotionless fuck. Demanding he get his head out of his ass and realize he could love me.

Instead, I go to my room, and study until I'm too tired to think.

The next day, it's the same.

All week, it's the same.

Come Friday, I'm worn thin. My stomach in knots. My heart is achy. Avoiding Pete doesn't do anything to change my feelings. It only deepens the hole in my gut.

I reheat a plate of leftovers in the fridge and collapse on the couch, ready to give in to my exhaustion. I'm not due anywhere until eleven the day after tomorrow. Sleeping until ten-thirty Sunday is making a lot of sense.

My phone rings. Whoever it is, I'll call back.

It rings again.

Then again.

I push myself off my couch. Where the hell is that thing? It takes three more ring cycles for me to find my phone in my backpack.

Incoming call from Madison.

My chest tightens. All the missed calls are from her. This must be important.

I steel my nerves as I answer the call. "Hello."

"Jess..." Her voice breaks. "I know you don't want to talk to me yet, but it's important."

My instincts push me to soothe her. Something is wrong. Something bad. "What is it?"

"I... I want to say I'm sorry again. I know that's not enough, but I am. It was wrong of me to be with Nathan at all. It was worse that it was so fast. I should have put you first. You've always been my best friend."

Her voice is earnest.

"I miss you," she says. "Long Island isn't the same without you."

"I miss you too." I miss talking to her. I want to talk to her right now. To tell her how much it hurts that Pete will never love me.

"Really?" The happiness drains from her voice. "It's um... I looked into everything with Dad."

That doesn't sound good. My chest tightens. Deep breaths do nothing to soothe me. There's no running from this. I have to rip off the bandage. "What happened?"

Her voice drops to a whisper. "I found a bottle of vodka in Dad's room. It was empty."

Fuck. All my muscles tense at once. He's drinking again.

How long has he been drinking?

I need the facts before I panic. "When did you find it?"

"This morning. It was in the bottom of his bathroom trash can. It's new. I emptied all the trash last week."

"Did you ask him about it?"

"He said he had a woman over. That it was hers." Her voice is weak, like she doesn't believe herself. "It's possible."

I press my fingers into the back of the phone. "It's not."

"Maybe... it's a slip. Maybe he'll get over it." Her voice wavers. "Jessie, I don't know what to do."

"We can't do anything. He's almost sixty. If he wants to drink, he's going to do it." I take a deep breath. I know the words are true. I know there's nothing I can do if he doesn't want to help himself.

Still, my legs go weak. I grab onto the nearest thing—the wall—and use it to brace myself.

I'm empty.

It's eighty degrees outside but I'm freezing.

"You don't mean that." She chokes back a sob. "There must be something."

There's not. "He only went to rehab the first time because of Aunt Zoe. If he doesn't want to get better—" My stomach clenches. I can't feel my feet. "If he doesn't want to get better, there's nothing we can do."

The hope drains from her voice. "Do you think he wants to get better?"

"I don't know." I take a deep breath, trying to figure out the answer. It won't come. I don't have a clue how this will go. But I know it's out of my hands. I have to be okay with that. "I'll think of something, Maddie. Give me some time."

"Okay."

"We'll do something. It might not work, but we will do something."

"Okay."

"We'll talk later."

"I love you," she says.

"I love you too."

I hang up the call and drop the phone on the couch.

Dad is drinking again.

What the hell am I going to do?

The microwave beeps. That must be the tenth beep. None of the other ones made it to my ears.

The food smells like nothing. Something with chicken, rice, and spinach. I'm sure it's delicious but it smells like nothing.

The forks are in the cabinet. I pour a glass of water. It tastes like nothing. Or is that how water always tastes?

My chest is tight. Has it always been this hard to breathe? Has the air always felt this heavy and cold?

I fill the glass again. I can't sit in this house. I can't decide which is harder—moving or standing still. There's the back-yard. It's only a dozen feet away. I pull the glass door open, ready for my thoughts to tear me into pieces.

Pete is here, sitting on the edge of the pool, his legs in the water, his hands curled around his e-reader.

He looks up at me. The aqua glow of the pool casts high-lights over his concerned expression. Thankfully, he says nothing. Simply nods a hello like we're polite and courteous roommates and nothing more.

I sit at the patio table and dig my fork into my food.

It tastes like nothing.

His attention stays on me as I eat in silence. No napkins. Fuck it, I wipe my hands on my skirt. It needs a wash anyway.

Dad is drinking. This is it. I can't watch him destroy himself. If he decides against getting help, I have to walk away.

He'll die on his own.

Probably in a pile of his own vomit, reeking of beer.

Tears sting my cheeks. I turn away from Pete. I only need to hold it together for the one minute it takes to get to my room.

I grab the edges of my seat and push myself to my feet. My knees buckle. I can't stand. I can barely breathe.

If I do nothing, Daddy is going to die.

I try to choke back my sob. It gets through. I pull my legs to my chest and bury my head between my knees.

Wet footsteps move closer. Then his arms are around me. I want them to feel awful, like an invasion, but they don't. They're warm and comforting.

Pete pulls me off the chair, into his lap.

His lips go to my ear. "It's gonna be okay. Jess, you're gonna be okay."

"You heard everything?"

"Yeah."

"Then how can you say that?" I dig my fingers into his soft cotton t-shirt. That too feels warm and comforting. "You promised you wouldn't lie to me."

"I'm not."

"You need to go." I tell myself to bring my hands back to my lap but the damn things won't cooperate with me. "I can't take you acting like my boyfriend anymore."

"I'm not leaving you to cry alone."

"Sometimes you have to be cruel to be kind."

His voice drops to a whisper. "Look me in the eyes and tell me you want me to go and I will."

"It's for the best."

"For who?"

"For my heart. So it doesn't break when you wake up tomorrow and tell me you'll never love me."

His voice softens. "I'm not going to say that."

What the hell does that mean?

I can't stomach his mixed messages. "I can't figure out

your intentions right now, Pete. Whatever you want, whatever you're doing, you're going to have to spell it out."

He shifts so we're eye to eye. His deep brown eyes are filled with concern. Like he's miserable that I'm miserable.

He does care about me.

His voice is steady. "I want to hold you. If you want something else, tell me."

He knows I want nothing else. He knows I want him to lend me those comforting arms every time I need solace.

"My dad is gonna die. If I don't do anything, he's gonna die." I stare back into his eyes. "How am I ever going to live with myself?"

"One day at a time." He finds the tie holding together my French braid and pulls it out. "You told your sister you can't save him unless he wants help. You believe that?"

"Yeah."

"You deserve to be happy, Jess." His gaze goes to the ground then it meets mine. "I'm not going to let you make yourself miserable."

"There's only a week and a half left of this non-relationship. You don't have a say over what I do."

He stares back into my eyes. "I blamed myself for my dad's accident. But trying to help him—" He takes my hand and brings it to his thigh. He presses it against his jeans so hard I can feel the outline of a scar through the denim. "Every time, I was the one who got hurt. I'm not going to let you get ground to nothing trying to save someone else."

"What if I'm kinda not really dating this guy who keeps playing with my feelings. What will you do then?"

His lips curl into a smile. "Kick his ass."

"How does that work?"

"Not sure yet."

"I think I'm falling in love with you."

His expression gets intense. "Are you there yet?"

I laugh. That response is ridiculous, but it's perfect too. "You sound like a kid on a road trip."

He runs his fingers through my hair. "Tell me when you're there."

"But... what about... isn't this doomed to not be forever? Aren't you set on not falling in love?"

"I was." His eyes turn down. "I can't promise shit, Jess. I've been doubting myself since I found out my ex was fucking my best friend. The only two people who knew me as a guy and not a celebrity and they thought nothing of betraying me. What the fuck does that say about me? Been trying everything to make the doubt stop. Only thing that works is being with you."

Something inside me melts. I make him stop doubting himself. It's very difficult to tell my feelings to slow down. This isn't a confession of love. It started with *I can't promise shit*.

But it feels like one.

His eyes meet mine. "Thing is—I'm not a gentleman. Once I decide I want you to be mine, that's it. I'm going to do everything it takes. Even if you're better off with some guy who isn't fucked up."

"I like that you're fucked up." I drag my fingers over the soft skin of his neck, sinking into his body. "We can be fucked up together."

He smiles.

I melt. That smile is the most beautiful thing in the history of the world. "Besides, that guy probably wouldn't have sexy tattoos."

Pete laughs. "Probably won't be a millionaire."

"Certainly won't be as good a musician as you are."

He nods.

"Probably won't kiss as well as you do. Remind me about that."

"That's your line?" He cocks a brow, shaking his head like he finds my story ridiculous.

"You don't like it?"

"No, I do. But I'd rather you ask for what you want."

I press my fingertips into his skin. "Kiss me."

Pete slides his hand to the back of my head and pulls me into a deep, slow kiss. Mmm. For the first time all week, I feel good.

The pain around me fades as I sink into the sensations in my body. His lips are soft. His tongue is aggressive. His arms are hard against mine.

I blink my eyes open and stare back at Pete. "He definitely won't kiss as well as you do."

"You think that's good, just see how well I fuck."

"That's a worse line than mine."

He smiles. "You saying you don't want to?"

"No." I slide my hands through his short, thick hair. "I want to. Soon." My eyes rake over him, slowly. He looks tired. Like he's as worn out as I am. "Have you been as miserable as I have this week?"

He nods. "Yeah."

I stare into his eyes. They're filled with affection. "So that whole thing about not wanting a relationship... not wanting to fall in love. You changed your mind?"

"Getting there."

Okay. He still doesn't know how he feels. Right now, I can live with that. I can live with anything but the sinking feeling that I'm sentencing my dad to death.

"I don't want to think anymore," I say. "Help me stop."

He pulls us to our feet. His eyes lock with mine as he presses his palm flat against my lower back. "You won't even know what day it is."

Chapter Thirty

Pete pushes his bedroom door open so hard the knob leaves a dent on the wall.

He shakes his head. "Fuck it."

"You're leaving this place soon, aren't you?"

"No thinking and no talking." He slides his hands under my ass. In one smooth movement, he lifts me and throws me on the bed.

His eyes rake over me, slowly, like he's never seen me before. Like he's never seen a woman before.

"I like when you talk," I breathe. "I like it a lot."

"I know." He stares back at me, intense and demanding. His voice is just as hungry as his eyes. "Take off your top."

I undo the buttons of my blouse. His eyes go wider with every one. I'm not in the mood to tease him. I want to be possessed by him. Now.

But the way he's looking at me makes my sex clench with delight. I slow. He stays standing. His eyes stay fixed on me.

Finally, I push the shirt off my shoulders. Hands back, chest out—I'm confident, seductive.

"Now the skirt," he breathes.

Mmm. My hands are shaky when they get to my waist.

I unzip the garment and slide it to my knees.

Pete's hands are at my ankles. He pulls the skirt off my feet and hurls it to the floor like the garment did him some wrong. "Now the panties."

"Kiss me first."

He climbs onto the bed. In an instant, his body is on top of mine. I sink into the not quite firm enough foam mattress. His lips press against mine. They're soft. They taste like him. And like whiskey. Was he drinking alone?

His tongue slides into my mouth. The taste is there too.

Pete breaks the kiss. His palms go flat against my shoulders, pinning me to the bed. "You're thinking."

"You taste like whiskey."

"Have one drink most nights."

"I'm not mad. Just... it distracted me."

He plays with the straps of my bra, his eyes fixed on mine. "No thinking."

I'm confident and seductive. I can do this. "Make me stop."

His lips curl into a smile. "You baiting me, baby?"

My heart thuds against my chest. He called me baby again.

"Fuck. Sorry." He shifts his hips, pressing his hard-on against my crotch. "Hard to think in this state."

"Don't be sorry. I like it. If you mean it." I stare back into his deep brown eyes. I can't have this conversation right now, but I can't deal with him calling me by a pet name if he's going to dial back his affection tomorrow. "Only say it if you mean it."

He nods. "Don't move."

I can't move. He's straddling me, his knees planted outside my hips. The weight of his body presses me into the bed.

Even if I could move, I wouldn't want to. His cock is pressed against my clit. My underwear and his jeans are in the way.

He reaches for something in the bedside drawer. I rock my hips. Instantly, his palm presses against my shoulder.

"Don't move." His voice gets firmer. It's a command.

My sex clenches. I like him commanding me.

I nod a yes.

He pulls a bottle of lube from the drawer. And a vibrator. It's a long, cylindrical thing—sleek, black, classy.

"Is that new?" I ask.

"Yeah." He tosses both on the bed then shifts back, so all his weight is on top of me.

"What's that for?" I ask.

He cocks a brow. *You'll see.* "Take off your bra."

I arch my back so I can reach it. With a flick and shimmy, it's gone.

His eyes rake over me again. This time, it's slower, like he's soaking in every inch of my skin.

His fingertips skim my glasses. His eyes lock with mine as he pulls the frames off. He's endlessly patient about folding them and setting them on the bedside table.

Is he going to call me baby again?

Does he mean it?

I'm thinking. I've got to do something to make it stop.

I bring my hands to my chest and play with my nipples. It's not nearly as good as when he does it, but it still sends flicks of lust to my core.

He takes my wrists, one in each hand, and brings my arms over my head.

"You want me to tease you?" His voice gets low, hungry.

"Yes," I groan.

"Gonna do it till you beg me to stop." He pins my arms to the bed.

My sex clenches. He presses his lips to mine for a quick second then they're gone. It's barely a kiss.

He does it again.

Again.

I go for the back of his head, to pull him closer, but his hands stay on my wrists.

His lips brush against mine. Again. Again. I can barely taste them. Barely feel their softness.

I arch my hips, pressing our bodies together. He's still hard. He's so fucking hard but he stays firmly in place.

His hands stay tight against my wrists as he teases me with almost kiss after almost kiss.

I press my thighs together. Anything I can do to contain the ache in my core. He's barely getting started. I'm not sure I can handle this.

It feels like an hour passes. More likely, it takes thirty seconds for him to finally kiss me properly. My lips part. Relief floods my limbs as our tongues dance.

Who knew a kiss could make me this fucking hot?

The man is a tease, but he delivers. Pete kisses me long and hard before he moves his beautiful torture to my neck. His lips press against my skin, feather soft. Then harder. Wetter. His tongue flicks over my collarbone. His lips brush my areola.

Almost.

He kisses his way to my other breast. Again, he teases, his mouth everywhere but my nipple. The moment he releases my wrists, my hands go to his hair.

I don't guide him. Only dig my hands into his locks. He's driving tonight and I'm along for a hell of a ride.

Tension builds in my core. Maybe it's possible to come from anticipation. It sure as hell feels like it.

A sigh escapes my lips. I need more of him.

Finally, his tongue flicks my nipple. Fuck yes.

Pete looks up at me. "You want me sucking on your tits?"

I groan a yes.

He draws circles around my nipple with his soft, flat tongue. Then his whole mouth is on me, sucking on me so hard I scream.

"Don't stop." I tug at his hair. "Promise you won't stop."

He moves to my other nipple and takes it between his lips, sucking hard. My sex clenches. This feels fucking good, but I need more.

Need him.

He presses his lips against my stomach. "You want my tongue in your cunt?"

"Yes," I groan.

"Good. Want you coming on my face. The first time."

"What about the second time?"

"Haven't decided."

He kisses his way down my stomach. Still, he teases. One hand pins my leg to the bed. The other goes straight to my inner thigh. He watches me, gauging my reactions as he rubs my skin with his thumb. Closer and closer and closer.

My breath hitches. I nod a yes. Please. Now.

His expression is intense. As merciless as he is with his teasing, I trust him with my body. Trust him to get me off.

His thumb brushes against my clit. My sigh of relief goes all the way to my toes. I'm already close. A few motions of his finger and I'm at the edge.

"Pete," I breathe. "I'm going to come."

He pulls his thumb away, pins my other leg to the bed. Then his mouth is on me, his tongue lapping at my lips, plunging in my core, flicking against my clit.

"Pete," I groan. "You feel good. Promise you won't stop."

He presses his lips to my thigh. "Not until you beg me to."

With his next flick, I go over the edge. The tension is so

heavy I can barely breathe. It hurts in the best possible way. A wave of pleasure crashes into me as I come.

"Pete." I tug at his hair but it does nothing to contain my orgasm. God damn, he's amazing at this.

His mouth stays on me. He's more aggressive, his motions focused on my clit. Is it even possible to come again? I feel spent. It's intense enough it hurts. Not enough for me to ask him to stop. Begging him—out of the question.

My legs sink into the bed. My hands sink into his hair. A few more licks and I'm at the edge again. This orgasm is hard and fast.

He doesn't relent. Keeps licking me. Keeps pushing me closer and closer to the edge. It's too much. Too intense. It hurts.

"Stop. Please. I can't take anymore." I tug at his hair.

He shifts, kissing his way back up my body. This time, there's no teasing. His lips sink into mine. His tongue plunges into my mouth.

Mmm. I groan into his mouth. Dig my hands into the hard muscles of his back.

He takes my hand and brings it to his cock. Damn, does it feel like I've been deprived of this. Soft skin but he's rock hard. I rub his tip with my thumb, soaking in the feeling of his shudder against my hips.

Pete breaks the kiss. He stares into my eyes, confident and needy at the same time. "Where do you want my cock, baby?"

He called me baby again.

It's difficult to think in this state. But his expression—there's no frustration, no confusion, no doubt. He means it.

"Here?" He slides his thumb into my mouth. His other hand goes between my legs. "Here?" Then his hand is flat on the flesh of my ass. "Or you want me to finally fuck that gorgeous ass of yours?"

"I've never... will it hurt?"

"A little." He stares back at me. "If you don't answer, I'm deciding for you."

I nod. "Yes. I want to... want you..."

"Want my cock in your ass?"

My cheeks flush. "Yes."

He shifts to the side of the bed and rearranges me so I'm on my hands and knees. "Spread your legs, baby."

My insides melt. How can it feel so sweet—him telling me he's going to fuck me in the ass?

I move as much as I can.

He lets out a sigh of pleasure. "Fucking beautiful."

I groan.

He grabs the vibrator and the lube and places them next to his ankle. His voice is steady, reassuring. "I'll ease you into it." He squeezes the lube. "Trust me."

I do. God how I trust him.

His finger brushes against my anus. That's enough to surprise me—my ex never even mentioned an interest—but I'm not tense or scared.

I'm excited.

I want him somewhere no one else has been.

He spreads my knees wider. Spreads my cheeks apart. Slowly, his finger slips inside me.

I let out a sharp gasp. It's different. Intense. I take deep breaths, until it feels more good than surprising.

"Keep going," I groan.

He slides his finger deeper. I lose track of everything but the sensation. I trust him to gauge my reactions. Trust him with my body.

He takes his time warming me up. More lube. A second finger. Even more lube. Then his hand is gone and his cock is nudging against my ass.

Slowly, he slides inside me.

My knees go wider, my body opening for him. The physical sensation is intense but it's nothing compared to the feeling of offering myself to him.

He's slow about going deeper.

It's different. Really fucking different. After a few more slow thrusts, I forget about comparisons and focus on the pleasure spreading through my body. On the sounds of his groans. Of his nails digging into my thigh.

The weight on the bed shifts as his clean hand grabs something. There's a buzz. The vibrator.

Pete presses it against my clit. A shock of pleasure goes through me. I groan. My knees threaten to buckle.

"You want this in your cunt, baby?" He drags the toy over my sex, until it's teasing me.

"Yes," I groan.

He teases. Again. Again. Again. All the while, he fucks my ass with those same slow strokes.

Finally, he slides the toy inside my core. I'm filled everywhere. It's intense. Naughty. I can't place one sensation or another. Only pleasure.

Pete groans. "God damn. You feel fucking amazing."

The hand on his hip leads me over him, so I'm fucking him and the toy at once. My sex clenches. I'm so God damn filled. It's overwhelming.

Within moments, I'm at the edge. There. I grip at the sheets as I come, the toy still inside me.

"Say my name," he demands.

I scream it.

His voice gets low, his groans guttural. He's close. I turn back to watch the pleasure fill his face. It's a beautiful sight, his eyes rolling back in his head, his lips parting, first with a sigh and then with my name again and again.

He moves faster. Just barely. I can feel his cock pulsing as he comes. It's different. More like I'm at his mercy.

When he's done, he collapses next to me. He kisses my neck as he presses the still vibrating toy against my hip. "You want another?"

"Not right now."

He turns off the toy and pulls me off the bed. "I'll give you a shower to recuperate."

His lips curl into a smile. He's teasing but I have no doubt he'll deliver.

We take a long, hot shower together. He presses his body against mine, pinning me to the wall, kissing me hard. It's wonderfully slippery and wet and the perfect clean to how damn naughty I feel.

I'm about to turn the water off when he slides his hands around my hips and brings his lips to my ear.

"Changed my mind," he groans. "I want to feel you come on my hand again."

I can't argue with that.

Chapter Thirty-One

Sunday, Meg, Kara, and I hit half a dozen stores in search of the perfect dress. Meg settles on a short, hot pink number with matching wedges. She'll be taller than everyone in attendance, including her boyfriend, but she doesn't seem to mind. Kara is perfectly demure in a clingy navy dress that hugs every one of her enviable curves.

And I end up in a long, chiffon, pastel purple gown. It's the kind of girly thing I would have skipped to avoid one of Nathan's not quite kidding *why don't you dress like a grown up* taunts.

Fuck him. I like it.

When I get home, dinner is waiting. Take out Thai food. And, better yet, Pete has the entire collection of *The Hunger Games* movies ready.

I melt into the couch all night, wake up in his bed, in his arms. I have to hustle to get to class on time, but I don't mind rushing. I don't mind squeezing in my homework when he's busy with wedding prep. It feels amazing being with him. Like we're a normal couple.

It feels amazing enough that I let myself forget about my dad, about next week, about everything but being with Pete.

⊗⊗⊗

I MEET KARA AT THE AIRPORT FRIDAY AFTERNOON. Everyone else flew to Maui yesterday. The guys are rock stars —they can keep to whatever schedule they want. Meg skipped her Thursday classes. Willow took the entire week off. She is the bride to be.

Kara and I weren't willing to skip class. I'm not sure if that makes us admirably devoted or tragically workaholic.

She waits until we're settled in our first class—Tom insisted—seats to launch into real discussion.

"Are you excited?" she asks.

I nod. "Tom seems like a great guy. And Willow too. She almost cried over how happy she was that Pete was happy with me."

She smiles. "I almost cried. Pete's a great guy. And you two are adorable. Not just because you're all blond and blue-eyed and he's all tall, dark, and handsome. He lights up around you. He's gaga."

"I don't know about that."

"Trust me. He is."

How is it everyone knows my relationship better than I do?

"Thanks." I find my Kindle in my purse and pick out a YA novel about a princess finding love. "I hope you're right."

"Do you have any doubts?"

Shit. Not going there. But I don't want to lie either. I'm tired of tip toeing around things. "We haven't talked much about the future."

"You know musicians. They live in the moment. He'll

figure it out. And if he doesn't—" She shows off her thick wedge shoe.

"I'm not sure you could take Pete."

She laughs. "No, I'm sure I couldn't." She shifts back into her seat. "Guys, they can be damn stupid sometimes. Don't let him run away from what he wants."

I nod. But she has it all wrong. Pete isn't a gentleman. He doesn't walk away when he wants something.

If he walks, it will be because he doesn't want me.

🌸

THE HAWAIIAN AIR IS SWEET AND STICKY. IT'S LATE. VERY late. But the warm air has me wide awake.

Even the airport parking lot is beautiful. The sky is a glorious shade of blue and there are tall, tropical trees everywhere.

We take a cab to the hotel and go directly to room 3045, Drew's room, for a combined bachelor/bachelorette party.

The massive room is mostly dark except for the light coming from the TV. Everyone in the band, plus Meg and Willow, is sitting on a couch or on the floor. The bride and groom to be are fawning all over each other. It's not very bachelor party. But it is cute.

There's a karaoke machine hooked up to the TV.

Meg stands to take her turn. She waves hello to us then waves us over. "Join me!"

"Water first," I say.

Kara nods. But before she can make it to the bathroom, Drew has her in a tight embrace. She's on her tip toes. He's leaning down. They have quite the height difference.

"Missed you, baby. It's been too long," she purrs.

"It's been a day." Tom shakes his head. "He's trying to upstage me."

"You're about to spend the week banging his sister. Let him have a moment," Miles says.

"Come on, Jess." Meg motions *come here*. "You must know this one. It's Lady Gaga."

"Then I know it." I take the other mic and join her in the sexy pop song.

When we're finished, we bow. Everyone claps.

Pete is still on the opposite couch, watching me with affection in his eyes. I swallow hard. Even if we're closer to a couple than to nothing, I need to keep attention off us and on the bride and groom to be. It's their day. I'm not stealing the spotlight.

I move to the couch. He looks up at me, sliding his arms around my hips then pulling me into his lap. My legs have a mind of their own. My knees plant outside his thighs. My hands go to his shoulders.

"Flight okay?" He finds the tie holding my French braid together and pulls it out.

My sex clenches. Usually, he does that before he touches me. "About as good as a flight can be. I'm exhausted."

"Sorry, Jess, but you're fucked tonight. You have to do whatever I say." Tom smirks. "Or whatever Willow says."

"What if I tell her to go to bed?" Willow asks.

"You'd really disrespect me like that, kid?"

She laughs.

On the other couch, Meg is in Miles's lap, cooing as he presses his lips against her neck. They look like they're about to fuck right here.

Meg pulls back with a sigh.

Miles adjusts her so they're in a less compromising position. "You gonna sing backup on the next single, babe?"

"No way in hell," she says.

He laughs. "A cover? You sure you can live up to the original. Hear that guy kills it."

She rolls her eyes but she's clearly enjoying his ribbing.

"A cover, you say." Tom pushes himself to his feet. He looks at Pete. "You want to take this one or should I?"

"You," Pete says. "I'll get the next one."

Miles groans, but there's a hint of delight in his voice. "It hurts Drew more than it hurts me—that polyphonic melody."

"I've heard the stories." Willow folds her arms. "No punching. Tom needs to be beautiful in pictures." She looks at Tom. "And don't punch Drew. He's my maid of honor. He needs to be even more beautiful."

Kara jumps in. "Oh, what do you say, baby? Will you wear some eyeliner tomorrow?" She runs her hand through his hair.

He looks at her like she's ridiculous.

Tom shakes his head. "Still can't accept he's in an emo band."

"Don't bait him!" Kara glares at Tom. "I want my baby in eyeliner."

Drew shakes his head but he's smiling. He looks to Kara then to Willow. "Whatever the bride wants."

Kara presses her hands together and throws Willow a pleading look. The girls giggle over Drew's obvious discomfort.

The giggles fade as Tom steps up to the mic. The man commands the attention of a room. It's easy to see why he's the closest thing the band has to a ring leader.

Tom winks at Willow. "This is for you, kid."

She laughs with glee. Her eyes get wide. That's true love. It's as clear as day.

Tom steps onto the coffee table. He does his best impression of Miles's throaty, breathy singing as he moves through the song. Come the second verse, he rips off his shirt and claws at his chest tattoo. It's a funny, and accurate, impression. By the time he's done, everyone is in stitches. Even Miles.

Pete turns to me. "You seduced?"

"What if I am?" I ask.

"Have to win you over." He plays with the bottom of my skirt.

"Ahem." Tom shakes his head with mock outrage. He nods to the mic as if to say *your turn*.

Pete smiles as he takes the mic. He programs in the next song, another Sinful Serenade number, and steps up on the table.

His eyes lock with mine. He motions to the mic. "Hold this for me for a sec."

I do.

He pulls his shirt over his head, stretching long and lean, showing off his chiseled torso.

"That's better." Pete takes the mic back. "Can't sing in a shirt. Where would all the pain in my soul go?" He winks at Miles. "Usually, I'd dedicate this to Mr. Webb, but this time, it's for the lovely Ms. James."

I take a seat and watch him perform. He's more animated than he was at Miles's place. He does a great job mocking Miles's breathy style, better than Tom did.

But there's more to the song than mocking.

I can feel the pain in his soul.

I fall back onto the couch.

He finishes the song to great applause. His eyes go to Willow. "Bride to be's request."

"Do another. Please!" She claps her hands together. "Pretty, pretty please."

"Anything for my adoring fans." He winks at Miles. Then at me.

Then he's back on the table, singing another Sinful Serenade song in a lovingly mocking way.

Every ounce of my attention is on him. The passion in his deep brown eyes. The exaggerated movements of his lips and tongue. The way he rakes his hand over his chest. It's an imitation of Miles but it's sexy in its own way.

When he's done, I'm thoroughly seduced.

"Oooo, my choice still?" Willow asks.

Everyone nods.

She claps her hands together in excitement. "Drew! Please!!!"

The guitarist groans.

"You're my favorite brother," she says. "This time tomorrow, Pete will be my brother-in-law, so you'll finally have competition."

"No competition. I win, hands down," Pete says.

Drew rolls his eyes but he's smiling. The guy isn't as uptight as he lets on.

Kara coos. "I'm going to have to drag you to the bedroom after this."

His eyes light up. He grabs the mic right out of Pete's hand.

Pete laughs, good natured. Happy.

It makes me all gooey, how happy he is.

He slides back onto the couch next to me. His arm goes around my waist. He leans in to whisper in my ear. "I'm glad you're here."

Chapter Thirty-Two

Our hotel room is down the hall. It's the same model as Drew's—a suite with a private bedroom and a big common area. The walls and floor are beige. The furniture is an intense shade of aqua.

I draw the curtains, pull open the door to the balcony, and let in the sticky sweet early morning air. Sunrise streaks the horizon.

It's humid and warm, like summer nights back in New York. For a moment, the thought of home doesn't sting. There were good times there, before Mom left, and after too.

Pete places his body behind mine. It should feel like too much—the warmth of him—but it's just as comforting in the sticky air as it is coming out of the freezing ocean.

He brings his mouth to my ear. "What are you thinking?"

"Nothing important. Little things Madison and I did in the summers, like sunbathing in the backyard, or cozying up to our neighbor so we could use his pool. That was all her. I never really tried to seek out male attention."

He brings his hands to my hips and pulls my ass against his crotch. A small sigh escapes his lips.

It's nice feeling appreciated.

"You miss her, huh?" he asks.

"She's a lot of fun. The kind of person who shakes things up. She cares, too, about Dad. She hasn't given up hope yet, I guess."

He nestles his chin into the crook of my neck. "Have you?"

"One more try. Then it's done."

"And if he won't get help?"

"Then he's out of my life. Forever." I swallow hard. The heaviness doesn't come. It must be black magic, the way Pete's arms keep me light. The thought of losing Dad hurts, but it doesn't drag me down. With Pete holding me, I know I'll survive. "Hey. It's a wedding. Your brother's wedding. Let's talk about happy stuff."

"Are you happy?"

I turn and slide my arms around his waist. "Give me another hug and I will be."

He pulls me into a tight embrace. Front to front this time. This is just as comforting.

"I like when you ask for what you want." His voice drops, low and hungry.

"That is what I said, that I wanted to be assertive."

"Do it again."

Tell me you love me. "Kiss me."

He leans down and presses his lips to mine. It's not patient. In a moment, his tongue is in my mouth, exploring it like it's the first time.

When our kiss breaks, I say the first thing that makes it to my lips. "You still taste like whiskey."

"I can brush my teeth."

"It's okay. It was a bachelor party. Sort of."

Pete smiles. "Wish you'd met Tom this time last year. If that guy saw this, he'd flip his shit."

"That the bachelor party was you guys sitting around doing karaoke or that he's getting married?"

"Both."

"And your bachelor party?" My heart pangs at the thought of Pete marrying someone else. I go to my suitcase in search of pajamas. I need to get comfortable if I'm discussing something so painful. "All strippers and blow?"

He chuckles. "You know me too well."

I find a t-shirt and cotton shorts and take them to the bed.

Pete stays on the other side of the room. "You sure you're okay?"

"Sure? No." I do away with my tank top. Then my bra. The hunger in his eyes chases away the uneasy feeling in my gut. "They're really in love, Tom and Willow."

"Yeah."

I pull my t-shirt over my head. Can't have this conversation topless. It's revealing enough. "Is that what you were like with Cindy?"

The happiness drains from his expression. He doesn't look angry. More confused.

"You really want to talk about my ex-girlfriend right now?" he asks.

I slide out of my skirt. "Kind of."

His eyes stay on my bare thighs. They get wide as I do away with the panties too. "Not interested in using my mouth for conversation at the moment."

"I'm changing." I slide my pajama bottoms on. "See?"

"You know what you're doing."

Maybe. "Were you?"

"I did love her, yeah."

"You've never told me about it. About what happened. Not in detail."

"Not an exciting story." His eyes turn down. "Not much to tell."

"Tell me anyway." I pat the spot next to me. "I want to hear it."

His eyes stay on the carpet as he moves to the bed. He sits. Then his eyes are on me, raking over me. "Not exactly in the mood to talk."

"What if I say please?"

"Maybe."

"Pretty, pretty please."

"Fuck. The extra 'pretty' is my weakness." His eyes meet mine. "You want the whole story?"

"Yes."

He nods. "Feel like I should ask for something in return."

"You don't have to bait me to get my clothes off."

"I know." His eyes turn down. "Thought you wanted happy."

"Why don't you want to tell me?"

He doesn't reply. Instead, he settles into the bed. "We got together senior year of high school. Just after Mom was in recovery. Her being sick... I barely held it together. After that, I wanted to seize the day. All that shit. Cindy was cute. She liked me. Not sure we had much in common besides a mutual love of Michael Crichton."

"Really?"

"He's more than *Jurassic Park*. You ever read *Prey*? *Timeline*? Shit's addictive."

"Just... I thought you were all about facts and information. He's a little—"

"I was seventeen." He smiles. "It's not like *The Hunger Games* has consistent world building."

"You did not just insult *The Hunger Games*!"

"And if I did?" He raises a brow, baiting me.

"I'll shoot an arrow through your traitorous heart."

He smiles. "I like you assertive."

"Me too." Might as well push it further. I cozy up to the spot next to him. "You haven't distracted me, you know."

Pete nods. He takes a long time composing his next thought. "I did love her. We didn't talk much, but I've never been one for conversation."

"You talk to me."

"Yeah. It's different with you."

"How?"

"Actually have something to say."

My heart sings. Does he realize what he's doing to me? No, he must not. He's still focused inward, pulling his thoughts together.

He continues. "She liked listening to me play. Not bass but the guitar. Should have been the first sign." He laughs but there's a sadness to it. "I'd look at her art. She was a painter. Does graphic design now. Advertising. She's good. Always was. She got into Columbia, full scholarship. I told her to go. Not like I'm gonna get in the way of her future."

"Reasonable."

"Yeah. I didn't see the point of college. Didn't really have a chance. Knew the only thing I wanted to do was play bass. Stayed home. With Mom. And Tom. Sinful Serenade was only half formed. Didn't have Drew yet." His face scrunches in concentration. "Maybe. Dates blur together. We got serious pretty soon after I graduated."

"You look cute thinking."

"Don't tempt me to take those shorts off, Jess. It's hard enough as is."

My cheeks flush. "Okay. No more comments about how cute you are. Unless you put on your glasses. Then I have to jump you."

He cocks a brow. "What if we lived together and I wore them to bed every night?"

"We do live together."

"But if we shared a bed. Would you jump me every night when you saw me reading in my glasses?"

Mmm. I want him already. But I'm not getting derailed. Especially not with how hard my heart is pounding over this hypothetical living together, sleeping in the same bed scenario.

I clear my throat. "I suppose I'd have to have sex with you every night. If that works for your schedule."

He smiles. "I'll rearrange some things."

Pete leans in to kiss me. I get warm all over.

He pulls back. His eyes turn down as he speaks. "We were young and stupid. She never told me she wanted me to follow her. I never told her it would gut me to be away from Tom and Ophelia. We never shared like that. Waited for the frustrations to build up until feelings were insults."

I press my fingers into my thighs so I won't move too close. It's not enough. I need to be close to him. "Did you fight a lot?"

"Normal amount. The particulars aren't that exciting. Long distance meant we got to live in bubbles. I had my life. She had hers. Then we had this bubble just for the two of us. The three of them didn't connect. She couldn't go to my shows. I didn't know her friends, couldn't follow the gossip." His brow furrows. "It's hard to explain."

But it makes sense. "I think I understand. It's like having a pen pal. You communicate but it's not as natural as being in the same place as someone."

He looks at his hands, thinking. "When our lives did connect, when the bubbles broke, things didn't make sense. If she was home for the summer, we didn't know what to do together. The quick intense bursts—that was normal. A weekend to squeeze in everything we could. Or a long phone call that ends with... You want to hear this part?" He motions to his crotch.

"As long as you're not going to say the sex was better with her."

"Fuck no."

My lips curl into a smile. It's not possible to stay on the other side of the bed. I move close enough to take his hand.

Pete chuckles. "Phone sex was amazing. But when we were actually together... not as much."

"Fantasy trumps reality."

"Or I'm that good."

My cheeks flush.

"It was nice having somebody to call at the end of the day. Even if it was clear we were growing in different directions. By the time we finished our first tour, I felt like the only people who knew me were the guys in the band, Mom, and Cindy."

"And your friend, the one who slept with her?"

"Yeah. And him. I couldn't let go of that. The bigger the band got, the less I connected with everybody else. People always wanted to use me somehow. Or they put me on this pedestal. Soon as we were on the radio, all our musician friends were too jealous to be happy for us. I get it. It's hard seeing someone else with everything you want. But it meant nobody knew me. Nobody gets what it's like to be on the road five months a year. To lose track of where you are one day. It's easy to talk about, but to feel it... hearing your music playing at some store, seeing your picture in a tabloid, catching strangers talking about you... It's a mind-fuck. Guess that's not eloquent."

"It is, in a certain way."

He nods. "The bigger the band got, the more I needed that Pete and Cindy bubble. That was my only normalcy. That and Mom." His lips curl into a smile. "She always tells us we're not as good as Fleetwood Mac. Stuff like that. To keep us humble."

"Yeah?"

His smile spreads ear to ear. "You heard what she said about our last single?"

"No."

"Said it would be better if we went country with it. Should have heard her and Tom go at it."

His eyes meet mine. There's something on the tip of his tongue. Then he swallows and it's gone. He blinks and the vulnerability in his eyes is gone too.

"Want to hold you right now, but I'm pretty sure it means I'm not getting to the end of this story," he says.

"No. Keep going. I want to know... I can tell it hurt you a lot, what happened."

"Yeah."

"Did you love her all that time?"

"Hard to say. Not sure what love is supposed to feel like anymore."

"You love your brother. Your mom."

"It's not the same."

"You see Tom and Willow–"

"It's different from the outside. I know what love looks like. But I'm not sure what it feels like here—" He presses his palm to his chest, over his heart.

"You're lucky you're as hot as you are or that would be cheesy as hell."

"You saying you don't want to fuck me?"

"Absolutely not." I shift a little closer. "But you haven't finished your story."

"Fucking me is a lot more entertaining than this story."

"True. But I still like the story."

His lips curl into a half smile. It's short lived. He shifts back into the bed, happiness falling off his face.

"How did you find out?" I ask. "That she was sleeping with your friend."

"Things had been weird. We were on a break for a while. Shit was busy on both our sides and I think we realized we were holding on to something that wasn't quite there. I was ready to break it for good but she begged me to take her back. I was about to go on tour. Wanted some normalcy. Seemed like a good idea." He swallows. "My first trip to see her, she made excuses to avoid being alone. Left early. Claimed she had to work the next day. But Kyle, he made a point of seeing me the next day. We met at some bar. He was eaten up with guilt. I knew something was up but not what."

"What happened?"

"He blurted it out. Made all these excuses about how they couldn't help it. They were in love." His voice fills with frustration. "And it's not like it could work, me being famous and her being a regular person. It's not like I had any concept of what their lives were like. Fuck, they were ready to get married. He had a ring and everything. He looked at me, asked for my forgiveness, but he didn't apologize."

"No?"

"He talked about how it hurt him, how bad he felt, but no apology. I couldn't deal. Told him he could get out of my face or have my fist in his. He kept up the bullshit, so I hit him. It escalated. We got kicked out of the bar. That was that."

"Have you talked to either of them since?"

"No."

"Did he ever apologize?"

Pete shrugs. "Doesn't matter. Don't want to talk to someone who would do that to me. But I kept thinking... these are the only two people who knew me as Pete, the guy and not the minor celebrity, and my trust meant nothing to them. My feelings meant nothing to them. Kept thinking. Fuck, still keep thinking I must be lacking in some way."

I can't resist touching him any more. I shift into his lap, run my fingers over the skin on his cheek. "You're not lacking. You're amazing."

"Sure you're not under the influence of orgasms?"

I nod. "No... if you were wearing your glasses... that would be a different story."

"You like them that much?"

"Yes."

"Can't return the favor—" He taps my glasses. "They'll get in the way when you're coming on my face."

Mmm. "I'll forgive you. This time."

He smiles.

I press my palm against his chest. "Does it still hurt?"

"Not as much... still don't know who to trust."

"You can trust me. I would never hurt you like that. I know Pete, the guy, and I like him better than anybody else I know."

"Jess—"

"I'm not saying... I don't want to talk about that yet." I stare back into his eyes. "But my feelings for you—they have nothing to do with you being rich or famous."

"My cock?"

My cheeks flush. "I'm only human."

He's deflecting, but I feel the shift in the energy. We have a long day tomorrow. We should have some fun now.

I pull my shirt over my head. "You're gonna have to stand up if you want me to keep my glasses on."

His pupils dilate. There. He's under my thumb.

"Will you put yours on? For this part?"

He cocks a brow. "This part?"

"You really want to make me say it?"

"Fuck yeah."

"I'm going to suck you off. Then you're going to eat me

out. Then, you'll be hard again, and you're going to throw me on the bed and fuck me."

My cheeks flush. Did I really say all that? I don't feel embarrassed. Just exhilarated.

He smiles. "Fuck am I a good teacher."

Chapter Thirty-Three

I
n the morning, we order room service and eat breakfast in bed. Pete leaves a little after noon to tend to his best man duties. Surely, it can't take the groom more than an hour to get ready. He wears a suit, combs his hair, done.

I take a long shower, dress, and join Meg and Kara to do my makeup. Apparently, Willow is getting ready alone. Well, with her maid of honor, Drew. We giggle over the thought of the overprotective guitarist helping his sister with her hair and makeup.

The hours pass quickly. The girls are drinking champagne. For once, I indulge. Without lunch or dinner in my stomach, I get tipsy quickly.

At six, we put the finishing touches on our makeup and take a cab to the ceremony site—the beach, a few miles north of the hotel. Everything is set up on the sand. It's beautiful— an altar decked with hot pink flowers, white folding chairs lined with turquoise ribbon, rose petals lining the aisle.

I only recognize a few people. Flutters fill my stomach. I'm nervous for them. Kara and Meg make chit chat, mostly speculation about Willow's dress—no one has seen it except Ophelia.

The sun sinks into the horizon until the sky is streaked with hot pink. The seats are full. It's time for the ceremony. A coordinator tells everyone to stand. Music plays.

The procession starts. First, Pete and Drew. The best man and the maid of honor. They aren't quite arm in arm, but they're close enough people could talk. It doesn't seem to bother Drew. He's beaming.

Pete too. His smile is ear to ear. His eyes catch mine. He winks. I'm not sure what it means. Only that it makes me warm all over.

Damn does he look good in that dark navy suit. It brings out the flecks of lightness in his deep brown eyes.

Then it's Tom, arm in arm with Ophelia. Her hair is turquoise. Her dress is pink. Despite her recent health scare, she looks strong and bad ass. She holds onto Tom, her face beaming with pride. There isn't a hint of disbelief. For all I've heard of Tom's manwhore reputation, there's no doubt in anyone's mind that he's happier with Willow.

Actually, the drummer is nervous. He adjusts his grey suit as he takes his place at the altar. His eyes turn to the aisle. Then they're wide with enthusiasm, his cheeks pink. Still nervous but mostly excited.

His eyes are fixed on Willow. Damn is it impossible to look anywhere else. She's a pretty girl, but she goes far beyond that today. She glows like the setting sun. It's nothing about her elegant faux updo or her soft, natural makeup. It's not even her off-the-shoulders chiffon dress. Okay, the dress doesn't hurt. The wind blows it in every direction. It flashes hints of her hot pink wedges. She looks like an angel. Well, with the pink tipped hair it's more like a punk rock angel.

Mostly, she looks happy.

I've never seen a group of people this happy. Something warm and salty stings my eye. A tear.

A happy one.

I cry through the entire ceremony, utterly in awe of the happiness around me.

Pete may not know what love feels like, but I do.

This, is love.

❦

CHAMPAGNE AND HAPPINESS IS A DANGEROUS COMBINATION. Everything is a blur of joy and love. We pose for photographs on the sand. Then we're at the cozy reception, eating an amazing vegetarian pasta dish with twenty of Tom and Willow's closet friends.

Come time to cut the cake, I drink another glass of champagne. It pairs strangely with the rich chocolate flavor, but I enjoy feeling like part of the celebration. Truth is, I don't need the champagne to feel bubbly and light. I only need today.

Pete wipes the chocolate frosting from my lips with his thumb. Then his thumb is in my mouth and I'm interested in more than the love of another couple. He looks sexy in his suit. Good thing he's not wearing his glasses. I'd have to take him right here at the reception.

It would be tacky, having sex at another couple's wedding.

Instead, I pull him onto the dance floor. My dance skills are pitiful, but I have fun moving my body with his. Okay, I admit it. At this point, I'm drunk.

The songs blur together. It feels right, in his arms, part of the family.

It's everything I want.

He's everything I want.

The words jump into my throat. I kiss him so they won't

get out. He tastes good, like chocolate and champagne. We go back to dancing. Everyone is happy. But tired.

It's almost midnight when the bride and groom take their exit. Another toast—this time I hold off. They skip their champagne. Instead, they go straight to their limo.

Miles mumbles something about the odds on them making it to the suite before consummating their marriage. No one is willing to bet against them having sex in the limo.

"Mmm. That's giving me ideas." Pete slides his hands to my hips and pulls my body into his.

Thank God. I surrender completely to his kiss. There isn't a single thought in my brain. Only a desperate need to be one with him again.

Okay, it's not just sex motivating me. I want our bodies connected. Want to be sure of exactly what he's thinking and feeling if even for a moment.

We're the first to leave, but that doesn't bother me. The walk to the hotel, through the lobby is a blur. Then we're in the elevator.

I can see us in the mirrored walls. Him in his suit, his hair still perfect. Me in my long lilac dress. I'm breathless watching him sink his lips into my neck, pull my shoulder strap aside so my breast spills out of my dress.

"Fuck, Jess," he groans. "Need to be inside you now."

The elevator door dings. Our floor. I need him inside me now, but I'll wait until we're in the hotel room.

"Only one minute," I say. "You looked amazing."

"You too."

I run my fingers through his hair. "And happy."

"You too."

"Really?"

"Yeah." He nods.

There, we're at our door. Pete pulls my body into his. In

one smooth motion, he presses me against the door. The weight of his body sinks into mine. He's hard.

"I was. I am. It was beautiful. I can feel it when I look at them." I press my palms against his. "I can feel what love is. Can you?"

He looks at me curiously then shifts his hips to press his hard-on against me. "Can't think much in this state."

Yes. That makes sense. I step aside so he can unlock the door. The key slides into it. The electric lock beeps green. Unlocked. He turns the key, presses the door open.

The words jump into my throat. I try to swallow them down—I want to have him one more time first—but they won't go. Damn alcohol has my inhibitions at zero.

"Pete, I didn't just feel their love. I..." My hands fall to my sides. "I love you. I'm in love with you."

Chapter Thirty-Four

⁂

The door slams into the frame.

Pete takes a step backwards. He stares at me, his brow knit with confusion. That isn't an *I love you too* expression.

He looks like he's been side-swiped.

We stand there staring at each other. It feels like an hour passes. It can't be more than thirty seconds but it feels like an eternity.

My stomach drops. I'm glad I said it, I am, but it doesn't feel good, him staring at me like I slapped him.

When he speaks, his voice is low, unsteady. "I still don't know what that feels like."

"If you loved me, you would know. You would feel it. I feel it every time I look at you."

His eyes go to the floor. "Let's talk inside."

"I don't think I want to talk."

"Whatever you want."

"Are you going to love me one day?"

"Don't want to promise you something unless I'm sure."

There's acid in my throat. Cake, champagne, and rejection

is another powerful combination. Only it sucks.

Sadness fills Pete's eyes. He wants to love me. It's almost sweet that he wants to love me but he can't.

I step inside. Not to talk. But to change, pack my things, go somewhere else.

The door slams shut. He tries to slide his arms around me but I break from his touch.

"We should cool things off for a while." I take a deep breath. This is awful but it's necessary if I want to survive the wave of feelings crashing over me. "I'll find some other place to stay. We can talk in a few weeks."

"No."

"What do you mean no?"

"No." He grabs my hand, pulls my body into his. "You're staying at the house. Even if it means I have to leave."

"You're getting kicked out in a few weeks anyway," I say.

"I can get around that."

"Pete... don't make this harder than it has to be."

He says nothing but he keeps my body against his. My breath hitches. I like his body. Even if I don't have his heart. It's tempting to ask him to throw me on the bed one last time.

To taste his sweet lips, to feel him driving deep inside me as our bodies connect, everything right in the universe.

A few minutes of bliss might be worth the emptiness I'll feel after.

I don't know what to say. I guess he doesn't either. Five minutes must pass. Ten.

Neither of us breaks the silence. No. It's the ringing of a phone. My phone. It's three A.M. in LA, almost four. But that means it's already morning in New York.

It rings all the way to voicemail.

"I want to be around you," he says.

"I want you to love me, but we don't always get what we

want." My heart rises up into my throat. Dammit. I feel free and caged at once. My love sends me soaring high. His non-response sends me crashing back to earth.

My phone rings again.

Again.

Again.

Fine. I find it on the bedside table. Sure enough, it's Madison. Pete is still staring at me. I rub my forehead to stave off the impending headache.

"Your sister?" he asks. His voice is soft, sweet, like he's only thinking of me again.

I nod. "I better take this." I pull off my glasses so I can better rub my temples. Damn. Running out of time. I pick up the phone and hold it to my ear. "What's wrong?"

"Dad is in the hospital."

My hand falls back to my side. There's no fighting the headache now. "What happened?"

"He was drinking. I found him... like before. The doctor said he'll be okay in a few days. But..."

"I'll leave as soon as I can."

"I'm sorry, Jess. If you want to leave him to drink himself to death, I understand. You're trying to have a life. I want one too." She chokes back a sob. "I wish I knew what to do. You're better at this."

"That's okay. I'll text you my flight info."

"I'll pick you up at the airport."

"You don't have to."

"Please. I want to." Her voice breaks. "I called Zoe. She's flying up from Florida today."

"Good." My head throbs. I fall back onto the bed, pressing my eyes together. I try to blink back tears but it's impossible. These aren't happy tears. I'm terrified. "I'll see you soon. I love you."

"I love you too."

My hands fall to my sides. The phone falling on the bed. This is happening too fast. But at least everything is clear now. Pete doesn't love me. Dad isn't getting better. Madison needs my help.

The weight shifts on the bed. His arms are around me again. I'm limp, pliable. He pulls my body into his. Clarity, what clarity? I can't walk away from him. Not when he feels this good.

"Your dad?" he asks.

I nod. "He should be okay, but..."

"I want to come with you."

I want him to come with me. But I'm not sure I can take it. I wait for my tears to quiet then for the fear in my stomach to settle down.

I wait until I can meet his gaze. "You aren't a gentleman."

He nods.

"So if I ask you not to come, and you want me, you'll fight for me."

"Don't play a game. Tell me what you want."

"I want my dad to be sober. I want law school to be easier. I want my own house on the beach and my own fancy Tesla, but I want mine to be silver. I want the biggest cup of coffee in the world. And I want you to love me." I wipe my eyes. "Can't have any of that. Might as well want to live on Mars."

His eyes fill with frustration. "I want to come with you."

"Please don't make me say it again. It was pathetic enough the first two times."

"It wasn't pathetic. It was brave." He goes for one of the bobby pins holding together my updo.

Dammit, how can he say things like that, like he admires me for telling him I love him? I can't breathe. I can't think. Every part of me hurts. I don't know which is worse—my dad in the hospital or Pete admiring me for confessing my feelings.

"Please stop touching me. I need to get my shit together. And I can't do it if you're touching me, if the only thing I can think about is how much I wish things were different between us."

He sighs but he does shift back. "How long will it take you to pack?"

"Half hour."

"Do it. I'll book your flight."

I nod, but I make a long stopover in the bathroom to unpin my hair and wash the makeup off my face.

Pete takes charge. He sits me down on the bed, has me drink a glass of water. Then there's a snack in my hands and he's telling me to eat.

Then he's unzipping my dress, sliding it down my body.

"Try to sleep," he whispers. "First available flight is four hours from now."

He helps me out of my clothes and into my pajamas. This isn't how I want him undressing me. But it still feels nice, his hands on my body.

He presses his lips to my forehead.

I want to ask him to join me. I want his arms around me, his voice in my ear, him convincing me it's going to be okay.

But only if it's what he wants.

He's not a gentleman. If he wants me, he'll get into this bed with me, hold my body against his.

I pull the covers over my head, press my eyelids together, and fall asleep alone.

᭞᭞᭞

I WAKE TO THE SMELL OF COFFEE AND PETE'S HANDS ON MY shoulders. It feels good and awful at the same time, him touching me.

"Too early for room service," he says. "I'll give you cash to get something at the airport."

I nod. Judging from the still dark sky, it's too early for any reasonable activities.

The room is totally stripped. Everything is packed. But the miserable look on his face tells me he hasn't changed his mind about coming with me. About loving me.

I let him lead the way through the lobby, into a cab, to the airport. He keeps his distance in the backseat. It's too much distance. I hate every inch we're apart.

He helps me out of the cab, helps me with my suitcase. Then we're at the self-checkout, he's printing out my boarding pass. First class. Nonstop. That ticket must have cost a fortune.

"I'll pay you back somehow," I say.

"Not a chance." His hand lingers on my shoulder. His eyes meet mine. "Are you sure?"

"About?"

"That you want to go alone?"

"Pete, you've already told me how it is. You fight for what you want. You're not fighting. You don't have to spell it out."

"That's not it—"

"I'm leaving now."

"I'm gonna kiss you. If you don't want that, tell me now."

I do want that. One last time. One piece of comfort to take with me. I nod a yes. Then his lips are on mine. They're frantic and hungry. I can feel the affection in his kiss.

That's love.

How can he not feel it?

When the kiss breaks, I'm dizzy. I take a step backwards. "I hope you figure out what you want."

For a minute he stares at me. He opens his mouth like he's about to say something. But all he does is nod goodbye.

Chapter Thirty-Five

I t's almost midnight in New York, but I'm wide awake. Two sleeping pills plus one incredibly reclining seat equals few hours of conscious thought.

I text my sister and go in search of coffee. But there's no time for caffeine. She's already here. Waiting.

I go straight to the drop off/pick up area. There she is, in her shiny red car. Madison has always been flashy.

Her face lights up when she sees me. She climbs out of the driver's seat and rushes to pull me into a hug. "I've missed you so much, Jessie. Was your flight okay?"

"For a twelve hour flight." My instincts tell me to push her away, but I don't. I hug her tighter. I'm tired of hating her. I want my best friend back. "It will take a while for me to get over how much it hurt, you betraying my trust like that."

"I understand. I'm sorry. Really, Jessie. I feel awful. I've thought about calling you every night since you left. Couldn't admit it to myself for a while. And then, well, you seemed like you were doing so well. Starting school and... whatever was happening with... I thought maybe he'd come with you if he was your boyfriend. But I understand if you don't want to talk about it. It's not like I deserve to be your shoulder again. Well, I know it's not like I was ever your shoulder. You've always been the strong one."

Yeah, I have. I've always carried everything around on my shoulders, never let anyone help. Until Pete...

Look how well that went.

As much as my heart aches, I'm glad I talked to Pete. Even if he never figures out that he loved me.

It will fucking suck, but it won't take away how light he makes me feel. Made me feel.

I better tell Madison. Between getting dumped and Dad drinking himself into the hospital, I'm going to overflow.

"Let's talk at home," I say. "Will they let us into the hospital?"

Madison puts my suitcase in the backseat. We get into the car.

Her eyes go to the time on the clock. "It's well past visiting hours but there is a nurse who likes me." She checks her reflection and adjusts her top for maximum cleavage.

❧

EXCEPT FOR THE EMERGENCY ROOM, THE HOSPITAL IS quiet. Madison leads me right to the wing where Dad is recovering. There's a small waiting area but the lights are off.

It's clearly not visiting hours.

The nurse at the station is an older woman.

Madison pouts. "Guess he's off already. Can't hurt to ask her." She moves to the reception desk and offers the nurse a pleading look.

The nurse shakes her head. They speak for a few moments then the nurse calls me over.

"Are you Jessica James?" she asks.

I nod.

Immediately, she starts explaining Dad's condition. He's no longer at risk of alcohol poisoning, but his liver is damaged. Any future drinking is risky, even a glass of wine at dinner.

When she's done with the medical technicalities, she hands me a stack of brochures. "There are excellent treatment programs in the area."

Madison picks the polish off her red nails. "What if he won't go?"

"Then he can drink himself to death alone."

She bites her nail. "Jessie... I can't."

"You can." I nod a thank you to the nurse and walk my sister back to her car. I take her keys, take over driving duty. "It's going to hurt, but you can do it. We can both do it. I hope we don't have to but we can."

❦

AT HOME, I MAKE COFFEE AND BREAKFAST. DINNER. Whatever this meal counts as. Hash browns, oranges, scrambled eggs with vegetables.

"I missed you so much I stole your *Hunger Games* poster." She stirs sugar into her coffee and sips it. Her face scrunches in distaste. "Don't know how you drink this stuff."

"You want tea?"

"I'm okay." She pushes her short blond hair behind her ears. "Plus, when it came out you were dating Pete Steele... seemed weird having his picture hanging in my room."

"It's a little weird."

"It made me feel bad. Knowing I hurt you." She attempts another sip of her coffee. "You tensed up when I said his name."

Figures. "We... broke up. Or maybe it's a fight. I don't know. We were barely together. Hard for it to be a break up."

"You want to talk about it?" she asks.

I do, actually. I want it off my shoulders. I nod. "On the couch. With proper background noise."

She laughs. "Let me guess. *The Hunger Games*. No, *Divergent*."

"Please. There's only Katniss. An imitation won't do."

She sticks her tongue out. I laugh. Then, we're both in stitches. The bar for comedy gold is lower when you've been in three time zones in two days.

"I've got it," she says. "Please. Let me."

For once, I let my sister lead. I take a spot on the couch. She gets me another cup of coffee, fixed the way I like it, a glass of water, a blanket.

She plops next to me. Once the movie is streaming, she turns to me. "You look heartbroken. What happened?"

I tell her everything. Even the part about it being pretend.

Then she tells me everything about her ugly breakup with Nathan. Turns out, he's still a controlling asshole underneath his charming exterior.

We talk about Mom and Dad—good times and bad—until Madison falls asleep on the couch. Only a few more hours until the hospital opens. I finish the marathon on my own.

By the end, I'm half asleep and I'm not watching the movie. I replay every ugly moment of the not exactly a breakup. When I can't take it anymore, I go to my room, unpack, put on my pajamas.

The doorbell rings.

This used to happen all the time. Dad would get drunk and make a scene. The neighbors would stop by, sometimes to check on us, sometimes to chew him out. Back then, I always lied. Always covered for him.

Not anymore.

No matter who that is, I'm going to be totally honest.

There are footsteps downstairs. Madison must be up.

"Hello," she says to the door.

I move to the hallway, poised to jump in if necessary.

She shrieks. "Really?"

I can't hear the person on the other side.

Madison pulls the door open and motions for the person to come in.

It's not a neighbor.

It's Pete.

Chapter Thirty-Six

P ete is at my door.

He's here.

He's taking what he wants.

God help me, he's wearing his glasses. He looks as yummy as ever in a black t-shirt and dark jeans.

My knees knock together. I try to speak but words don't come out.

He looks at Madison. "You must be Madison."

She nods. "Y-y-you're Pete Steele."

"Yeah." His eyes narrow. "You fucked Jess's boyfriend after he pulled that shit about asking her to choose between him and law school."

"Y-y-yes."

"What the fuck, Madison? Why did you hurt her like that?"

"I wasn't thinking. We... we already talked. I apologized." She motions to me at the top of the stairs. "She said she forgives me."

Pete looks up at me. "Do you?"

My mouth refuses to make words. I nod.

His lips curl into a smile. I melt. It's still the greatest sight in the world, that smile.

His expression gets intense and protective as he turns back to Madison. "You know how some guys write songs about how their ex-girlfriends deserve to burn in hell?"

"Y-y-yes."

"I'm giving you slack for hurting Jess cause I did the same thing. Hurt her again and there's gonna be a new Sinful Serenade song called *Madison is a Bitch*. And that's only gonna be the start of how much I make your life miserable."

"I... I didn't mean to. I'm sorry." She bites her lip. "I didn't do it on purpose. And you need to talk to her. She loves you. She was crying. This time, you're the one who hurt her. She told me everything. It sounds like you've had your head up your ass, but Jess loves you too much to see it that way."

He chuckles. "You have a backbone, huh?"

"Yeah." She clears her throat. "You've been an idiot. Make it up to her or I'm going to be the one making your life miserable."

He smiles. "Fair deal."

"Good." She folds her arms over her chest.

He nods an okay to Madison then all his attention is on me. "Were you crying over me?"

"Hard to pin point an exact source." I play with my pajama bottoms. "You were top two."

He smiles.

"You threatened my sister."

"Too much?"

"No. You... you're fighting for me."

He nods. "This is nothing."

"What's something?"

"You're gonna say it's cheesy."

"That's okay."

He moves all the way up the stairs. Until he's one step

below me. It puts us almost eye to eye. I'm still a few inches above him.

He stares into my eyes. "I love you, real or not real?"

Pete pulls his t-shirt down and points to his chest. His skin is red from a new tattoo.

It's an arrow with the word *real* in the middle of it.

It's the *Hunger Games* couple's tattoo I told him I wanted. Half of it.

My fingers go to his chest. Then I'm staring into his eyes. "Can I?"

"Yeah."

I trace the lines of the ink. "When did you do this?"

"Soon as your plane left." He presses his hand to his heart. "Well, soon as the tattoo parlor opened."

I trace it again and again. "Why?"

"Same reason I got my other ink."

"You felt something in your soul?"

"Yeah." He takes another step. "And more than that. I stayed at the airport. Watched your plane take off. The second it was gone, I felt it. This emptiness in my chest that had been filled before. Kept thinking about you hurting by yourself. It tore me in half."

"I tore you in half?"

He ascends the last stair. His arms slide around my waist. "Don't feel the emptiness anymore. Not when I'm holding you. I only feel right. That's love." His eyes meet mine. He brushes his hand through my hair. "I love you."

It's a good thing he's holding me as tightly as he is, because I'm reasonably certain I've lost all feeling in my legs.

His fingers find the back of my neck. "Jess, I'm in love with you."

"You're wearing your glasses."

He nods.

"For me?"

"Don't play fair when I want something."

"Good." I rise to my tip toes and press my lips to his.

I can feel it too. How much he loves me. How much I love him. We kiss long, slow, and deep.

I look back into his eyes. "Say it again."

"I love you, Jess."

"I love you too."

"I told you not to run from your feelings, but I was a fucking hypocrite. I was running from this, from how much I cared about you. Still didn't quite believe I had more to offer than my money or my fame. Or my body."

I run my fingers over the tattoo again. "It's a very nice body."

He smiles.

"It's mine now. You marked it for me."

"Yeah. And for Katniss."

"This is so much better than my name." I stare back into his eyes. "Can we stop talking now?"

"Fuck yes." His hands go to my ass. "Which room is yours?"

I point to my door.

In one smooth motion, he lifts me into his arms. I wrap my legs around his waist, holding on tight.

Pete kicks my door open. He lays me on the bed. It's small but that only means we're pressed closer together.

There's no patience in his kiss. Or in mine. I'm greedy about exploring his mouth with my tongue. About pulling his shirt over his head and pressing my palm against his chest.

He shimmies out of his jeans and boxers then does away with my tank top and shorts. I'm naked. I'm pretty sure my door is halfway open but I don't give a flying fuck.

His hand slides between my legs. "You're already wet, baby."

I nod. "No teasing today. I need you inside me."

"Need to be inside you."

He shifts our positions so he's flat on his back and I'm on top of him.

No teasing, no patience. I press my hands against his chest and position my body on top of his.

Pete's hands go to my hips. His eyes are locked on mine, filled not just with lust but with love too.

No teasing, he pulls my body over his, pushing his cock deep inside me.

My body cries out with relief. Pete is mine. I'm his.

It's perfect.

I ride him until I'm panting and dripping with sweat. Every inch of my body is on fire with pleasure. Is it possible to feel an orgasm in your soul? This one is hitting somewhere deep.

"You ready to come, baby?" He brings his hand to my inner thigh.

"If I can come with you."

"Fuck yeah." He rubs my clit with his thumb. His other hand goes between my shoulder blades, pulling our bodies closer.

My God, those fingers. He loves me and he has magic fingers. And he's mine.

I cry out his name as I come. He's there a few moments later. His lips lock on mine, all the love and affection in the universe pouring back and forth between us.

He stays inside me as he pulls us onto our sides.

I nestle my back against his chest, soaking in the sound of his breath and his heartbeat.

"I still have to deal with everything with my dad," I whisper.

"I'll hold your hand the whole time."

"Really?"

He murmurs a yes into my ear.

"Say it again."

"You ready to come, baby?" His fingers trail over my hip. "I can arrange that."

"No. Well, after you say you love me."

"I love you."

"I love you too."

He slides his hand between my legs and makes good on his promise.

❧

ONCE AGAIN, PETE TAKES CHARGE. HE'S INCREDIBLE AT getting shit done. He sends me to shower, makes coffee, calls Aunt Zoe and arranges a meeting time.

He even makes breakfast. Sort of. There are bowls of cereal and milk on the table.

It's good he knows his limitations.

He drives us to the hospital in his luxury rental car. It's visiting hours, but we need to wait for Aunt Zoe. We all need to be on the same page. Dad gets one more chance, that's it.

Nervous energy races through my body. I soak in all the comfort Pete can give me. It's a lot of comfort. He rubs my back, holds me, whispers in my ear that it's gonna be okay.

Finally, Aunt Zoe arrives. She looks less polished than she usually does. Her short brown bob is messy. Her cardigan is wrinkled.

"How are my favorite girls—" She hugs Madison then me. "Given the circumstances?"

"Okay, given the circumstances." I motion to Pete. "This is my boyfriend, Pete."

He looks at me and raises a brow. "I'm your boyfriend?"

"You aren't?

"No. I am. Just glad you knew."

Aunt Zoe looks at us with confusion. *The kids today*. She introduces herself then sits between me and Madison.

"There's really no question." I pull the brochures from my purse. "We have to tell Dad he has two choices—he can get treatment or he can deal with this alone. But it only works if all three of us are willing to pull the plug."

Pete rubs my back. It's easier getting through this with him here, knowing I have back up. I'm not light but I'm not heavy either.

"I can do it." I can't bring myself to look at my aunt or my sister as I make the claim. There's no way they're going to believe me. I clear my throat and look into Aunt Zoe's hazel eyes. "I don't want Dad to die alone, but I'm not watching him drink himself to death. Period."

Zoe purses her lips. She looks to Madison then to me. She nods. "I agree."

Madison nods. "Me too. But what do we do?"

"Let me lead." I push myself to my feet. Okay. I can do this.

Pete squeezes my hand as we walk to the hospital room. The hallway is a strange mix of beige and blue. The yellow fluorescent lights do little to make the place look more attractive.

The door is open, so I knock on the frame. "Dad?"

"Jessie." His is equal parts weak and ashamed. He knows he's been caught. "What are you doing here?"

I step inside the room. His grey hair is matted to his forehead. His blue eyes, usually full of life, are tired. And he's pale. Really pale.

He looks like he's going to break. My instincts beg me to throw away this plan and do whatever it takes to make him smile. But I'm not that person anymore.

I have to do this. Even if it means I lose Dad.

"Daddy, I'm sorry," I say. "But I don't have time for small talk. You're drinking again."

He says nothing but the guilt registers all over his face.

Madison squeaks. She bites her nails, one by one. Aunt Zoe wears a pretty strong poker face but there's frustration in her eyes. She's scared too. He's her brother. Of course she's scared.

I place the brochures on his tray table. "I love you, Daddy, but I'm not going to stay in your life if you keep drinking."

"Jessie, honey, I just took it a little far this time—"

My stomach clenches. His expression is vulnerable. His lips are pale.

My knees knock together. This is hard.

Pete brings his mouth to my ear. "You can do this, baby." He squeezes me.

That helps.

I take a deep breath and adopt my most confident posture. "If you want us to stay in your life, you need to get treatment. You can pick a program that works for you, but it's not negotiable." I stare into Dad's eyes. "If you decide not to go into treatment, that's it. I'm not going to pick up your calls. I'm not going to visit. I'm not going to invite you to my wedding. I'm out of your life. Madison and Aunt Zoe feel the same way."

"Sweetie, I don't know where this is coming from," he says.

God, if he keeps deflecting, if he keeps insisting every-thing is fine—this might be the last time I see Dad.

"Yes you do." I stare back at him. Okay, one last bit of confidence then I can break. "I'm leaving now, and I'm not going to talk to you until you're in treatment. I'm not going to take any excuses. Okay?"

He stares at me like I'm betraying him.

Okay, he hates me. I can take that. It's better than helping him destroy himself.

"Call when you decide to great treatment." My eyes go to the floor. "I hope you do, Daddy. I hope you get healthy, because it really will kill me watching you drink yourself to death."

A tear rolls down my cheeks. I can't fight it anymore. Again, I let Pete lead. He takes me to the waiting area and wraps his arms around me.

"I've cried more in the last three months than I have the last three years." I squeeze him back. "I'm sorry."

"You apologizing for your feelings?"

"No... Almost."

"Don't. I'm glad you're crying." He laughs. "Don't mean it like that."

"What a horrible boyfriend," I tease. "You're supposed to like it when I'm happy."

He looks down at me, his eyes brimming with affection. "I'm glad you're letting it out." He pats his shoulder. "This is yours, whenever you need it."

I run my fingertips over his other shoulder. "What about that one?"

"That one too."

"What about..." I drag my fingers down his chest and stomach.

"Don't tempt me, baby." He motions to a door on the opposite side of the hallway. "One more word and I'm dragging you to that closet."

My lips curl into a smile. "But is it?"

"You really have to ask?"

I shake my head.

Chapter Thirty-Seven

There's no word from Dad all day.

Or the next day.

I resign myself to defeat and let Pete schedule a flight home.

I'm about to go to bed when my phone flashes with a new message. Dad's cell phone. How did I miss that?

"Maddie, come here," I call.

"Are you decent?" she yells back.

I am. Pete is only wearing boxers. Mmm. Can't get distracted. This is more important than my libido.

"Yeah." I pull up the message ready to put it on speaker.

Pete slides his arms around me. He pulls us onto the bed, me on his lap. His warm skin presses against my bare shoulders and arms. What is it about a lover's touch that makes it feel like everything is going to be okay?

Madison steps into the room with a huff. She looks at us and shakes her head. "You're disgustingly cute. I hate it."

"Thanks." I smile despite the voicemail's potential to destroy me. "I prefer revoltingly adorable."

Pete chuckles. He leans in to whisper. "Ready?"

I nod and press the play button.

Dad's voice fills the room. It's stronger. More assured.

"Hey Jessie, Maddie. I thought a lot with you gone. You know, you girls were the only light in my life after your mom left. I shouldn't have put you through my drinking. Shouldn't be doing it again. I'm about to check in to a treatment center in Albany. I'll have them call to confirm. I'm not allowed visitors for three weeks, but I hope you'll be there soon. I love you, sweetie. You, too, Maddie."

The line clicks.

It's gonna be okay.

Pete whispers in my ear. "Want me to confirm that?"

I nod.

He takes my phone and makes a call. He nods, smiles. "First week you can visit is the week before Thanksgiving."

"Can you get tickets?" I ask.

He nods.

I hug my sister. "It's gonna be okay."

"Yeah it is," she says.

It might be hard, but it's gonna be okay.

Pete waits for me to release Madison then he pulls me into a tight, deep hug.

"Proud of you," he mumbles into my forehead.

I nod.

"Might be hard, all the rehab shit."

"I know. But we have three weeks to be happy." I look up at him. "And I know I'll be happy as long as I'm with you."

"I love you, baby."

"I love you too."

Epilogue

The doorbell rings.

I only barely manage to hold onto my mug of coffee. This day has been great so far. Hell, it's the best Thanksgiving I can remember. There's no place to go but down.

Ophelia nods to the door. "I'll get that. Stay put, sweetheart."

She pushes herself off the couch. It's across from the one I'm sharing with Pete. There's a coffee table between them. Between the trays of snacks and the mugs of coffee, there's barely a free inch of the table.

From their spot on the couch opposite ours, Tom and Willow try to act as if they're not staring at me.

I must look as anxious as I feel.

"Breathe, baby." Pete leans in close and rubs my shoulder. "You can do this."

I nod. Of course I can do this. It's not like it's a huge deal, our families sharing a holiday together. And not any holiday— the one about gratitude and sitting around a table with nowhere to hide.

"Your dad looked great when we saw him," Pete says. "Remember?"

"He did." Some of the tension in my shoulders eases. Dad looked great when we visited. But that was halfway through rehab. Now he's out, on his own, taking care of himself.

"You're worried about him?" Pete asks.

I lean in to whisper in his ear. "What if he's already slipped?"

"You really think that happened?"

"No, but..."

His deep brown eyes find mine. The certainty in them soothes me.

Pete pulls me into a tight hug. "You're gonna be okay, baby. I promise."

The front door opens. It's too far to hear exact words, but that's Madison's voice. She's greeting Ophelia. And there's Dad.

I push myself to my feet. I can do this.

Pete motions to Tom and Willow. The three of them stand at once. Then Madison is bouncing into the room. Her short hair hangs in front of her eyes.

"Jessie. Your dress is gorgeous." She throws her arms around me. "I've missed you so much."

"I've missed you too." I pull back and hug my dad. "How have things been?"

"Difficult, but good." He smiles.

He looks good. I can't believe how quickly the time has passed. It feels like just yesterday I was getting on a plane to get as far away from home as possible. And now I'm here, at Ophelia's place in Orange County, surrounded by my family, new and old.

Home is still in flux—the label is kicking us out of the Hollywood place—but I trust Pete when he says he's got it under control. The man really gets shit done.

Ophelia motions for everyone to sit. Madison and Dad introduce themselves. He asks them to call him Mark instead of Mr. James.

It's going well.

It's going to be okay.

"Can I help with dinner?" Madison offers.

"No. We're ordering delivery. No one in the family cooks." She motions to the kitchen. "Would you like some coffee?"

"No thank you." Madison turns to Dad. "You?"

"Yes, please. Thank you." He settles into the armchair with a half-awkward, half-welcoming expression.

"Anyone else?" Ophelia offers.

I hold up my cup. She takes it with a smile then she's in the kitchen, refilling our beverages.

Tom shouts to his mother. "Willow cooks." He points to Willow's wedding ring. "You saying she isn't family?"

Ophelia returns to the room. She shakes her head at Tom. "Don't be ridiculous, Tom. You know Willow is as welcome as you are." She hands Dad his cup. "Cream and sugar are on the table. Almond milk in the fridge if you'd like that."

"Jess cooks," Pete offers.

"She's family," Willow says. "Even if it's not legal... not yet... I'm sure soon they'll be... soon... Nevermind."

Tom laughs. "Kid, you might as well spell it out and say, you're sure they'll get married soon."

"Leave your wife alone. It's bad enough she has to live with you," Ophelia teases.

Tom presses his forehead against Willows. "You're my wife."

She drags her fingers over his wedding band. "You're my husband."

They kiss. Thankfully, it's more sweet than steamy.

Ophelia clears her throat and turns to Madison and Dad. "How was your flight?"

"Good. Long." Madison smiles. "So, who is going to fill me in on all the gossip about my sister?"

Tom lights up. He and Pete share a look.

Pete nods then he turns to Madison. "What exactly do you want to know?"

⚜

THE AFTERNOON IS PERFECT. DINNER IS PERFECT. IT'S AN incredibly untraditional spread of Indian food. It's all vegetarian, so Willow won't feel left out.

It's sweet how much Ophelia cares about us feeling accepted. She's warm, welcoming, and take no shit at once. Come evening, she practically kicks us out of the house. I hug Dad and Madison goodbye. They're staying at a nearby hotel. We have plans to show them around Los Angeles tomorrow.

But, tonight is ours.

After we say our goodbyes, Pete slides his arm around my waist. He practically drags me outside.

The dark sky is dotted with stars. The moon is a thin sliver of silver. We're in the suburbs, surrounded by the light of houses and shopping centers, but I can see so much more details of the stars than I can in Hollywood.

"You secretly miss the suburbs, baby?" he asks.

"No." I pull him closer, soaking in the warmth of his body. It's cold out here. "I miss the stars."

"Let's go look at them."

"We caught a ride here with Tom and Willow." I stare into his eyes, trying to figure out what the spark of mischief in them means. "Explain yourself."

"You trust me?"

"You know I do."

"Then follow me."

I nod an okay and follow him around the corner. The next block is a cul-de-sac lined with perfectly symmetrical two-story, four-bedroom houses.

It doesn't seem like the kind of place that suits Ophelia, but her home is as warm, inviting, and bad ass as she is.

Pete pulls something from the front pocket of his jeans. Keys. He taps them and a car's beep echoes through the air.

Where did that come from?

I stare at my boyfriend.

He smiles back at me then he motions to a car parked on street, some fifteen feet in font of us. Its lights flash as its electric lock disengages.

Pete hands me the keys. "It's yours."

"What?"

He leads me to the car. It's the same as his. A Tesla. A very expensive luxury electric car.

Only it's silver.

"When I asked you what you wanted, you said you wanted a silver Tesla." His eyes fill with affection. "Now you have it."

"But it's so expensive."

"You said you wanted it, so I got it for you."

My heart melts. I slide my arms around his waist. His cotton hoodie is soft and thick but I can still feel the warmth of his body under it.

"Your dad is sober too." He presses his palm between my shoulder blades, pulling me closer.

"And you love me."

"Only two things left. The house on the beach and the cup of coffee."

My tongue is in knots. This is too perfect for words. I murmur something that vaguely resembles a yes.

"Guessing you don't want a giant cup of coffee right now," he says.

"No."

"I'll buy you one first thing tomorrow." He squeezes me tighter. "And you wanted law school to be easier. Can't do much about that. Well... I'm trying something."

"You're being mysterious."

"Yeah." He steps back and leads me to the driver's side door. "Let's take her for a spin. I'll show you a great make-out spot."

I press the keys between my palms. "Okay, but my car is a boy."

He chuckles as we get in the car. "What's his name?"

"Hmmm. Steele."

"Baby, that's a little myopic."

"But you're the only person I want to sit on."

He shakes his head. "You're lucky you look as hot as you do in your glasses, because that was terrible."

I push the bridge of my glasses up my nose. "Okay. How about Peeta?"

"Peeta is perfect."

I secure my seat belt and turn the car on. The electric engine barely whispers. It's quiet. And it's mine.

Damn, it's like the car handles better being mine. I pull onto the street and follow Pete's directions. Traffic is light. The streets are wide. It feels like I zoom through every green light.

Twenty minutes later, we're turning on a quiet, curvy street. It takes us to the top of a hill. The twinkling lights of the suburbs surround us. And past those, there's the dark blue of the ocean.

It's beautiful. And empty.

The perfect make-out spot.

I turn off the engine and undo my seatbelt.

Pete turns to me. "Should we christen Peeta or is he shy?"

A laugh escapes my lips. "No. He's into it. He digs threesomes."

Pete chuckles. He pats his lap.

I don't need to be asked twice. I climb over the center console. My knees plant outside his thighs. It already feels so good, the weight of my body sinking into his.

He looks up at me. His fingers trail over my jaw and my cheek. He takes off my glasses, folds them, and places them in the center console. "Let me see it again."

My lips curl into a smile. Okay, time to tease him back. "You want me topless, ask."

"You're wearing a dress."

"Technicalities." I pull the zipper to my waist and pull the dress over my head. It's difficult positioning myself so Pete can see the tattoo on my shoulder blade. It's my half of our couples tattoo—an arrow with the words *real or not real* in the center.

He traces its lines again and again. "How did I get so lucky, you falling in love with me?"

I turn so we're face to face. "I'm the lucky one." I lean in to kiss him.

Affection flows from his lips to mine and back again. It's still overwhelming, how lucky I am, how amazing this relationship is, how much he loves me.

I don't have a hint of patience today. I've been busy with school. He's been busy with work on the new album. We're both adamant about putting nose to the grindstone Monday through Friday then spending our weekends together.

It's Thursday. I haven't touched him properly since Sunday. Even after months together, four days without touching feels like an eternity.

I unhook my bra and let it fall aside. The starlight flows in through the windows. We're as good as alone here. It's safe to do this, to do whatever I want to him.

His hands go to my hips. He pulls my panties to my knees.

I'm not waiting. I unzip his hoodie and slide it off his shoulders. Then the t-shirt. His jeans prove more difficult. I can't manage to get the button.

He takes my hands and brings them to his shoulders. Then his lips are on mine. His tongue is in my mouth. His kiss is greedy. Mine is too. I run my fingertips over every inch of his skin I can—his shoulders, his chest, his stomach, the back of his neck.

My hands find his hair. I hold his mouth against mine, kissing him hard and deep. The intimacy of it takes my breath away. I have to pull back to stare into his eyes.

That look in his eyes—that's love. It pours into my soul. It fills the car.

This space is ours.

The world is ours.

He's mine and I'm his.

Our bodies need to be joined. Now.

"I want you inside me," I breathe.

His eyes cloud with desire. He shifts off his jeans and boxers. In one swift motion, he pulls my body onto his.

I let out a sharp gasp as he plunges deep inside me. His mouth goes to my nipples. His hands go to my hips, guiding me over him.

He knows exactly how to play me, knows my body better than I do. I dig my fingers into his shoulders and surrender to his guidance. The car isn't exactly roomy—I bump my head against the roof a dozen times—but I don't want anything else.

This moment, right now, the two of us together, is perfect.

The motions of his soft, wet mouth send pangs of desire to my core. I get closer. Dig my nails into his skin. My lips part with a sigh.

"Look at me," I breathe. "Watch me come."

He groans as he kisses his way up my chest, neck, lips. After one long, deep kiss, he pulls away.

His eyes fix on mine.

His hand goes to my shoulder blade, right over the lines of my tattoo.

I hold his gaze for as long as I can. His deep brown eyes are as intense as ever. They're wide with desire, affection, love.

Pleasure wells up inside me. I dig my nails into his skin. I let a sigh fall off my lips. Then it's his name.

Still, I keep my eyes glued to his. Damn, I love the way he looks at me like he's never seen anything better.

With the next thrust, I come. I groan his name as pleasure spreads to every inch of my body.

Pete presses his lips against my neck. He kisses his way to my ear. Then he's sucking on my earlobe.

He moves faster, harder. I can tell from the way he's groaning that he's almost there. I can see it in the shaking of his shoulders.

I dig my fingers into his hair and take in every second of his orgasm. The way he groans against my skin, the way his nails dig into my back, the way his muscles tense and relax.

There. He moans my name as he comes.

We collapse into the slightly reclined seat. It's messy and it's cramped, but it's perfect.

Whenever I'm with him, life is perfect.

⚜

I TAKE PACIFIC COAST HIGHWAY BACK TO LOS ANGELES.

For miles and miles, the road curves along the ocean. I roll the windows down and let in the cool evening air. We're going so fast the rushing air leaves no room for conversation.

But that's okay. Pete squeezing my hand is all the communication I need.

I'm about to turn onto the 105—taking it to the 110 to the 101 is the fastest way back to Hollywood—but Pete stops me.

"Stay on Lincoln." He calls the highway by the name of the street it turns into.

"But this isn't where you live."

"Trust me."

My heartbeat picks up. A lightness passes through my chest and stomach. This is a surprise. And it's something good.

I check his expression just to be sure. He's smiling ear to ear. I'm not sure I've ever seen him this happy and free.

He motions to the dash. "Eyes on the road. Don't want to die before we... you'll see."

I nearly squeal. It's hard to maintain an even grip on the steering wheel. Somehow, I manage it. We stay on Lincoln/Pacific Coast Highway though Marina Del Rey. We're just into Venice Beach when Pete tells me to turn onto a side street.

What the hell is he up to? We're near Tom and Willow's place. Half a mile away, less even. Are we going to see them? It's possible. For a while, we take the route that would lead us to their house. Then we're turning south instead of north.

Not their place.

The streets are narrow and they're packed with cars. I give up on figuring out exactly what it is we're doing so I can focus on navigation. After a few turns, we're there.

Pete points to a reserved parking spot next to a black luxury car. No, it's a black Tesla.

It's *his* black Tesla.

And it's in front of a beautiful two-story house on the beach. It looks a lot like Tom and Willow's pace, only it's more rectangular, more modern. The walls are white, the roof is flat, the blue tinted windows are wide.

There are succulents everywhere. The gated garden is lined with them. And the balcony.

Pete laughs. "Of course you're looking at the cacti."

"I like them." I turn back to him. "That's your car."

He nods.

"So this..."

"It's ours."

It's ours. I practically jump out of the car. "Give me the keys."

He laughs again. "There are more cacti on the rooftop deck."

There's a rooftop deck.

And there's the beach. It's right there. Ten feet away. Less. The backyard is on the sand.

It's the last thing I wanted, a house on the beach. My eyes meet his. He smiles and nods.

He bought me a house on the beach.

I have everything I want.

He locks the car and leads me inside. It's beautiful and clean and furnished with just enough.

"There are three bedrooms. One is ours. One is your office. One is my practice room." He presses his lips to my forehead. "Of course, you're always welcome to listen."

I nod. It's still overwhelming. He bought me a car and a house on the beach. "This place looks expensive."

"Real estate is an investment."

That's true.

"I know what you'll say, Jess. You'll say it's mine. And you're partially right. According to the state of California, this place is mine." He stares into my eyes. "But the second we get married, then the state will recognize it's ours."

Pete's talking about getting married. Am I dead? Is this heaven? It doesn't seem possible for this to be happening.

"That something you want?" he asks.

"If you're proposing you better get down on one knee and pull out a giant rock."

He laughs. "Since when are you showy?"

"Since all my classmates rolled their eyes at how my boyfriend is in a band."

"You ever tell them the band?"

"No."

He runs his fingertips through my hair. Then his lips are on mine. Mmm, he tastes good. All the excitement in my chest pours through my lips to his.

I feel steadier when he's around, like I can do anything.

He pulls back and looks into my eyes. "That's petty, wanting to make your classmates jealous. I expect better from you."

"Please, you'll pick out something at least four carats if I don't guide you."

"Maybe." His smile spreads ear to ear. "Is that what you want?"

I nod. That's everything I want.

Good. He drops to one knee.

No.

He's not...

He looks up at me, an ocean of affection in his eyes.

Oh my God, he is. He's really doing this.

Pete takes my hand. His eyes fix on mine. "I don't ever want to run away from my feelings again. I love you more than anything. I know I want you forever." He pulls a ring box from his pocket and flips it open. "Jess James, will you marry me?"

"Yes. Of course."

He slides the ring onto my finger. It's a round solitaire on a platinum band. It's huge but it's elegant and classic too.

It's perfect.

He smiles. "Now, *I* have everything I want."

Want More Sinful Serenade?

Sinful Ever After, book five in the Sinful Serenade series, is available now.

It follows all four Sinful Serenade couples. The book is a collection of four novella length epilogues, one for each couple.

The Sinful Serenade guys will also be appearing in the spin off series, *Dangerous Noise*, coming late 2016.

Sign up for the Crystal Kaswell mailing list to get exclusive alternate POV scenes from all four Sinful Serenade novels! You'll also get exclusive teasers and news on new releases and sales.

Sinful Serenade
Sing Your Heart Out - Miles
Strum Your Heart Out - Drew
Rock Your Heart Out - Tom
Play Your Heart Out - Pete
Sinful Ever After – series sequel

Author's Note

Thank you so much for reading *Play Your Heart Out.* I hope you loved Pete and Jess's story as much as I did, and I hope you love Sinful Serenade as much as I do. They (and the rest of the Sinful Serenade couples) are back in Sinful Ever After.

If you enjoyed the story, please help other readers find it by leaving an honest review on Amazon or Goodreads.

Want news about new releases and sales before anyone else? How about exclusive sneak peeks and bonus scenes? Sign up for the Crystal Kaswell mailing list.

If you love to review and want to get books before anyone else, join the Crystal Kaswell ARC team.

Want to talk books? I love hearing from my readers. Contact me through Facebook, Twitter, or email.

You can find more of my books here.

Acknowledgments

My first thanks goes to my husband, who not only tolerates but loves all my weird quirks (even my rants about grammar). The second goes to my father for always encouraging me to follow my dreams and especially for taking me to the book store when I was supposed to be grounded.

Skyla at Indigo Chick Designs, thank you for the lovely covers! Tonya, you are the best developmental editor out there. Thank you for always pushing me to take the draft to the next level. To my critique partner and fellow rock star addict, Athena Wright, thank you so much for the notes (but thank you even more for listening to my terrible song title puns and telling me they are comedy gold). And, of course, thank you to Giselle at Xpresso book tours and to all the bloggers who are helping to promote this book. And to all my beta readers and my ARC team, a million thank!

Karine, I don't have the words to thank you, and not just for fostering my obsession with *that* band and *that* musician. You were a great friend at a time when I desperately needed support. Sinful Serenade would not exist without you, and I wouldn't be the person I am today without our friendship. I will always wish you the best. Wherever you are, whatever you are doing, I hope you are happy and fulfilled.

As always, my biggest thanks goes to my readers. Thank you for taking a chance on Sinful Serenade. I hope you'll be back for *Sinful Ever After*. I know I'm not ready to let go of Miles, Drew, Tom, and Pete yet.

PLAY YOUR HEART OUT

First edition. May 24, 2016.

Written by Crystal Kaswell.

Cover by Indigo Chick Designs

Also by Crystal Kaswell

Sinful Serenade
Sing Your Heart Out - Miles
Strum Your Heart Out - Drew
Rock Your Heart Out - Tom
Play Your Heart Out - Pete
Sinful Ever After – series sequel

Dangerous Noise
Dangerous Kiss - Ethan
Dangerous Crush – Kit
Dangerous Rock – Joel
Dangerous Fling – Mal
Dangerous Encore - series sequel

Inked Hearts
Tempting - Brendon
Playing - Walker
Pretend You're Mine - Ryan
Hating You, Loving You - Dean - coming summer 2018
Breaking the Rules - Hunter - coming fall 2018

Sign up for the Crystal Kaswell mailing list to get the *Play Your Heart Out* alternate POV scene.

Made in the USA
San Bernardino, CA
09 September 2018